The
SECRET OF JI:

SIX HEIRS

Forthcoming titles by Pierre Grimbert in The Secret of Ji series:

The Orphan Oath
Shadow of the Ancients
The Eternal Guide

The SECRET OF JI:

SIX HEIRS

PIERRE GRIMBERT

TRANSLATED BY
MATT ROSS AND ERIC LAMB

amazon crossing

The Secret of Ji: Six Heirs was first published in 1996 by Les éditions Mnémos as *Le Secret de Ji Volume 1: Six héritiers*. Translated from French by Matt Ross and Eric Lamb. Published in English by AmazonCrossing in 2013.

Published by AmazonCrossing
P.O. Box 400818
Las Vegas, NV 89140

ISBN-13: 9781612184593
ISBN-10: 1612184596
Library of Congress Control Number: 2012941518

To my clan.
You're not in the story, but you've always been there.

Author's Note

At the end of the book, the reader will find a "Short Anecdotal Encyclopedia of the Known World," a glossary that defines certain terms used by the narrator and provides supplementary details that don't appear in the story, without giving the story away, of course—far from it!

Therefore, the reading of the "Short Anecdotal Encyclopedia" can be done in parallel with the story, at moments the reader finds opportune.

CONTENTS

PROLOGUE

My name is Léti. I come from Eza, the fifth-largest village in the southern province of the Kaul Matriarchy. One hundred and eighteen years ago, an unknown man presented himself to the Council of Mothers, saying he carried a message of the utmost importance. He claimed his name was Nol, and that he did not come as an ambassador from any of the known nations. However, many among the Mothers thought him a Levantine: a Wallatte, Thalitte, Solene, or some other inhabitant of the Levant. And so it was with suspicion that they prepared to listen to him.

Nol expressed himself with ease. He observed the customs and rules of the Council as though he had spent his whole life in Kaul. The Mothers returned his respect, listening to his speech without interrupting him, as Tradition demanded.

The debates of the Council were not recorded in that era, which is why it is difficult to give an exact transcription of their words. Here is an approximation:

Honored Mothers, I stand before you with good intentions. The wisdom of the Council members is legendary, and I hope to earn the honor of your trust, though I must keep secret a great number of things.

I cannot say why I am here, nor where I come from. I am bringing my message to all of the rulers of the known world, and

I can only hope to convince them to lend credence to utterances I know to be strange.

At last, here is my declaration:

For a purpose that I cannot make known, I ask that you choose one person from your people, one who is reputed to be among the wisest, and one worthy of representing you. I will meet her on the Island of Ji at dawn on the Day of the Owl, along with the emissaries from the other nations. We will be safe thereafter, so there is no need to bring too great an escort. They cannot accompany us on our voyage anyway.

The wise one whom you choose will only be absent for a few dékades. A boat shall await her return at the same place, on the Day of the Earth.

What will happen upon her return is not yet written. I can only tell you that an important decision will have been made, and that the outcome will be shared with you.

I have finished and I sense your questions. Do not ask them in vain, Honored Mothers, as I cannot answer them.

Nol was still questioned, of course, but he maintained his silence as he had promised. Once he had departed, the Mothers discussed which action to take. Some of the younger ones, whose husbands were still fighting alongside the Lorelien troops, demanded that they hunt down the stranger, or hold him prisoner until they learned more. Others thought they had been confronted by a harmless madman, and that nothing should be done in response to the incident.

Only some of them, driven more by curiosity than by anything else, judged that sending an emissary to Ji would not cost much and that it would be the best way to shed light on the mystery. They proceeded to vote, and it was this wise proposal to send an emissary that was finally agreed upon, under the condition that Nol indeed transmit his "message" to the other nations.

Confirmation came from the Junine ambassador, who some days later reported a similar encounter between Nol and an assembly of barons from the Small Kingdoms.

Then it was time to choose the emissary. It seemed obvious to the Mothers that the wisest people of the Matriarchy were members of the Council. Furthermore, choosing one of their own allowed them to act with total secrecy.

All of them turned respectfully toward the Ancestress, who was the wisest of all. Fortunately, shrewd as she was, she knew she was too old for this adventure. Hence, she asked for volunteers to come forward, not those who called themselves Wisest, which would have been vain, but those who considered themselves to be the most devoted. Four Mothers offered to represent Kaul, and Tiramis was elected from among them.

Tiramis is my ancestress; she is the mother of the mother of the mother of my mother—the grandmother of my grandmother.

It was decided that a man would accompany her for protection. They chose Yon, who was the third son of the Ancestress and who they knew to be strong and devoted. To convince Nol to accept the second emissary, Yon was put forth as the representative of the masculine population of Kaul, which could have been true after all. As a final measure of security, they decided that only one schooner would distantly follow the strange man and the other Sages.

On the Day of the Owl, Tiramis and Yon landed on the Island of Ji, just off the Lorelien coast. It was a small, uninhabited land that could be circled on foot in a single day. It had very little vegetation, only rocks upon rocks, and sand between them.

Nol, looking solemn, but seemingly satisfied by the number of people who had come, was waiting for them on the beach. Tiramis knew some of them by sight or reputation, and a Goranese chamberlain, a self-proclaimed master of ceremonies, took on the responsibility of introducing her to the others.

There was King Arkane of Junine, the representative of the Baronies; young Prince Vanamel of the Grand Empire of Goran and his councilor, His Excellency Saat the Treasurer, the two of them representing, of course, the Grand Empire; Chief Ssa-Vez, who had come from the distant Jezeba; His Excellency Rafa Derkel de Griteh; Duke Reyan Kercyan, sent by King Bondrian, of Lorelia; His Excellency Maz Achem, representing Ith; His Excellency Moboq the Wise, representing King Qarbal of Arkary; and finally Their Excellencies the Honored Mother Tiramis and Yon of Kaul, representatives of the Matriarchy. Each of these distinguished luminaries had arrived with considerable pomp—especially Prince Vanamel—such that the only strip of beach free of rocks was overrun with banners and makeshift camps, decorated with colorful pennants, which swarms of servants and soldiers in all liveries skirted or shuffled past.

Nol welcomed each emissary, thanking them for their trust, which was a good omen, and informed them that he would wait until nightfall for the arrival of the other emissaries. He offered no additional information.

Rafa de Griteh objected to the unequal representation of the nations present. To resolve this misunderstanding, Nol asked if the Grand Empire of Goran and the Kaul Matriarchy had some reason to each send two emissaries. Tiramis gave him the half-truth about Yon representing the men of Kaul, and Prince Vanamel protested that because the Grand Empire was much bigger than most of the others, it was fitting that it should be represented by two people. His Excellency Moboq the Wise, for whom the debates had been translated, objected in his own right that Arkary was much larger still than the Grand Empire, and that King Qarbal should have sent three or four representatives. Nol made a discouraged face and cut short the dissension by making it clear that a superior number of emissaries would not give a particular advantage to any nation in any case; the limit was simply a question of practicality. Rafa de Griteh declared himself to be satisfied. At that moment, no one seriously wanted to contradict Nol.

The stranger spoke everyone's native tongue with disconcerting ease. He listened to everyone, but firmly and politely swept away the objections of these nobles who had all come to recognize him as an extraordinary person. When he had seen the last of them and declared a desire to meditate alone, they all stifled their impatience and watched respectfully as he slipped away.

When night came, Nol regretfully declared that neither the Land of Beauty nor Romine had sent an emissary, and that these two kingdoms would not be represented. Some also remarked that not a single Eastian diplomat was present, but they did not know what to conclude from that.

The stranger invited the Sages to follow him, and set out on foot through the rocky labyrinth that was the Island of Ji. After a brief moment of confusion—they had all been expecting to go by sea—Tiramis followed him and Yon, then Duke Kercyan, then the rest, all in lockstep.

Various officials, guards, and servants remained on the beach, unsure of what to do. Then they hastily put several ships to sea, thinking that the emissaries might embark from the other side of the island.

At first, the crews, who were practically adversaries, quickly organized themselves to patrol their own sectors. But no unknown embarkation point was discovered that night.

In the gray light of morning, armed men were sent to the interior of the island. The soldiers scoured the labyrinth all day, and continued through the following day, finding nothing save some grottoes used as warehouses by nondescript Lorelien smugglers.

By the end of the fourth day they had lost all hope of finding the emissaries' trail. One by one the delegations regretfully left the island, each suspecting the other nations to have concealed some information about this strange adventure, or worse: to be behind it all.

Four dékades passed, and no ransom was demanded. Some had suggested abduction, though that notion was slowly abandoned. The Day of the Earth arrived, the boats were sent to the island once more, and in the palaces, those left behind began to hope for the imminent return of their Sages.

On the dawn of the Day of the Bear, one dékade and a half after the Day of the Earth, seven people emerged from the rocks, stumbling along the same path that they had taken two moons earlier. The soldiers who were on guard watched incredulously as an exhausted Duke Reyan, eyes empty of all expression, and Rafa de Griteh, his hair burned and face blackened, carried King Arkane of Junine on a makeshift stretcher. There was a wound on his head and a red tourniquet pressed over the stump that was his left arm. They saw His Excellence Yon of Kaul staggering as he carried an unconscious Honored Mother Tiramis in his arms. Finally, they saw Their Excellencies Maz Achem of Ith and Moboq of Arkary limping as they finished the march.

Prince Vanamel, Saat the Treasurer, and Ssa-Vez of Jezeba were missing from the roll call.

Nol the Strange did not return, either.

Ramur was a happy man, for it had been a good day. Not yet the third Day of the Lorelien Fair and he had already sold more than two-thirds of his cargo of Lineh spices. And he hadn't even needed to haggle.

A full purse at his side, he headed toward the city center with a smug swagger. He was hoping to celebrate his success in a fitting manner, and maybe make one or two more sales, if the occasion presented itself.

Maybe he would go down to the less respectable neighborhoods to see if a certain young woman he met every year was still generous with her charms.

Of course Ramur gave a thought to Dona, the Goddess of Pleasure and Opulence, his favorite divinity by far. He promised himself to make an offering to her cult later, as a thank you for his good luck. Perhaps during the next moon, upon his return to

Lineh. Or better yet, in three moons, after the harvests. It was better to honor Dona all at once, he thought, after several good ventures, than to waste—no, what he really meant was than to *disturb*—her priests with insignificant offerings.

If he were honest with himself, he knew he wasn't going to make an offering until he wound up at death's door. That way, he could enjoy his possessions as long as possible. He also recognized that he was loath to give his terces to the representatives of a cult that wouldn't hesitate to steal them.

Despite the arrival of the Season of Winds and the coming darkness, the sun shone brightly on Ramur and he gave it a smile. His smile was one of his gifts. Experience had taught him that people were less inclined to haggle with someone with a friendly face.

He wasn't very far from the city center by now, and the mob, which had thinned out at the edge of the fair near the old port, began to grow thick. Out of habit, Ramur kept a hand on his purse, carefully watching everyone who crossed his path. Thanks to his vigilance, he had avoided pickpockets until now, but it only took a few moments of negligence to find oneself relieved of a few hundred terces.

Several times he had seen pockets picked from behind his stall, but he wasn't about to interfere. People should mind their own business. It wasn't as if someone would return his purse to him, if it happened to disappear.

The crowd was becoming quite sizable, and many of the onlookers he passed seemed more frenzied than usual. He began to regret leaving his hired hand at the door. If one of these poor souls decided to make some money off a corpse, it could easily be his...

A man walking in the opposite direction bumped into him. Ramur quickly turned and followed the man with his eyes, taking a rapid inventory of his purse and jewelry as he did so.

The tactless man wore common priest's robes. The hood covered his face so completely that Ramur couldn't see the color of his hair, or if he had any at all.

Ramur's terces were still in their place, but the alarm had been raised, and he regretfully gave up the simple pleasure of parading about with a fat purse at his side. He started untying it to slip it under his clothes when he was knocked again, only a few moments later, this time from behind. His hands clenched the decorated cloth bag, while a painful sting set his back aflame.

The man who ran into him this time looked exactly like the first one. He simply whispered in Ramur's ear, "My name is Zokin. Tell it to Zuïa."

As if paralyzed, Ramur watched Zokin leave, his eyes wide open but unseeing, his hands still clutching the purse to his chest. With horror, he realized the implications of what he had just heard. Then his vision clouded, his legs gave way, and he collapsed.

He was dead before he hit the ground.

Upon the return of the Sages, once the initial moment of astonishment had passed, each delegation wanted to interrogate its own emissary. Rafa de Griteh declared with an aggressive tone that it was out of the question to separate them.

Not right away.

He walked over to the Ithare tents, where he locked himself away with his companions and two Eurydian priests trained in the art of healing. The priests dressed the wounds of the injured in respectful silence. It wasn't until Rafa had walked a few steps outside their retreat that he was questioned about the missing Sages.

He responded simply that they had died, giving no other details.

During the days that followed, the survivors didn't mingle much with the colorful crowd of kings, barons, and other such notables who had come for the event. They kept silent or simply claimed not to remember anything when questioned. Eventually, it was only this last response that was given.

The nations in mourning—Goran and Jezeba—quickly packed up their belongings and left the island on bad terms with the others. One could imagine that a new war between Goran and Lorelia was possible, but Emperor Mazrel seemed to have held Prince Vanamel in such low esteem that he could not justify the reopening of hostilities.

One by one, each of the Sages returned home. They were interrogated again separately, but responded only with silence. Several of their liege lords took them to have a prolonged influenza.

They relieved Maz Achem of all his responsibilities at the Grand Temple. Thereafter, he abandoned all religious activity and left Ith.

Rafa de Griteh was dismissed from military command, which was a major humiliation, for he had been the personal strategist to the king. He stayed in the army regardless and served so well that in his final years his title and honor were restored.

Arkane of Junine, himself a king, experienced only public disapproval from his peers in the other Baronies. Knowing that the power of the Lesser Kingdoms was in their union, he prevented any disagreement by abdicating the throne in favor of his son.

Moboq the Wise returned to Arkary, simply announcing that it would be better if everyone ignored what had happened. As he was a Sage, everyone accepted his decision and quickly forgot the incident.

Reyan Kercyan was most wronged. They took away his title of Duke. They took his land. And he was publicly disgraced. He did not sink into a depression as one might have expected, but continued to live in Lorelia anyway, where he survived as a merchant.

For her own part, Tiramis left the Council of Mothers. She merely declared that the Matriarchy wasn't in danger and that she never again wanted to be questioned on the subject. The Ancestress herself asked that everyone respect this request; it was useless to revive these seemingly terrible memories.

Tiramis took Yon in Union the next year. Yon is my ancestor, the grandfather of my grandmother.

They moved here 118 years ago, to this same small southern province where I live.

To everyone else, Nol and the emissaries are forgotten. There may be a few people who know some of the story, but they would have trouble distinguishing between the facts and the stories that are occasionally told.

I have not forgotten. The heirs have not forgotten.

Something wasn't right.

Nort' had always possessed a sort of sixth sense that had saved him many times before, and this latest feeling of alarm was clanging louder than the six hundred bells of Leem.

Ever since the apogee, he'd felt that he was being watched. Nort' had always attracted looks, generally feminine ones, with his imposing muscular frame, but this was something else. Someone was watching him.

Nort' guarded the western door to the imperial gardens of Goran, standing with the most military bearing possible, arms tense at his sides, hand firm on his halberd. He usually performed his duty with an exceptional patience, but today he was ill at ease.

He examined the passersby, then examined the closest windows in an attempt to expose his spy. He shot a glance at his two subordinates, frozen in the same posture, hoping that one or the other shared his fears. But they apparently had nothing on their mind except the changing of the guard.

An old, filthy man clothed only in rags approached them, presenting an equally soiled cup in his wrinkled hands. *A foreigner, no doubt,* he thought to himself, *maybe a Lorelien.* The man broke into a series of pleas in a mix of Ithare and Goranese when Nort', with a wave of his hand, had his subordinates unceremoniously sweep him away.

This episode brought him back to the task at hand and made him temporarily forget his worries. It was hot at the end of the day, and Nort' began to look forward to the change. His right arm was tired, and more than anything, he wanted to drop that cursed halberd, which was killing his shoulder. He also couldn't wait to walk a bit. He was a former trooper and never really got used to the guard's long decidays of forced immobility. Finally, his patience was rewarded: he was relieved to hear the six bells ring briefly from somewhere behind him in the palace, marking the end of the sixth deciday. The door opened, exposing three military men dressed in thicker clothes for the night guard. There was the necessary orchestra of exchanging halberds, then the ritual salute, and the new guards took their place.

Nort' decided not to mention his feelings to the night guard. Nort' saw no real reason to inform them, and he would be roundly mocked if he confided his childish fears to the veteran warriors.

He decided not to return immediately to the guards' barracks since he had some free time. But the feeling of being watched stopped his long-awaited stroll before it could really begin. He couldn't be at ease until this cursed foreboding, which stuck with him like a bad hangover, passed.

If he had to, Nort' was prepared to start a little skirmish with some strangers to soothe his unease.

Yet he felt himself walking quite fast, muttering with a hand glued to the hilt of his broadsword, and staring down each passerby he came across with an evil eye. He stopped, took a long breath, and began his walk again at a more moderate pace.

He rarely lost his composure so easily. "By Mishra, if something must happen, then let it happen now, gods damn it!" he grumbled.

He heard an eruption of voices behind him. Turning around, Nort' saw a mob of Goranese men fleeing something that wasn't yet recognizable. Then the human mass split in two, making way for two Züu killers.

The Züu killers!

They didn't need to show any discretion here in Goran, where their influence and reputation were well known. Nort' saw the scarlet tunics, the vermillion headbands encircling shaved heads, the damned daggers—long and thin as needles—gleaming in their hands. And, more than anything, their eyes. They were the eyes of fanatics, ready to do anything to achieve their end: to slaughter their prey.

They were coming his way, but that didn't mean anything, as Nort' was in the middle of the street. He drew his broadsword while slowly sliding to his left. Then it hit him: they were there for him.

The two killers had seen his every move. Nort' remembered those looks now; they had been watching him all day, faceless until now.

They were no more than a few steps away from him and approaching rapidly, practically running. Nort' saw the glistening of the daggers, the murderous eyes, and the curious crowd that wouldn't interfere for all the world. A savage hatred rose up in his chest, and he let out a roar as he leaped toward the two men; his skin would come at a dear price.

But instead, it was given freely; a third assassin he hadn't seen came at him from behind.

His cry died in his throat as the poisoned needle shot through him, and he silently collapsed at his murderers' feet.

———∞∞∞———

Some moons after their return, the surviving Sages felt the urge to reunite. The old King Arkane of Junine was the first to act on this desire by inviting all of them to the most beautiful of the Lesser Kingdoms. The chosen date was the Day of the Owl: as such, they would commemorate the day that they had all left in single file, following Nol the Strange.

Even though Arkane was one-handed, aging, and more or less ostracized by his peers, he was still a powerful individual, and finding his old friends wasn't difficult. Everyone responded to his call, even Moboq, who was the farthest away and had to travel for two dékades.

They were warmly welcomed. The ancient king, seeing them all reunited and joyous in his personal palace, declared that there was one fortunate outcome of their adventure, at least: friendship.

They spoke of their personal fates, of the events after that "voyage." They all empathized with the others' misfortunes, particularly those of Rafa, Maz Achem, and Reyan Kercyan. But no one pitied their own situation; they all simply stated the facts, without appearing to regret the mutual silence that had caused it all.

Later, free from spying eyes, each emissary renewed their vow to keep the secret, no matter what happened beyond the suffering, dishonor, and solitude that they had already felt.

They left each other, promising to reunite again, which they did the next year, and two years later, then regularly every two years. King Arkane was not at their fourth meeting; he was the first among them to disappear. But three new people participated: Tiramis and Yon had a daughter, and Maz Achem, although aging himself, had taken his Union with one of his previous students, who quickly gave him a son. He came with his young wife and child, and no one voiced any objection.

Thomé of Junine, whom King Arkane had abdicated in favor of, asked to represent his father. He knew nothing of the secret, but wanted to pay homage to the thing that had been most important in his father's eyes. Of course his request was accepted.

The arrival of these new characters in the group changed the style of the gatherings; what began as rather serious occasions eventually became family celebrations. The nations stopped sending spies to reveal the secret, which was never brought up again.

In their own time, Moboq the Wise, Rafa de Griteh, and Reyan Kercyan had wives and children. The gatherings of the growing group became more and more organized. Since everyone came from faraway lands, they decided to set the meeting every three years in Berce, a Lorelien city, which was the closest point to the Island of Ji and an approximate midpoint between all of their homes.

Over the years, the old ones died out. The majority of their descendants continued to reunite to celebrate this event they knew nearly nothing about. Sometimes, when the night was dark enough, the ancestors brought the oldest of the children to the island. There, they shared a part of their knowledge, then took a solemn vow of silence. Perhaps they should not have done this.

A secret, can it always remain so?

This year is the year of the gathering. The Day of the Owl is only three dékades away. This will be my fifteenth year, and they will bring me to the island.

Those who have gone come back different, more solemn, more serious. Sadder.

I don't really want to know. But I want to be a part of the heirs, see my adoptive cousins, uncles, and aunts again, and pay homage to Tiramis, to Yon, and to all my ancestors since them, all the way up to my own missing mother.

In three dékades, we will meet for the gathering of the heirs, and I will go to the island.

BOOK I:
THE ROAD TO BERCE

Bowbaq awoke soundlessly. He kept his eyes shut for a few moments, then reluctantly opened them. It was dark; morning was still far away. He brought the covers and pelts up to his chin and stretched out comfortably, resting his hands behind his head.

Wos sounded anxious. Bowbaq heard the animal fidgeting in his pen. More than likely the wolves had ventured too close to his humble cottage. The man debated whether or not to get up, and eventually decided to stay under the warm covers. Wos had always been too nervous, and the wolves too timid and clever to attack a steppe pony in full health.

Bowbaq tossed and turned in his bed; he missed his wife. As usual, Ipsen had left with their two children to spend the Season of Snows with her home clan. At first, he was always happy to rediscover his freedom. But after a few dékades, loneliness began to weigh on him. Perhaps he could go visit his own people? It was

1

too late now to catch up to Ipsen, but his own native village was only a few days' ride away.

Wos whinnied. What a pain that pony could be! Bowbaq thought of all those times when "Master" Wos acted all high and mighty, thinking himself too imperial to pull a sleigh, caring only for grand, daring rides. Yes, he was quite the noble, adventurous steed.

Letting out a sigh, Bowbaq resigned himself to checking on his mount. He reluctantly threw off his covers and went over to the chimney.

The coals in the fireplace were still red; he realized that he must have been sleeping for only a few centidays. But still, a biting cold had already infiltrated the tiny cottage, and the small drafts coming through the cracks in the walls suggested the temperature outside was even colder.

He piled on a few logs to get the fire going again. Then he prepared to go out, haphazardly throwing on all his furs without fastening the ties. Finally, he grabbed his walking stick and cracked the door open.

Immediately, he felt the biting cold on his face. It seemed a calm night compared to the blizzard and the heavy snowfall of recent days. He closed the door carefully behind him and set out toward the back of the cottage where the pen was. It was nearly as light as day out; the moon was full and its light reflected off the immaculate landscape.

In spite of his large size, Bowbaq's step was hindered by the thick layer of snow that covered the ground, and it took him several millidays to reach the fence. The pony was waiting for him there, stamping his hooves impatiently. He began chattering to Bowbaq as soon as he was in sight.

"*Stranger hunt us. Stranger come. Hunt us. Stranger. Many. Come hunt us. Stranger. Many.*"

Bowbaq rubbed his eyes as he trudged the last few steps. Wos's abilities were truly amazing for a herd animal. It was rare for a pony to communicate with such ease. But he lacked restraint and calm, which gave predators the advantage. His words invaded Bowbaq's mind with an indecipherable, buzzing disorder.

As he lifted his head, he gazed hard into the animal's eyes and reached for his mind, as he often did. He spoke to him without saying a word, directly from mind to mind, making an effort to choose simple words and concepts that the pony could understand.

"Safety. Stranger weak. Frightened of us."

Then he formed a mental picture of a wolf and transferred it to the animal's mind.

"Stranger small. We big."

Wos reared and sent a few nervous kicks into the air. Neither Bowbaq's gentle strokes nor his simple words reassured the pony.

"No. No. No. Not him. Him small. Not him. Not dangerous. No. Stranger big. Dangerous. Many. Hunt us. Come. No. Not him. Dangerous."

The animal was visibly panic-stricken at his master's ignorance. Despite his gift, Wos couldn't really tell what it was that he feared; he only knew he was afraid.

Bowbaq tried to reach the pony's hindbrain, but to no avail. Not wolves? What then? An insomniac bear, running behind on his hibernation schedule? But Wos spoke of many. Bowbaq lamented the fact that animals didn't know how to count. Many could be a whole lot.

Foxes? Anators? Maybe even a pack of spotted lions? If Mir were there, Wos—and Bowbaq himself—would be a lot less worried. Bowbaq had raised the lion cub since birth, and he was very proud, as was his whole clan, to be friends with a genuine adult wildcat. But Mir was serving as Ipsen's and the children's escort for their journey, and they must have been dozens of leagues away from the cabin.

The night wasn't going to be as pleasant as expected. Closing his mind to the pony's fanatic babbling, he retraced his steps back to the house. He wasn't that worried. The predators must have simply been passing through, or roaming around, not daring to venture too close to the house, which would be even more true once he lit some logs and took position with his bow, on guard for any ill-intentioned creature. It was still rather vexing to find himself on a night watch, even though he had been careful to build his cottage far from concentrations of known predators.

Back inside, Bowbaq gathered all the things he needed for his watch: a flint lighter, some kindling and a few dry logs, his bow and quiver, an ivory dagger that he slipped through his belt, and finally a bottle of fermented fruits along with a hardy piece of smoked ham. He wrapped it all in a thick skin that he planned on using as a blanket later, fastened the ties of his furs, and went back out.

As he closed the door behind him, he noticed that instead of quieting down, Wos's whinnies had gotten louder.

Suddenly he heard a sharp snap accompanied by a vibration near his head.

Reflexively, he pinned himself against the doorway, shielding his face. Then his eyes found the source of the noise.

A crossbow bolt had pierced the wooden doorframe, barely a foot from his head. Bowbaq thought he could still see it quivering.

Dropping his makeshift bag, he threw himself facedown on the ground just in time to dodge a second projectile, which grazed his hat and stuck violently in the door. On all fours, he scrambled behind a white mound a few yards from the house that he knew to be a dead stump covered in snow. He took cover behind it and immediately drew his ivory dagger, grasping it white-knuckled.

The only audible sounds were those made by Wos and Bowbaq's own labored breathing. He tried hard to slow his breath while at the same time focusing all of his attention on his attacker. Where was he? Who was he? How many were there?

It takes more than a few moments to reload a crossbow, which meant one of two possibilities: either the man had at least two of them, or he wasn't alone. Unfortunately, his conversation with Wos tipped the scale in favor of the second option. Were they pillagers? Warriors from an enemy clan? Wanderers?

Bowbaq's mind was racing in all directions. He focused his scattered thoughts on one thing: escape. Everything else could be cleared up later...or not.

If he managed to make it back to the house, get the door open, and lock it behind him, he could defend himself better. There was no shortage of weapons in the house, and he could hold off his enemies at least until morning. Unless they set fire to the cottage. In any case, the house seemed leagues away, and Bowbaq kicked himself for not having had the presence of mind to lunge through the door right away!

Time flowed by like water in a river, and he knew that each wasted moment gave his enemies the advantage. It wouldn't be long before they surrounded him, if they hadn't already done so. If he could at least recover his bow, maybe he'd be able to prevent an attack from one side. But all his enemies would have to do is sit down next to a fire with a watchman and wait a couple of decidays until their prey froze to death.

Bowbaq then came to the horrific realization that if Wos hadn't woken him up, he would already be dead. His attackers showed no apparent signs of hesitation. They surely would have taken him by surprise and murdered him while he was still sleeping.

Wos. If only the pony weren't fenced in, he could call for him and escape. He mentally retraced his steps from the pen, but the pen was even farther away than the house. What was there to do?

Maybe…there was a wall on the south side—the other possible direction—that ran along a ditch used for drainage during snow melts. It was definitely filled with ice and snow during this time of year, but the bottom would still be at least a foot below ground level.

But it certainly wasn't very big. After shedding some of his most cumbersome furs, he had to be able to crawl through it—for a dozen yards or so at least—and get out of range of the crossbow quickly enough that his attackers wouldn't have the time to get closer.

He didn't take the time to search for alternatives and threw off his first few layers of fur without even untying them. A glacial breeze bored through him right away, and he hoped that he wasn't going to escape his attackers only to freeze to death on the way to his nearest neighbor's.

The most difficult part was going to be those few feet that stood between him and the ditch. He slipped his dagger into his boot and squatted, tensing his muscles in a spring position. He took a deep breath and leaped into the little strip of sunken earth that ran along the wall. His hands and knees sunk into a foot and a half of snow. He hastily brushed himself off and scurried toward the back of the house, expecting to feel the painful sting of a bolt at any moment.

He wasn't sure, but he thought he heard at least one bow snap during his leap. He didn't stop to check if a new fletched shaft was protruding from his cottage. He was, however, sure that he was hearing shouts. A man, who must have been only about thirty yards away, was barking orders in an unfamiliar language.

He came to the end of the little trench. His knees and elbows were drenched and chilled to the bone, and the rest of his body was scarcely warmer. He lifted his head a bit and quickly scanned all around. Two men were rushing toward him from different directions. One of them was holding a small spear and the other a curved blade. They were covered in furs from head to toe, but they didn't seem at all weighed down by the excess clothing. They wore large latticework sifters strapped to their feet, like the ones the Tolensk Arques used, which allowed them to run almost unhindered despite the deep snow.

Bowbaq realized that his chances were dwindling; he decided to go for it. He bolted upright in the ditch, then dashed across the short distance that remained between him and the pen.

He felt a burst of pain near his left shoulder, where the third man's bolt had just lodged itself. With his last bit of energy, he climbed over the fence railing and let himself collapse to the ground on the other side. He crossed the field to the stable, where he found Wos waiting impatiently for him.

Bowbaq knew that, at any moment, the bowman was going to take another shot or one of the others was going to block his exit. He threw open the gate and went over to the pony to mount him.

But Wos didn't see eye to eye with his master. As soon as the way was large enough for him, Wos dashed through the open gate, leaving Bowbaq alone and helpless.

Incredulously, he watched as the animal galloped away, deaf to his hopeless and furious cries.

The idiot wasn't even going in the right direction.

It looked like Wos was going to gallop right past the spearman, but then, at the last moment, he changed directions and charged him violently. The surprised enemy was thrown to the ground by two heavy blows from the giant pony's massive hooves. Wos diligently trampled him for a few more moments, then lifted his head and charged the second man.

After a brief moment of surprise, it was Bowbaq's turn to spring into action. He went back across the field, climbed over the fence again, and leaped knee-deep into the snow. Then he stumbled his way over to the body of the spearman.

The second round with his next adversary seemed harder for Wos. The second man was making impressive twirls with his sword, making it impossible for the pony to get near enough to be dangerous. At least Wos would keep him occupied for a while, thought Bowbaq. The third man was now in sight and was completely focused on reloading his crossbow.

The corpse of the man with the spear was not a pretty sight. Wos had delivered so many blows to his face and neck that he'd nearly been decapitated. Breathing hard, Bowbaq stifled his urge to vomit. He had almost finished stripping the long weapon from the corpse when a roar rang out, one that he recognized immediately.

The lion, Mir, was there. A hundred yards away, he stood proudly on the edge of the snow-covered forest like a statue.

His roar ended in a low and continuous growl that was audible even from such a distance. His mane was puffed out, doubling his size, and his hair stood on end all along his spine, from his shoulders to the tip of his tail. At the moment, his yellowish spots had somewhat faded, and his whole body was white as alabaster. The only contrast with the white snow were his two fiery eyes and his muzzle, blood red and bone ivory.

Mir advanced two graceful steps. Then his growl went silent and, after a moment of stillness, he broke into a series of rapid pounces toward the scene of the battle.

Just as immediately as they had frozen at Mir's appearance, Bowbaq and Wos snapped back into action. Wos decided to back off and make way for Mir, who was now heading straight for the man with the sword. The lion pinned the swordsman to the ground. Even without seeing anything more, Bowbaq knew from the screams that he had one less enemy.

He himself was taking large strides toward the third man, who didn't look to be giving up, despite the unfavorable turn of events. Bowbaq had never loaded a crossbow, and he wondered if he would have enough time to make it to his enemy before the man shot a bolt right into his forehead.

What if Bowbaq stopped to throw his stolen spear?

No.

It was a sure shot; he could hit anything from that distance.

No. He wouldn't kill the bowman.

But it would save his life. He could see Ipsen, his children, and his friends again...

No. Bowbaq had resolved to never voluntarily take the life of another man. He had sworn the oath.

But the time he spent lost in thought had already sealed his fate either way. With a cry of joy, the man snapped the small arrow into the groove and aimed his weapon, his target just a few yards in front of him and running straight for him.

Bowbaq closed his eyes and lunged forward at full force. He heard the fatal sound of the crossbow loosed at the same time that he felt the handle of the spear collide violently with something.

Stretched out on the snow, he awaited the arrival of the pain from the crossbow bolt he must have taken. But only the first one, still stuck in his left shoulder, was afflicting him.

He lifted his head just in time to see his enemy getting ready to whack him with his now useless weapon. Bowbaq rolled over, letting out a cry of pain as his shoulder grazed the ground, got to his knees, and swept his spear through the air in a horizontal movement. The wooden handle met the stranger's head, bringing him to the ground.

Bowbaq sat up fuming and pressed the sharp spear to his attacker's chest. The man sitting on the ground pulled back his hood, took off his face mask, and uncovered his bald head. He was quite young—younger than Bowbaq anyway, perhaps in his thirties. He wasn't an Arque; he didn't look like he was from the Upper Kingdoms either.

The man touched his aching temple and found blood. He shot a mean look at Bowbaq, who felt a little pang in his heart as he recognized the severity of the wound that he'd given the man. If his blow had been any stronger, he may well have broken his oath.

Mir came over to his side, and Bowbaq patted the lion's flank with one hand. The stranger stood up and, although it wasn't a sudden movement, the lion let out a threatening growl. With a squeeze of his hand, Bowbaq restrained the lion from finishing the bowman off.

"Who are you?" Bowbaq asked.

The man didn't answer and instead rapidly removed his furs. Bowbaq repeated his question but was ignored once again. When the stranger ceased his undressing, he was left in a lightweight red tunic and a thin band of the same color tied around his forehead. He had also taken off his shoes and was barefoot.

"I don't intend to kill you. I only want to know who you are," Bowbaq tried again, this time in the Ithare language.

The man calmly rested his arms at his side and lifted his head, closing his eyes as if in a contemplative state of prayer.

"Sir! Is this what you want? Do you truly wish to die now? Here? Like this?"

Suddenly, quicker than lightning, the stranger pushed away the spear and pounced on Bowbaq, brandishing a sharp dagger at least a foot long. Once again, Mir was quicker, and with a single blow, his monstrous paw threw the man five yards away. The lion was on top of him in two pounces and unceremoniously ripped out his jugular, not heeding Bowbaq's orders.

The Arque, who had always detested violence, was wracked with emotion. He let himself fall to the ground, and sat there for a moment with his face buried in the palms of his hands.

A rough tongue licked his fingers, and the stink of the lion's breath filled his nostrils. Bowbaq patted Mir absentmindedly, with a hand still over his eyes; images from the recent scenes invaded his memory. He had an urge to recoil while looking upon the peaceful face of the lion, which was just a foot from his own. His immaculate mane, his inquisitive eyes. His muzzle dripping red with the blood of his victims.

Bowbaq stood back up. Even though he was grateful that Mir and Wos had intervened, even though he owed his life to them, he had indirectly contributed to the death of the three men, and he didn't have to be at peace with that.

The large lion's words drifted into his mind: *"The man be safe? The man hurt."*

Bobwaq realized that he had almost completely forgotten about the bolt stuck in his shoulder. The pain had ebbed by then, and the wound was bleeding much less severely. He pulled gently at the feathers to gauge the depth of the perforation and grimaced when his body protested against the rough treatment. It was all the same; if he didn't take it out quickly, it was going to be even more painful later.

"I heal. Me happy see Mir."

The lion approved with a click of his jaw and disappeared without another word into the forest. Bowbaq knew that he had nothing to fear that night: nothing and no one would get past the lion's barricade. He made sure that Wos was doing all right and made it back to the house.

The heat of the fire welcomed him kindly. He carefully took off his drenched clothes, mindful not to brush against the jutting crossbow bolt. When the wound was finally bare, he put one of his gloves in his mouth, held his breath, and in one quick movement pulled the foreign object out.

He didn't bite down on the glove. He dropped it, letting out a wail. Panting, applying pressure to his wound with a cloth, he stared at the bolt laid out in front of him and saw with relief that it had come out in one piece.

Once the bleeding had slowed, he cleaned the wound generously with alcohol and applied a compress. Then, after a moment of thought, he also cleaned his throat generously.

He felt a lot better now that he was treated and warmed up. At last he felt up to searching for the answers to the questions he had been asking himself since he left the cabin.

Who were these men?

What did they want? Besides his death, of course.

Bowbaq didn't know a whole lot about anything outside of central Arkary. From what he could remember, he had never wronged anyone seriously enough to get three assassins sent for him. Or perhaps these men were acting on their own behalf. But they were obviously very misinformed, since the Arque didn't have any riches worthy of the name. Maybe they were mad? Fanatics in search of a sacrifice?

Or maybe…

His curiosity got the better of him, and he decided not to wait until morning to examine the dead bodies, as he'd originally planned. He got dressed again in dry clothes and went out.

Overcoming his misgivings, he first drew up on the man whom Wos killed. His skin had whitened, and a thin layer of frost was starting to form all over him. Bowbaq slipped his hands under the body and flipped it over. The stiff, frozen body made sickening crackling sounds as it was torn away from its frozen blanket. The Arque had no desire to think about what exactly made those sounds.

His brief search—he wanted desperately to have it done with—wasn't very fruitful. It didn't seem like the man had anything special on him, except for a red tunic and a dagger similar to the one the bowman had. Bowbaq moved on to the bowman.

Apparently, Mir had already taken a share of his guts. This time, the Arque wasn't able to hold back his nausea, and he let loose the contents of his stomach. The bowman was missing an entire arm, and most of his ribs were exposed. Bowbaq pulled himself together as best he could and searched through the pockets of the shredded tunic, which, surprisingly, were still intact.

This time, Bowbaq found something. His hand touched a piece of parchment, which he carefully removed. It was covered in blood, and folded in on itself at least six times. Once it was fully opened, there wasn't much of anything legible on it. Bowbaq didn't recognize the few symbols that had avoided the vermillion stains, but admittedly, he did not know how to read. He gave up and continued with his inspection.

When he shook the man's boots out, a small wooden flask half full of a sour-smelling liquid fell to the ground. Was it a drug?

Poison?

He shivered at this idea. What if the bolt had been poisoned?

Then he would have been dead already. Or maybe it was a slow-acting poison? Or perhaps his clothes had absorbed a portion of the fatal liquid?

Well, if he didn't die a few days on, he would never have an answer to these questions. He poured the liquid out into the snow and piled the man's clothes on top of his body.

He didn't discover much more from the examination of the third body; he found another dagger and the same scarlet tunic that the others wore. It was quite obvious that these men belonged to some sort of organization, military group, religious sect, or something.

Reluctantly, Bowbaq finally admitted the conclusion he had come to a while before: these men had come with a single obvious objective—to kill him. Him, and perhaps his family.

There were only two things that made Bowbaq special in any sort of way. First was his ability to read animal minds. He was *erjak*. But dozens of Arques had this gift, and it had even been discovered among some foreigners.

The second thing, though certainly not the least, was that he was a member of the heirs of Ji.

Bowbaq was a fourth-generation descendant of Moboq the Wise. Once he had brushed aside all his other theories, that was the only one that remained. Those men had tried to kill him because his great-great-grandfather had taken part in that strange adventure a century ago, an event that had been forgotten or remained unknown to almost everyone by now.

This was absolutely no time for hesitation: Bowbaq had to bring his family to safety and warn the other heirs of the fate that surely threatened them.

He immediately set himself to the preparations necessary before his departure. He wondered how he could rejoin Ipsen, as the glacier had closed off the route for two dékades, at least... Then he realized that this was hardly an obstacle for Mir.

Once he finished with his packing, he gathered his courage, the bodies, and their belongings. He showered the pile with oil and lit it on fire.

At that moment, Mir reappeared. He had found four ponies tied up to a tree not far from there. Bowbaq followed the lion while brooding on dark thoughts about the number four, but once they reached the spot, it turned out that one of the animals was only a pack pony.

The search through the saddlebags and other belongings he found there turned up dry. There was nothing but the clothing and equipment needed for a ride in a cold countryside. Bowbaq untied the ponies and led them to his pen, speaking soothing words to them the whole way to calm the nervousness they felt at being so close to the big lion. Then he freed them of their loads, which he quickly sorted through. The better half of it went into the fire; he kept the other half, which lacked any distinguishing markings.

Once he had put a harness on Wos, he went over to the wild-cat and gave him these instructions: *"My companion and my little ones are in danger. I need to protect them. But I cannot reach them. Does Mir understand?"*

"Understand. The pride in danger."

"That's it. Mir can protect them. Will he?"

"Humans with female and cubs of Man frighten by me. Want to kill me. Ipsen say come here. Not safe to leave."

"Mir is wise, but if he doesn't go, the family—the pride is dead. Mir must go."

The lion spun around a couple of times, obviously confused. Bowbaq knew how disconcerting the situation was for him. Animals don't understand the concept of choice, or rather, that of the future. Then Mir let out a brief roar and spoke. He had made his decision.

"I leave. Protect the pride because Man says."

He set off immediately. Relieved, Bowbaq saddled up and, with the four ponies behind him, headed off toward the south, hoping he was wrong about the gravity of the situation.

But the fire that burned until morning confirmed that he was not.

The Council meeting was shaping up to be a very long one indeed. As was custom, they dealt first with the simple daily affairs. And today it seemed that each of the twenty-eight Mothers, representing as many villages, had her share of proposals, claims, and questions to bring forward. Even the three Mothers responsible for the welfare of the capital, Kaul, who under normal circumstances monopolized this stage of the debates, appeared overwhelmed.

Corenn sunk into her chair in resignation. During the nineteen years that she had sat on the Council, she had learned patience. Fifteen years ago, she herself had ardently defended the local interests of a small town in the Matriarchy; now she worked on behalf of the entire State.

She was the Mother charged with Tradition; in other words, the guardian of institutions. For a few years now, since the death of her predecessor, Corenn's duty had been to uphold the State's integrity and to ensure respect from its citizens. Despite help from her subordinates, she herself was often on the road to soothe angered citizens in some village, to organize elections in another, or to ensure the proper use of power elsewhere still.

Her authority in the Matriarchy was so great that even at this very moment, right here at the Council, she could, for example, command silence from any of the elected Mothers for failure to comply with the right of seniority.

Her nomination by the Ancestress had prompted numerous protests at that time, especially on behalf of older women who believed they were the ones who rightfully deserved this permanent seat. But Corenn proved her effectiveness and her unfailing wisdom in exercising the judicial powers she commanded, managing the majority of the matters the Mothers brought to her by means of diplomacy alone. It was in this way, little by little, that she had earned the trust and often the friendship of her peers, especially after the Ancestress had placed each of the older Mothers in other important positions, such as the Mothers charged with Justice, the Treasury, and Resources.

After a while, everyone admitted that the Ancestress had made the right choice.

Corenn was also entrusted with a secondary duty, which was unofficial and known only to the permanent members of the Council.

She was responsible for spotting, among the countless Kauliens she met during her travels, those who seemed to demonstrate an aptitude for using magic. She herself was a mage, though she rarely called on her powers, which she deemed rather weak.

Each time something extraordinary was reported in one province or another, each time something seemingly impossible occurred, Corenn arrived on the scene. She made inquiries, observed, and, far too rarely for her liking, found an individual who might possess the talent.

Without revealing anything, she would then ask the individual his, or more often her, opinion on magic, the Matriarchy, and the idea of starting a new life. When the answers were satisfactory, which was generally the case, Corenn offered a trial, requesting the utmost discretion. Among the twenty individuals she had seen, only twice were the trials crowned with success.

In both of these cases, Corenn had passed on her knowledge to her recruits, both women. The Mother of Global Relations now employed them, needless to say, as spies. The Permanent Council's intention had been to bring together enough mages to restore the legendary grandeur of former Mothers; the objective still seemed far from being realized.

The debates followed one after another. The Tradition Corenn guarded required her to attend all of the meetings. But her intervention was rarely necessary; the majority of the matters brought forth during the Councils of Villages mainly had to do with food, trade, security, or other domestic themes. For fifteen years, it was always the same problems.

So she waited patiently, voting when a consultation was asked of her, and casting a stern look when a young Representative raised her voice a little too much in the presence of her elders, which was usually enough to restore a more respectful attitude from the tactless individual. Finally, the Mother of Recollection reread the decisions made that particular day, and reminded the Council of the matters they still needed to debate. The village representatives then left the enormous meeting room.

Only sixteen people stayed in the room: the Permanent Council, which now had to debate the important matters previously brought forth, in addition to matters concerning the whole of the country as well as its neighbors.

In the past, they had asked Corenn to report on her search for magicians. For a long time now, that no longer interested many members. And so they went straight to foreign affairs.

The discourse on trade, taxes, and international competition annoyed her even more than the village quarrels. Unfortunately, this part was the most time-consuming.

Then the Mother of Global Relations proudly announced the final ratification of a peace treaty with Romine. Everyone applauded and congratulated her. Though for some time now Romine had no longer deserved its title of High Kingdom and only had a very weak military force, it was still best to ensure neighborly relations.

They then discussed an increase in port traffic, a problem that had just been brought before the Council of Villages and hadn't been resolved. The Mothers attempted to draft a piece of legislation, but it quickly became clear that none of them were very knowledgeable on the subject. They decided to carry out a study and consult an expert, a task entrusted to the Memory committee. They would then revisit the matter.

Since they had already made significant progress in the day's agenda and the principal matters had already been looked over, the Ancestress suggested that they take up the remaining business the following dékade. Everyone accepted with relief, as they were weary from the string of meetings, which had gone from the third to the sixth deciday.

Corenn was gathering her things when Wyrmandis, the Mother of Justice, approached her.

"Do you know a Xan? He's a sculptor from Partacle, I believe."

Yes, she knew him well. He was the one in charge of organizing the upcoming meeting of the heirs. He and Corenn corresponded regularly; she truly admired the gentle and thoughtful man, one of the few who didn't consider the gift of magic a monstrous deformity, but rather a talent, a skill to be perfected.

"Yes, actually. How did you know?"

"I'm sorry to inform you, but he's dead."

Corenn was shaken. Wyrmandis waited a while, uncomfortably. She seemed to be waiting impatiently for the questions that Corenn was inevitably going to ask her.

"What happened to him?"

"He was killed in his own home, along with his wife and three children. I'm sorry," she repeated.

Ermeil too. Richa. Garolfo. And what was the youngest's name again? She couldn't remember anymore. Dead. All of them were dead.

"They didn't suffer. I believe they were sleeping when it happened. According to the information I received from Goran, they were poisoned."

Corenn swallowed painfully. Weakened by shock, her voice was merely a murmur.

"Poisoned? They were murdered?"

"Yes. In fact…"

Wyrmandis pulled her to the side and lowered her voice.

"It's almost certain that it was the Züu. That's why I received the information."

Corenn understood. The Züu hadn't set foot in Kaul for decades, and everyone wanted it to stay that way. The Justice committee was responsible for keeping a close watch on the murderers' activities the world over.

"But why? Why would the Züu have wanted to eliminate Xan and his family? Who would have wanted that?"

"I have no idea. I was hoping you could tell me. The Goranese are also baffled. Recently the Züu have been going after a number of people who are nothing like their usual targets, which include nobility, priests, and bourgeois."

A terrible suspicion suddenly came over Corenn, leaving her frozen in horror.

"Do you have the names of these people? Of the unusual victims, I mean."

"Yes, of course I do; they're included in my report. I can recite a few by memory: there was a Goranese soldier, a Lorelien nobleman, a Sailor from Lineh, or from Yiteh, I believe, and an herbalist from Pont..."

Corenn felt as if the ground had split open right under her feet. She knew all of them, personally or by name. Nort', Kercyan, Ramur, Sofi...almost all of them were her friends. And all of them were heirs of Ji.

Wyrmandis ended her morbid recital once she saw how pale her listener had gone. Corenn was swaying when she came to her senses and asked solemnly, "Please tell me, but only if you're absolutely certain...was a Kaulienne killed by the Züu? A young woman named Léti?"

"No, fortunately not one Kaulien has been killed. Not as of last night, in any case. What is it?"

The mage let out a sigh of relief, ignoring the question. Her little Léti, her only family, the light of her life, was unharmed. Léti was her cousin's daughter, but since her cousin's disappearance, she treated the girl as her own.

"I must leave at once. My niece is in danger, and"—she realized as she spoke—"so am I. Wyrmandis, I need that list as soon as possible. Can you have it brought to me in my quarters?"

Wyrmandis frowned as she listened to Corenn, answering her plea with a stare. This all seemed grave.

"You think the Züu are after you? The Züu? I think it would be best if you told me everything. I will do what's necessary to protect you."

"I can't," she replied, as she hurried off. "I may not get there in time."

She turned to Wyrmandis as she walked and said, "As for protecting us"—she shot a glance around the huge room, staring pointedly at the few fat-bellied soldiers who guarded the exits, the deserving veterans of the Matriarchy's small army—"you know that's impossible."

She practically ran through the long hallways leading to her personal quarters in the Grand House.

For the first time in a long time, the mage was afraid.

———

"By all the gods and their whores!"

Reyan was truly furious. He had deployed his entire seductive arsenal for this damsel. He had brought her to all of the fashionable places; he had bought her a meal, drinks, and, above all else, entry to the finest establishments in Lorelia. And the ungrateful wench had refused him hospitality and a little bit of tenderness for the night, flat out slamming the door in his face.

Things had looked so promising. At the end of the performance that day, he used his charmer's trick once again. Instead of the retort originally written by Barle—"I cannot because I love another, forget me!"—Reyan had declaimed, "I cannot because I love another; it is thee!" bringing some previously identified girl onstage, who was alone and certainly had an appealing physique.

Barle, the head of the acting troupe, had cried out in protest when his young actor followed such an inspiration for the first time. But he became more tolerant, given the comic success of this text bending. Fortunately, Barle had a good sense of spectacle.

After the show, Reyan had, as usual, offered his prey a drink. This decisive step taken, he showed her his caravan and presented her to each of his companions, nonchalantly mentioning his numerous voyages and his often totally fictional triumphs before the royal courts. Normally, at that point, his victory was sealed.

Seated in front of a goblet, Reyan had moved on to a performance of flattery, praising his companion's beauty, noble bearing, disposition, and other real or imaginary qualities. Perhaps she was an actress? She would surely become a great performer...

His efforts were followed, at last, by a nighttime stroll, punctuated by visits to bars and taverns, until the moment when he finally thought himself ready to conquer the beauty's bed.

Only this time, the evening was a failure, and he found himself walking alone in the dark. Just to make matters worse, a thunderstorm cracked overhead.

He violently stomped his foot into a deep puddle, splashing water everywhere. He was soaked anyway.

He didn't always have to use all of these strategies. Usually his youth, charm, and a few witty words could storm most feminine...ramparts. He was frustrated to have expended such efforts in vain. The woman was simply selfish, he decided, amused at the same time by his own bad faith. No other woman, no matter how insensitive, would have left him searching for a bed like this.

"Sleeping" with a harlot was out of the question. His days of such debauchery had certainly come and gone, even if he still had some friends in the Three-Steps Guild.

Barle had surely locked down the caravan, and it was better for his health to sleep out under the stars than to wake up Barle, who was getting surlier with age. That left the inns, but Reyan knew that he had spent enough terces for the night. No, he had another idea in mind.

Despite their slight disagreements, Mess wouldn't refuse his cousin some hospitality for the night. Especially if he could be made to recall that his house was, after all, their house, inherited in equal parts from their grandmother. Under this battering rain, he wanted just once to be recognized as a Kercyan. He wanted to be recognized as anything at all.

He stopped at a crossroad. Was it left or straight? Despite having grown up in Lorelia, he wasn't completely sure which way to go. Truth be told, he tried to take a shortcut, dipping off into the narrow alleyways of the old neighborhoods, and maybe he had overestimated his knowledge of the largest city in the known world.

Out of instinct, he went straight and was rewarded with the sight of the Cheesemakers' courtyard. The old family home wasn't very far, on the Money Changer's street, after the Small-Horse courtyard on his left.

A tremendous flash streaked across the sky, and thunder boomed shortly after. Reyan hurried his step.

Finally, he drew close to the building. It was certainly large, but ancient, very ancient. His great-great-grandfather, whose name he carried, had acquired the house more than a century ago, and it was already old in that time. For the young actor, it symbolized the fall of the Kercyan family, a story his parents had repeated over and over throughout his childhood. But tonight it represented, more than anything else, a roof over his head and an inviting bed.

The tricky part was going to be getting in without "disturbing" Mess, who wouldn't hesitate to turn him out, and Reyan had had enough doors slammed in his face for the night. So he would simply skip asking his cousin's permission to stay in his own house.

All he had to do was use the same entrance he had always used to sneak out without his grandmother knowing, to visit the brothels, seedy taverns, or other fine establishments of the Lorelien nightlife. Yes, at one time, he truly was depraved.

He hoisted himself onto the wall above the interior courtyard, accessible from Firebrand Street. In his time, their dog Baron guarded this courtyard, and Reyan had to remember to offer a treat to buy Baron's silence. Now anyone could enter; he was a bit annoyed by Mess's carelessness, though it made things easier for him.

The hardest part was to walk, as on a tightrope, the whole length of the wall, which rose higher until it joined the common room's little terrace. Some metallic spikes and miniature gargoyles were embedded in the top to discourage attempts of this type, but they typically did not present any true obstacles. But today it had rained, and the rock was slippery.

Reyan had fallen only once, one day when, on top of his habitual intoxication, he had chewed the dried roots of some plant imported from the Lower Kingdoms. He woke up a little before dawn, laid out on the cobblestones with Baron licking his face, and he'd had just enough time to slip into his room before his grandmother discovered him. He had never again smoked, breathed, or ingested any dubious plant or powder, no matter what its origins.

The darkness was illuminated by a lightning strike and he ducked, letting out a curse in the thunder. He could not let himself get picked up by the watchmen; he would have a difficult time explaining why he was breaking into his own house. Worse yet, Mess wouldn't necessarily confirm his story.

Finally, he reached the small terrace. The game was practically won; it was down to the final play. By gripping the decorative reliefs, he climbed the facade until he reached the little cornice two steps above him. All this seemed more difficult than it used to be. No doubt this was merely due to lack of practice. Then, once perched on the ledge, he pulled on the wooden shutter that covered the window to the third-floor hallway, praying to all the gods and their whores that Mess hadn't locked or closed it.

The wood scraped against the rock and the hinges creaked, but the shutter opened. Reyan hoped that the noise would be drowned out by that of the storm and wouldn't wake his cousin. He waited for another rumble of thunder before slipping into the house and closing the shutters behind him.

For a moment, he delighted in the simple pleasure of no more rain falling on his head. Then he listened closely for the sound of footsteps, but all he heard was the pitter-patter of water droplets dripping off his clothes onto the floor.

He took off his cape and his soaked shoes and rolled them up together. The bundle under his arm, he headed for his old bedroom. His cousin had no doubt kept it the same as always. It had been that way for a century, and Mess was attached to tradition, to their ancestor's historic patrimony and other drivel of the same sort meant to prevent moving even a stick of furniture.

He passed in front of two doors opening to empty rooms, and then, after a final turn in the hallway, he arrived at his destination.

Reyan noticed a strange odor wafting through the air; he glanced toward Mess's bedroom across the hall.

His door wasn't closed.

Perhaps his cousin was not at home? It would really be a shame to have put forth so much effort at discretion in an empty house! He wanted to know for sure, and approached the door.

The odor was immediately stronger and Reyan felt uneasy; a morbid idea began to form in his mind.

He pushed open the door with the back of his hand and reeled, pinching his nose shut.

A corpse was lying there. Mess.

A flash of lightning illuminated the room, and Reyan was certain. The odor was awful, penetrating, and he had to muster his courage before approaching the bed.

There were no obvious signs pointing to the cause of death. Mess's face didn't look tense, and he was wearing his nightclothes. Reyan could only conclude that it had happened in his sleep, and that someone had touched the body afterward.

Someone had laid him out on top of the covers. Someone had pushed his legs together, stretched his arms out, and tilted his head back slightly. Someone had pulled his clothes over his limbs. So why did they then abandon the body?

The odor became unbearable and Reyan turned away.

Thunder clapped and someone was in the doorway.

Someone, or something.

Reyan would keep each detail of this moment with him forever. A man with a dagger and wearing a scarlet tunic was watching him silently. He was bald and his face was painted: black eye sockets, black nose, black ears, all set against white face paint. Altogether, it had the morbid appearance of a human skull. A monstrous, expressionless skull, lifeless except for two blazing flames: the eyes of a demon.

The actor was well traveled and could recognize what stood before him. One of the messengers of Zuïa, a furious madman, a cursed Zü killer.

In the flash of light, the thing spoke. His voice was guttural and his pronunciation of Lorelien very odd. Reyan wondered, while reproaching himself for the detachment he felt now, at the hour of his demise, if this was part of the usual assassin mise-en-scène.

"Are you ready to appear before Zuïa?"

The actor didn't waste any time answering and charged at the intruder, throwing his cape and shoes at his face. He kicked the disoriented assassin and ran down the hallway.

His dagger. His poison dagger.

Did he touch it? No, he didn't think so.

He ran past his grandmother's old bedroom and then hurtled down the stairs to the second floor. The Zü was already on his heels, just three steps behind, maybe fewer. Reyan expected to feel that lethal steel penetrate his flesh at any moment, and the mental image gave him speed. He ran the length of the hallway in ten strides, came to the top of the staircase that would lead him to the ground floor, then threw himself down.

The Zü stumbled heavily over his body and flew right down the stairs. Reyan didn't waste any time perusing the result and stood up to run toward the other stairway, which he leaped halfway down. He jumped over the rail and landed on the ground as the Zü was getting up, apparently unscathed. The Zü started down the rest of the stairs, no doubt grumbling threats and insults all the way.

The actor was already making for a distant door, which he threw open and ran through. The library—there were weapons in the library. He pulled down the first one he saw, and the

Zü charged into the room, barely sidestepping an axe blow that Reyan had delivered too early.

The two men faced one another, each studying the other with the hope of surprising him in the darkness separating two lightning strikes. In normal combat, Reyan would have had the advantage with his weapon, but right now, with the help of the poison, the Zü would only have to touch him once to strike him down.

The actor never had much practice with weapons; he didn't even carry one. The training he received in his youth was limited to the classic swords of the Lorelien nobility: thirty-five-pound blades anyone would struggle to handle. This skill only came in handy during a performance.

Before playing with Barle, he was also a member of a little circus troupe, for which he performed a number—a pathetic one, at that—that involved throwing knives. But the weapons hanging on the walls here had nothing in common with the perfectly balanced knives from the circus. Maybe he could still try?

A flash revealed that the Zü had shifted to his left, and Reyan, surprised, reeled back with a cry. Luckily, the thunderstorm was at its peak, and the flashes followed each other quickly enough that the adversaries didn't lose sight of each other for very long.

Be that as it may, in this little game the assassin would have the upper hand sooner or later.

The room went dark again and the actor randomly struck in all directions, as he had been doing up until now, hoping to injure the Zü—or at least prevent him from coming closer. The scene was lit up, then hidden again.

The killer seemed to be enjoying the scene, teasing the actor left and right, closer and closer each time. Reyan realized suddenly that he was nothing but anonymous prey for the Zü, and this horrified him.

He made his decision and immediately put his plan into action.

The glow of a lightning strike gone, he launched his axe in what he supposed was the direction of the Zü and flung himself toward the wall. His fingers grabbed at a metallic object; he pulled it down immediately and found himself with a bastard sword in hand.

A clap of thunder filled the room: he didn't hear a cry or the fall of an axe. Calm restored, he listened, breathless in the fading light.

The intervals were getting longer, and this silent wait seemed to last an eternity.

The light returned to reveal a corpse. The axe had struck the Zü square in the forehead. Reyan drew near and mercilessly stabbed the point of the sword in the Zü's throat, just in case.

Armed with a crossbow, he went through the house cautiously, locking every door and checking every dark corner. Reassured, he came back to the assassin's body and searched him from head to toe.

He found a skeleton key, which he quickly slipped into his own pocket, a little wooden flask, a spool of thread, a little box containing a moist brown paste, a red headband, and, most importantly, a parchment. The little flask and the box must contain the poison and the antidote…or the antidote and the poison. He would figure that out later. The rest was insignificant, except for the paper, which he unfolded with care.

As he feared, he couldn't decipher it. Reyan knew and read several languages, but this one was not Lorelien, nor Ithare, nor Goranese, much less Romine. It was most likely Ramzü, given the bearer's nationality.

He recognized some words, however, which were always written the same way as long as the Ithare alphabet was used.

Mess Kercyan

Reyan Kercyan

And names of other people Reyan knew of, along with their presumed addresses. He knew their commonality right away.

First, they were all Lorelien.

Second, they were all the damned heirs of that damned island, Ji.

It seemed he wasn't through with the story that was ruining his life. All through his childhood, he had been told about Reyan the Elder, who preferred to lose everything rather than break an oath. But Reyan had never asked for that! Was the family truly happier being modest yet honorable?

Now someone was organizing a hunt. Had he asked to be the prey?

He kicked the body twice. It was pointless, but it made him feel better.

He pondered this for a bit longer and came to a decision.

If these Züu wanted him dead, his only chance was to fade into the wild. To exile himself for a few years, just until things settled down. To the Old Countries, maybe.

"Curses!"

He kicked the body again, and read through the parchment once more.

He vaguely knew some of these people. He had met them when his grandmother dragged him and Mess to one of those ridiculous gatherings. Presumably they were all in danger, or already dead.

But that wasn't his problem; it was theirs!

He let out a heavy sigh. He'd had better days. And his conscience wasn't done tormenting him…

He gathered up his battle trophies, then moved from room to room putting together a small pack. He brought everything upstairs to the second-floor window and prepared to go back out into the night; better to avoid the front door, which could be watched.

He changed his mind, came back to the library and chose two knives. One he slipped into his boot, the other in his belt. Then he retrieved the Zü's dagger and the bloody sword, for which he grabbed a scabbard. Loaded with these tools, he was glancing over the room one last time when a final idea came to him. He returned to the corpse and removed his clothes. An official Züu outfit could surely be useful for something.

And Reyan didn't know what the future might bring.

⸺⸻⸺

The Day of the Falcon began that morning.

The Day of the Promise was only a dékade away: the dékade of the Unsure.

Yan, fifteen years old and a modest fisherman from a small Kaulien village, realized that these ten days would earn their name as they never had before.

Though he had considered the problem from every angle, he didn't yet know how to strike up the courage to ask for Léti's hand.

He had seen enough celebrations of the Promise to know what was expected. The suitors seeking a Union had to obtain their loved one's agreement before nightfall, when the whole village would celebrate the engagements.

Of course, you could exchange vows at whatever time of the year you wished, but Yan knew how tied Léti was to traditions and that she would most certainly be infuriated if he dared to even discuss the subject on any day other than the ones set forth by the cult of Eurydis.

No, he really had to gather his courage. He had to ask for Léti's hand in the next dékade. Otherwise he would have to delay his plan until the following year.

Curses, curses...

He had never realized that these rituals, which amused him under normal circumstances, became so restrictive when one was actually faced with them. Proposal, Promise, Witness, Union—there were so many steps to complete, and in front of the whole village, just so he could live with Léti! Not to mention the mockery and bawdy sarcasm that came along with the Day of the Virgin, the Day of the Mushroom, and the Day of Children, which couldn't help but increase Yan's apprehension.

The dékade of the Unsure...No, he was sure that he wanted a Union with Léti, but he was just as sure that he didn't want to face all those trying moments!

And still, these problems were nothing compared to the biggest anxiety that ate at him: Would she accept?

It's true that since they were kids everyone had always considered them promised to one another. Léti's mother, Norine, had taken Yan in as an orphan and raised him until he was deemed too old to live in decency with the two women. He then returned to live in his parents' small house, but he still spent most of his time with his adoptive family, fishing for them, working for them, even preferring to maintain their house rather than his own, which fell into ruins a little more each day. When Norine had disappeared, he took care of Léti, who had taken ill, and nursed her back to health. Now they were both orphans. Yes, in everyone's eyes, they were already promised to one another.

In everyone's eyes, but in her eyes?

Yan knew himself to be a rather mediocre fisherman of little wealth, and he didn't think himself particularly handsome or charming. He didn't have any special talents, perhaps with the exception of knowing how to read a little; he had no family to rely on, and to others he came off as a somewhat lazy dreamer.

For him, Léti was the most beautiful woman in the world. He loved her strong will, her laugh, and her zest for life. Several women in her family had become Mothers; her aunt was a member of the Permanent Council, and it was likely that she too would be elected as a Mother in a few years. She lived in the biggest house in the village, which was furnished more lavishly than all the others combined. Yes, Léti was certainly too good for him.

Yan would have done anything to be more handsome, funnier, richer, more talented, and more interesting.

For instance, he had tried to improve the traditional methods for dive fishing by using the framework of an old crossbow to build a better harpoon. But he never perfected the weapon's use, and the villagers were uninterested, deeming it too dangerous and suitable only for lazy people.

He had also spent several days with a learned traveler, eagerly drinking in his knowledge of marine birds while serving as the traveler's guide to the more interesting coves and beaches. But when he told Léti that corioles migrate as far as Northern Arkary at the beginning of the Season of Fire, she asked him how knowing that could possibly benefit him. He was still searching for an answer.

He stopped fishing for a while and successively became the apprentice to the blacksmith, the carpenter, a farmer, the miller, and even the brewer. But he was forced to give up each time, aware of the mounting irritation from each master artisan that was caused by his suggestions. His only aim, according to them, was to do the least amount of work possible. The priest was the only person left in the village who was willing to take him on, but Yan politely declined his offer. He respected Eurydis and Brosda, but he was far from devoting his life to them.

In short, he now found himself with no prospects for his future, other than to take Léti in Union.

His life would be different then. Perhaps they would move to a new village or, at the very least, travel. Above all, he could finally accompany her to that mysterious gathering she attended every year with her mother and aunt. That alone would be an exciting experience—see new places, meet strangers and, better than that, foreigners! It really would be amazing.

Well, it would be amazing if he found the courage to propose and she accepted.

Yan decided that he had worried himself sufficiently for one day and stood up. Given the position of the sun, it must have already been a deciday that he had been lying on the beach brooding, and it was time he thought about the present: what were they going to eat for dinner?

He went to inspect the holes that he had dug in the sand that morning, where he had placed a basket woven in the shape of a labyrinth. The tide had risen and fallen, leaving behind a few crabs and shells in the trap. Over time, he liked crab less and less, but he would have to settle for it since he hadn't gone out with the fishermen. Besides, Léti had surely thought to prepare some dish herself.

He placed his catch into a basket and took the path back to the village. Although he had sought solitude, he hadn't gone very far and had just over a half league to cover.

He had only been gone since morning, but he still couldn't wait to see Léti again. He had never realized, before thinking about it, how much she meant to him. For as long as he could remember, they had never spent more than a few days apart.

He had this on his mind when he got closer to the hamlet. A gang of children rushed toward him as soon as he was in view. He greeted them with a smile, which soon faded.

"Léti's gone! Léti's gone!"

The children surrounded him, tugging on his clothing; every one of them wanted to reveal a secret, but each secret was the same.

"Léti's gone! Léti's gone!"

Something roared in Yan's ears. Gone? How could she have left? Sure, until this evening, maybe. She couldn't have *really* left.

He spotted the village Mother slowly making her way toward him. He was beside her in an instant. She talked to him in an artificially reassuring tone, but with a sincerely sympathetic hand on his shoulder.

"She left at the apogee. She looked for you everywhere to warn you, but no one knew where you were. It was her aunt, the one from the Council, who came for her. She arrived in the morning. I have the feeling it was something very serious, because they left in such a hurry."

"Léti was crying!" exclaimed one of the kids, innocently.

"Where did they go?"

"My boy, Corenn requested that no one follow them, and it's most certainly wise advice. It's better that way, for—"

"Which way did Léti go?" he asked one of the children.

Fifteen fingers pointed toward the east while a chorus echoed, "That way!" and "Léti went that way!"

"Yan, wait!" the Mother commanded.

But he was already out of earshot, in a sprint toward his house. He dumped out a canvas bag and rummaged through its contents for a waterskin, two tunics, a line and a few hooks, his old fishing knife, and some dried fruit. He picked up a harpoon, then was gone as fast as he came, running in the direction where the kids had pointed.

"It's useless, you'll never catch them! They left at the apogee, and they're on horseback!" the Mother cried after him.

Yan was already beyond the bounds of the village.

———— ∞ ————

Léti refused to believe it, though she knew it all was true. All her friends, all the heirs, her adopted cousins, uncles, aunts, grand-mothers, grandfathers, they were all dead. She remembered all of their names, seeing each face in her mind as she did, and grew even sadder thinking that she would never have enough tears for them all.

Her aunt Corenn seemed just as shaken, though a bit more reserved. She hadn't said a word since they had left. Léti knew that her aunt hadn't slept the night before, riding all night to reach her niece. She must be tired; anyone could see it in her face.

They both walked slowly, leading their horses by the reins. The two animals were also exhausted; they hadn't rested since the night before either.

Léti forced herself to ask, "How far do we have to go?"

Corenn seemed to snap out of it a little. Her gaze left the ground to move toward the horizon. She cleared her throat before responding.

"I'm not sure. As far as we can, anyway. We'll leave the path to sleep for a bit soon, but I want to get a little farther."

She turned toward her niece, forcing a smile.

"Is that all right?"

"Yes, yes," Léti assured her.

The more she thought about it, the more she preferred to keep on walking, to walk forever. It made her feel like she was escaping her sadness. She knew that when they stopped, all her torments would catch up with her. Maybe it was the same for her aunt?

Mixed with the grief of all the disappearances, the image of Yan repeatedly came back to haunt her. She regretted not being able to speak to him. What if she never saw him again?

A fresh stream of tears flooded her face and she let the sadness overtake her completely. She was so happy, just yesterday. Why? Why was all of this happening?

They progressed in silence, each of them lost in her own thoughts.

By the time they heard the horses approaching, it was too late. Panicked, Corenn shoved her niece and their horses toward the bushes at the edge of the path, as she had several times before, but she was not fast enough to escape the eyes of the three men who suddenly appeared from around a bend in the trail.

They slowed down their rapid pace in perfect unison, then came to a stop before meeting the two women with a silent stare. Léti immediately understood, without knowing why, that the men approaching her were the assassins. Her aunt knew too; Corenn's hand gripped her shoulder. Then Corenn stepped in front of her niece, and resolutely faced the strangers.

They were all wearing the same red-colored tunic and had shaved heads. They could have easily been mistaken for young, innocent priests of some harmless cult. So here they were, the famous Züu killers. They didn't seem so terrible at first glance. They wouldn't, so long as you ignored the horrible reputation that preceded them and their fanatical stare. And if you also ignored the various weapons that hung here and there on the sides of their horses, and the notorious daggers resting in their sheaths.

The tallest of the three pointed toward them, barking a quick order. His acolytes quickly jumped off their horses. Léti, incredulous and helpless, saw them grab their blades and calmly approach, one directly, the other moving at an angle to cut off any escape.

This wasn't happening. She wasn't going to die here, right here, right now, like this, stabbed on a dirt road. It wasn't possible.

She wanted to run, but her legs were paralyzed, as was the rest of her body. She wanted her aunt to flee, but she knew Corenn was too tired. This could not be happening. Not like this. They couldn't die like this.

The tall one gasped suddenly, and Léti found enough energy to lift her eyes toward him.

Blood ran from his mouth. An arrowhead stuck out of his chest.

The man grabbed at it clumsily, as if drunk. A second arrow emerged from his body as if by magic, a half foot above the other. The Zü's eyes rolled back and he slid off his horse.

Thirty yards away, a man in black lifted his bow. The two remaining killers immediately reacted and rushed for the bushes. One of them wasn't fast enough and let out a gurgle as an arrow passed through his throat. He collapsed, drowning in his own blood.

The two women hadn't moved an inch. Léti felt incapable of moving. Her eyes went from the man in black to the two corpses, from the corpses to the man in black, and she couldn't do anything but watch, transfixed by the battle that unfolded before her.

The stranger grabbed his sword and stuck it in the ground. Calmly, deftly, he aimed his bow toward the bushes in front of him. The Zü charged with fury, running straight at him; the arrow flew two fingers above his head. The stranger dropped the now useless weapon and hurriedly seized his blade. The two men faced each other, the assassin ready to pounce, his knees bent and his hand clenching his dagger, the man in black holding him off with his sword extended. Then, it happened in an instant.

The Zü launched himself so quickly that even though Léti was waiting for it, she was surprised. But the stranger reacted just as quickly, as if he had known what his adversary would try. His blade gleamed, and the Zü's hand was sliced and his stomach opened in a swift dance of steel. Léti saw the man's guts gush out onto his legs and the ground, despite his desperate efforts to hold them in with a bloody arm.

Her will gave way and she fainted in a heap.

―∞∞―

Yan felt his hope dwindling by the moment. It had been dark for a while now, and cutting through the scrubland of Southern Kaul no longer seemed like a good idea.

He had made a mistake. The light of the moon wasn't bright enough to illuminate the way; it couldn't break through the thick layer of foliage that hung above him most of the time. His legs, arms, and face were irritated, scratched, and even cut in areas by the brambles and the other plants that formed the dense maze of shrubbery, and he had fallen several times. He was only a few decidays into his trek, and he was already hurting all over; he was covered in mud, his clothes were torn to shreds, and his hair disheveled.

The worst was that he was beginning to doubt his bearings. Was he still headed in the right direction? Or was he lost?

On two separate occasions he had the feeling of passing the same spot twice. Navigate using the stars, sure. It was a lot easier when you could see them! In addition to the foliage, which was quite dense at times and reduced his field of vision, a haze had recently fallen, suggesting a heavy fog was on the way.

His foot caught on a root and he nearly fell again, but he just barely caught himself on a low-hanging branch that his hand happened to meet. This time he was lucky: it wasn't a thorny branch.

A family of margolins scurried away a few steps ahead. That had to have been the sixth time. The critters really had to be deaf not to hear him approaching. And to think of all the trouble he normally had trapping one!

Yan cursed himself for not thinking to bring the things necessary to build a fire. That should have been a priority during his rushed preparations, instead of the fruit or the fishing line. Everyone was right; he really was a good-for-nothing dreamer.

It was just what he needed now, to find himself face-to-face with a bear or a stray wolf. He would look really fierce with his fishing knife and his rusty harpoon.

He should have first gone to the neighboring village and got his hands on a horse. He should have found a weapon worthy of being called so. He should have taken the time to think, like he so often told others to do.

Léti must be far away. Perhaps even dead.

He delivered a furious blow with his harpoon to a wall of seda shrub that was blocking his way. A swarm of huge silvery flies took to the air, buzzing. A bat swooped in, gliding toward them, ready to make a dinner of them. Yan chased him off by waving his arms around like a madman. It was unfair, but the bat had frightened him.

He allowed himself a short break. In spite of the situation, a funny thought ran through his head: maybe Léti had already gone back to the village, and she was now worrying about him. If it were true, he would really be the King of Fools. But this idea was pleasant, since it implied a return to normal life.

Unfortunately, for now the only thing he could do was to carry on and try to find the trail.

He found it two centidays later, on the other side of a thick grove of broad-leaved trees. Relieved, he immediately scanned the horizon in both directions, hoping to make out the shapes of riders in the misty twilight. But, of course, he didn't see anything.

He was now faced with a decision. Either head back toward the village, praying that they hadn't yet made it this far, or continue east, hoping they had already stopped for the night. If they veered off the path before he caught up to them, it was likely he would never see them again.

This idea made his blood run cold, and he quickly set off toward the Lorelien border. The exhaustion of the strenuous trek was beginning to take a merciless toll on him, but he forced himself to ignore it. Besides, covering ground without stumbling on roots or trudging through thorny bushes made it much more tolerable.

The only challenge was to not lose the trail.

Rarely traveled, the trail wasn't always easy to make out. With the fog, Yan sometimes had a hard time telling the trail from the scrub. At one point, he convinced himself he had lost it again.

He ended up focusing his attention just a few steps ahead, walking with his gaze practically stuck to his feet.

He continued on that way for almost a league, when a detail, which he had nearly passed by, snapped him out of his daze.

He was just about to step on a fresh print left by a horse's hoof.

The surprising part wasn't the print itself, of course, on a road frequented by riders, but its direction.

He soon found others, quite a few even, leaving no doubt: two horses, maybe three, had recently pulled off the road into the thick scrub.

Taken by a wave of hope, Yan lunged down this new path, keeping his eye out for more clues hinting at a recent passage of animals. It was harder than he had thought, and several times he had to retrace his steps to correct his course, the darkness hardly helping matters.

During one of these moments, he realized that he might have made a mistake.

A low-hanging branch like any other, which he had brushed aside just as he had done so many times that night, didn't straighten back into its place, but fell.

A living plant that size doesn't just break.

When he examined it up close, he discovered a thin string tied to one end, more or less taut, which vanished into the bushes.

Genius. The other end of the string must have activated some sort of alarm. Yan had made enough hunting traps himself that he didn't need it spelled out.

He ran a few paces and hid. Who could possibly have put such a setup in place besides thieves? Besides people who didn't have good intentions? It wasn't Léti, or Corenn, in any case. So who was it?

Yan decided that he could live happily without knowing the answer, and began to cautiously make a wide loop back to the trail. He concentrated all his attention on being silent as he moved forward, frequently looking behind him.

Suddenly, he felt a shiver race down his spine. What if they had been attacked? Kidnapped? By those with evil intentions?

He needed reassurance. He had come this far for at least that.

After taking his knife out, he hid his bag under a branch. He also left behind his harpoon, which was too cumbersome. Then he went back to the string and began following it to its other end, cautiously keeping a bit of distance from it.

He continued for fifteen paces or so. The people at the other end had set themselves up rather far away; this did nothing but confirm his theory. As he moved forward, he heard more and more distinctly the characteristic crackling of a fire.

He abandoned the string's path and slipped away toward the camp. He covered the remaining distance practically at a crawl, with only one thing in mind: don't make a sound, whatever you do, don't make a sound.

The fire was burning at the bottom of a depression in the ground. It was surrounded so well by shrubs and seda bushes that it was impossible to see it even from twenty yards away. Three horses were tied up nearby, and two figures were lying on the ground, their backs facing Yan.

His heart leaped in his chest. He wasn't sure, but…yes, that body, there…It was Léti!

Something cold pressed against his throat. Out of the corner of his eye, he could make out the dull gleam of a blade clenched in a man's hand.

"Drop your knife. Put your hands up. Slowly," a calm voice whispered in his ear.

Yan complied, cursing himself. How did he always manage to mess things up?

The blade left his throat. For an instant he wondered if he should make a move. Not easy, in this position…

Something hit him on the back of the head and everything went black.

<hr />

"Maz Lana? Are you well?"

The priestess lifted her head. It was Rimon, the young novice, who had kindly come to comfort her. He had always been her best student as well as a loyal friend, and Lana knew she would pass on her title of Maz to him one day or another, if Eurydis allowed it.

"Yes, yes. Thank you."

"Is there anything I can do for you?"

"No, thank you. Not right now. I just need to be alone for a moment. To reflect."

"All right. I'll be outside your door. Don't hesitate to call for me if you need anything."

At the doorway, he added: "The Temple has sent a few officers. They're placing a guard around the building. You are safe."

"Very well, you can go now."

Rimon obeyed her meekly, with one last pitying look at his teacher. Sometimes Lana asked herself if she saw more than respect, more than friendship in the eyes of the young novice. But they both knew things would never go any further.

She stood and paced across the little cell that served as her home. Even though it was austere, modestly decorated, and only functionally furnished, her bedroom had always felt very comfortable. Its main appeal was the magnificent view from the window. The midday sun shimmered off the Alt's flowing waters, glistening on the Holy City's myriad domes and temples, warming the foothills before the high mountains of the Curtain range. It was such a beautiful city. Peaceful, pacifist, spared from the barbarism of the rest of the known world.

Lana closed her eyes to say a silent prayer. Wise Eurydis, why this new hardship? Hadn't she suffered enough from these recent struggles?

The morning's events invaded her memory despite her efforts to forget. She had just begun leading her disciples in a reflection on the vanity of wealth, a subject that she held particularly dear; such corruption is difficult to resist even for the wisest of the wise. They convened, as was their habit, in the gardens at the foot of Mount Fleuri, and peacefully debated the numerous references to vanity found in religious literature.

This type of teaching was open to anyone; it wasn't uncommon to see strangers sit in the circle with the order's members, out of intellectual interest or mere curiosity. So no one made any objection when a young man without a mask and wearing the common robe of a novice joined them.

The stranger kept silent, but avidly listened to each of the speakers, particularly the women. This hadn't escaped Lana, who, having merely been intrigued at the time, understood perfectly well now.

When the stranger was sure he knew who was leading the class, he jumped to his feet like a cat and leaped, brandishing a dagger.

Toward her.

Lana didn't make any movement to defend herself, and would never understand why. She saw the assassin approach her, very clearly, as if time had slowed down. And she simply told herself her earthly life was about to end.

Fortunately, or rather, unfortunately, some of her disciples reacted quickly enough to save her.

Finally, she allowed the tears to come, feeling them run down her cheeks. No one, no one deserved such a sacrifice.

Four were killed, simply grazed by that horrible dagger. Four young people who had always condemned violence. Four children who only aspired to serve Eurydis their whole lives.

Lopan, Vascal, Durenn.

Orphaëlle...

Lana let the pain overwhelm her. Poor Orphaëlle. So young, so innocent.

Tragically, the assassin realized his failure an instant after stabbing the young novice who had jumped in his path.

Halted, seized by several pairs of hands, he stabbed the terrifying weapon, which they were trying to wrest from him, straight into his own heart.

Lana had woken up in her cell, Rimon at her side. She didn't even remember fainting. He had told her the few things he knew: the Temple's officers had dispersed the curious crowd and then escorted those involved in the affair to their homes. Each of them would be questioned and placed under protection for a while.

They took justice very seriously in Ith.

Three knocks sounded at her door, and Lana went to open it, forcing herself to recover a dignified bearing. Self-pity was far from being a valued virtue in the Eurydis cult.

An old man looked at her compassionately. Short, thin, without a mask, dressed in a plain robe, and barefoot. Emaz Drékin.

"Your Excellence," she said, inviting him in.

"Come now, Lana. This is no time for protocol," he scolded gently, taking her in his delicate arms.

She returned his embrace, sobbing, her dignity ceding to emotion.

They released each other after a moment, and Lana closed the door behind them.

"Do you want an infusion?" she offered, trying to sound natural again.

"Another time, my child, another time. Before anything else, we must speak about important matters."

Lana agreed and went to sit at the small bench in front of her table, inviting the Emaz to do the same. She had a feeling that Drékin came not only as a friend, but also as a high-ranking leader of the Temple.

He sighed for a moment, searching for words, then launched into a discussion that, despite his calm tone, was nothing short of an interrogation.

"Lana, did you know this man?"

"No. Not at all."

Lana was making an effort not to burst into tears.

"Had you ever seen him before?"

"No, I don't think so. Not in my class, anyhow. Unless he was wearing a mask, of course."

The Emaz let the silence linger. He was still hesitant to speak about certain things.

"Do you know what the Züu are?" he asked her, finally.

Lana's eyes widened in fright. Yes, of course she knew. A sect of murderers who committed their crimes in the name of a judiciary goddess, that's who they were. In previous centuries, the Züu had systematically massacred all the Eurydians who disembarked on their island. How could she not know that, she who had studied the history of Ith?

"You think that...?"

She didn't finish her sentence.

"Sadly, yes. The officers found your name in a note on his body, and other details about you. It was written in Ramzü."

Lana let it sink in. She thought she had simply come across a demon. She understood now that the attempt was premeditated.

And that she was far from out of danger.

"Lana, what I ask of you now is very important. The Temple cannot allow for renewed opposition with the Züu, new martyrs, a new crusade. So, tell me why they are after you."

Lana thought for a moment, which seemed to be an eternity to the Emaz.

"Unfortunately, I do not know. I have no idea."

The old man looked disappointed.

"Ah, well. We couldn't have changed their minds anyhow, but we might have known how to protect you."

"What you're saying is awful! This means that they will try and try again until they succeed!"

"Perhaps not, my child, perhaps not. This is the other thing I must speak with you about. The Temple can arrange to shelter you, but at the price of a large sacrifice, one that you are not obliged to accept."

Lana prepared herself for the worst.

"Go on."

"Except for the young Rimon, all of your disciples are still wondering whether you've survived. The Temple has kept this information secret up until now..."

Lana was horrified.

"You aren't about to suggest that..."

"It's the best thing to do, my child. Consider it. Unfortunately, the young Orphaëlle perished in the attack. Don't let her sacrifice be in vain by dying in the next dékade."

Lana wondered how the Emaz could think such a thing. To take advantage of the young girl's misfortune.

"The witnesses will be unable to say who was killed," the Grand Priest continued. "For them, there was at least one masked woman among the victims. If we announce you are deceased, we won't need anything else to trick the Züu."

"I understand perfectly well, Your Excellency. I just need some time to think. This strategy will force me to leave Ith, won't it?"

"Unfortunately, for some time. Your salvation depends on it."

"My salvation."

Lana stood up and admired the landscape from her window with new eyes. It seemed to her already that it was the last time she would enjoy it.

"Because it is necessary, I will abandon everything I have. Everything that makes up my life. May Eurydis give me strength."

"Wise words," concluded the relieved Emaz, standing up. "It would hurt me immeasurably to lose you. We will figure out the details later; until then, I will make the arrangements I must for... for what we have decided."

He took his leave, briefly embracing her again.

Alone again, Lana argued with her conscience. She had lied to an Emaz. Blatantly. She knew why the Züu were looking for her. At least, she knew the basic cause.

Her ancestor Maz Achem, and his mysterious voyage to a small Lorelien island. The Island of Ji.

The Züu had only started her on a journey she had been planning for years.

But the Grand Temple couldn't know anything about that.

Yan slowly emerged from darkness, struggling with the throbbing pain in the back of his skull that was trying to drag him back down. He was lying on his back, and opening his eyes, all he could see was pale morning sky through the branches hanging above.

"He's waking up," announced a quavering voice. Yan's heart leaped in his chest: it was Léti's, unmistakably. He sat up too abruptly, bringing back the pain, and immediately passed out again.

When he came to, the sun was higher in the sky; it must have been the start of the third deciday. Yan propped himself up on his elbows, cautiously this time.

To his relief, he realized that he was not mistaken: Léti was sitting nearby, and she appeared to be in good health, with the exception of her eyes, reddened with tears. Her aunt was there too and stared at him disapprovingly. There was also a stranger dressed in black, facing him with an openly hostile expression on his face.

Even though he hadn't met many, Yan was almost certain that the stranger was a native of the Lower Kingdoms. He was rather short—shorter than him, at least—but the first adjective that came to mind looking at him was "imposing."

The second, definitely, was "dangerous."

He must have been in his forties, at least. That's what his appearance suggested: his leathery skin, already full of small wrinkles, his profound, somber gaze, and the gray strands among his dark head of hair. A thick mustache and an ugly scar drew crisscrossing lines on his face. He was quite obviously dressed for battle: pieces of leather solidly attached to one another, with flashes of metal here and there, from head to toe. This handmade outfit wasn't brand new anymore; it was worn at the joints, scuffed everywhere, and patched up in some places. The man carried, rather comfortably, a bare curved blade and a dagger at his waist. Yan thought to himself that he must handle those weapons just as naturally as he slipped on his tunic in the morning. And this imposing and dangerous man was staring right at him with a fiery look.

"You were told to stay in your village, were you not?" he scolded.

His strong accent was typical of the Lower Kingdoms.

Still in shock, Yan looked at Léti and her aunt with the hope of finding some support. But Léti was sobbing, her face buried in her palms, while her aunt seemed to be in agreement with the stranger. His head felt heavy. He worried that he might faint again.

"Who are you?" he managed. His throat was dry and his own speech sounded strange to his ears.

"This is Grigán," Corenn answered for the man in black. "He's...a cousin of mine. A very distant cousin."

Yan looked back at the strange man, who was nervously pacing as he stroked his mustache. This man was related to Léti?

"If it weren't for him, we would be dead by now," continued Corenn in a conciliatory tone. "He saved our lives yesterday. He won't harm you," she concluded loudly, turning to the warrior.

"We'll have to see about that," he grunted. "Are you alone? Does anyone know where you were headed? Were you followed?"

Yan's mind was clouded by the pain, and it took him some time to process all of the questions and to answer, which appeared to annoy the man—apparently called Grigán—even further.

"No, I'm alone, and I wasn't followed. I went through the scrubland. What's going on?"

The man in black stared at him for a moment.

"Are you sure?"

"If he says so, it's true. That's it. Yan isn't the type to lie, and he has no reason to."

Yan shot an appreciative look at Corenn for the unexpected intervention. But the man in black wasn't going to settle for that.

"How did you find us?"

"I spotted hoofprints at the edge of the trail. Because of the fog, I practically had my nose in the dirt."

"I think that's enough, Grigán."

"All right, all right. In any case, we can't waste any more time. We need to get back on the road as soon as possible. Which means now."

He made as if to retrieve the horses.

"And what about me, what am I to do?"

Yan wasn't at all happy with what the warrior had implied in his last comment.

"You? You can rest up if you wish; then you'll return to your village. You won't speak of this to anyone. Understood?"

It wasn't really a question.

Yan looked at Léti, who was sobbing silently. The Day of the Promise was near. This man had saved their life? Why were they in danger in the first place?

"No, I'm staying. I'm coming with you," he answered, in a voice he wished were louder.

Grigán let out a sigh of exasperation and took a few steps away from him. Yan was well aware that if it weren't for the presence of the two women, the warrior wouldn't waste his time with a boy who dared to argue with him, and would resort to more persuasive measures.

"Yan, I know you very well," attempted Corenn. "Perhaps better than you think. I've watched you grow up all these years, along with Léti. And I know you're doing this for her."

He remained silent, but avidly watched for Léti's reaction.

She didn't appear to react at all, apart from a sob that might have been louder than the others. Léti seemed to be in complete shock, overwhelmed, utterly closed off to her surroundings. Yan had seen her like this before, when Norine disappeared.

"By staying with us, you'll be putting her in danger," continued Corenn, softly. "As well as me, and Grigán, and others whom you don't know, whose survival isn't at all guaranteed and depends, in part, on ours. Not to mention, you'd put your own life in danger. Do you realize that you could have gotten yourself killed by Grigán last night? Do you see? Léti cries enough as it is, don't you think?"

The arguments were irrefutable, but Yan didn't want to admit it. He felt that, being the important diplomat she was, Corenn was trying to trick him like she would a child. The pain in his skull was throbbing more intensely, disturbing his thinking, and he got stuck on one idea: stay with Léti, stay with Léti.

"I have to come with you. I'm sorry," he added, with less resolve.

Corenn frowned, disappointed, and searched for something to say. Despite his strong will, Yan knew that in the end he would yield to reason. Or force. He had to find a way to convince them, rather than force himself in.

"The men who are after you don't know who I am. They don't even know that I'm with you. Surely, I can help you. I'm coming."

A moment of silence followed Yan's response. Then Grigán stepped away from the tree he was leaning against and quickly approached. Yan had a burning impulse to protect his face to avoid a potential blow, but that was definitely the last thing he should do if he really wanted to go with them.

The warrior squatted down next to him, stared him right in the eyes, and pointed an index finger at him. "All right, you can come. But make one false step, disobey me just once, and I'll make you regret it. And I hope you won't stick around too long."

Yan wondered whether that last remark was in reference to the likely dangers of the trip or to the promised punishment. It didn't matter; he was staying with Léti.

He agreed, completely sincere, and Grigán released him from his oppressive stare to have a word with Corenn.

Léti still hadn't moved and had kept on sobbing, her face buried in her hands. Last time this had happened—when her mother had disappeared—she had stayed like this for over a dékade. The next few days were shaping up to be just wonderful.

He realized that he hadn't spoken a word to her yet. He got up very slowly, staggered over to her, and half fell, half sat next to her. She appeared to rouse from her daze a little, threw her arms around his neck, and cried on his shoulder. He held her close to him. He'd earned that much at least.

"You will ride with her," Grigán came over to tell him. "We'll buy another horse as soon as possible."

"All right."

Yan had only ridden a horse twice in his life but didn't want to be a burden already.

"We must leave right away. We have to make it through Bénélia before tomorrow evening."

Léti stood and began gathering her things. Corenn did the same. It bothered him a little to see a Mother of the Permanent Council, one of the highest authorities in all of Kaul, obey this rather frightening stranger without question. He felt that she should be the one leading the group. But perhaps she simply shared his opinion, or maybe she was too tired to take charge.

Yan stood up then and found his own bag, his harpoon, and his fishing knife at the base of a tree. He remembered having left his things in the bushes before approaching the camp. Grigán must have been following him the whole time. He really had failed as a spy in all respects.

He went over to the horses and waited patiently for someone to tell him what to do. The man in black, busy balancing the loads, took Yan's pack and pulled out the six-foot-long harpoon.

"You have to leave this behind if you're coming. It's too cumbersome, too conspicuous, and it's useless."

He held the object out to him. Yan took it and obediently ditched it in a thorny bush. Grigán looked satisfied. He unstrapped one of the two bows he was carrying on his horse and held it out to the fisherman.

"Do you know how to use it?"

"Yes," Yan lied.

He had never held one before. But if lying would reassure the warrior...and with such a weapon, he could actually protect Léti.

"Good. Here are the arrows. Only shoot if I ask you to. And keep your distance. Never approach your target. Got it?"

"Yes."

Yan tried to appear comfortable, the quiver in one hand, the bow in the other. Curses! It was heavier than he'd thought. Could he really use it?

"Have you ever killed someone?"

"No."

By Eurydis, no, never! Did this man imagine he spent his time skewering people with his harpoon? Yan couldn't lie this time. He had never even been in a fight.

"Alright."

It seemed like Grigán had made up his mind. He turned around to load the last of the bags.

"I want a weapon too."

Léti stood in front of them with her arms crossed. She wasn't crying anymore, but her reddened face and eyes gave her a crazed look.

Grigán turned his back to her. He didn't seem inclined to give in to her demands.

"Women don't fight," he answered shortly and firmly.

Léti remained motionless in disbelief. Yan felt that she was on the verge of tears again; he held out his fishing knife.

"Here, just in case. But stay out of battle."

The man in black stared at them for a moment. Léti took the blade before he could intercept it and walked away. Yan wondered if he might have already brought an end to his career as a guardian knight, but the warrior nodded, turned back around, and led the horses away by the reins.

Corenn sent off the two young Kauliens behind Grigán, swept the camp with one last glance to make sure they hadn't forgotten anything, and followed the others toward the main trail.

She had the unmistakable feeling that it was the beginning of a very long journey.

———

A fat, somewhat reckless margolin was trying to squeeze his way into Bowbaq's reserve provisions. Bowbaq, feigning a nap, had spotted him a while ago.

It wasn't until the little glutton jumped on the pack, frantically tearing at the canvas with his teeth and claws that Bowbaq decided to intervene.

"Ho! What if I did the same to your den?"

The rodent stiffened and froze, then bolted faster than if he had been surrounded by a pack of wolves. There's no way he could have understood much from the threat, but the intrusion into his mind had driven him to panic.

That's how it always went the first time. Bowbaq remembered Mir's intensely aggressive reaction to his first attempt. Luckily, he had taken the precaution of tying her up first.

As for Wos, that was a different story. Bowbaq had been able to reach his mind before he had even come into the world. After that, the bond was much easier to maintain.

Poor Wos. Bowbaq was forced to abandon him around Cyr Heights. The giant pony, so at ease in the vast frozen expanse of Central Arkary, was already suffering cruelly in the mild climate of Northern Lorelia. He never would have made it to Berce.

Bowbaq had sent him back to Arque country, explaining that he would rejoin him soon, which had been no small feat since the animal only understood future in the immediate sense. So he had to lie, inventing something like: *"If Wos goes there, he see Bowbaq."* For the pony's peculiar perception of time, it would make little difference if he were there right away or a moon later.

So the *erjak* had been on foot since he crossed the Lorelien border. It didn't really bother him. He had often walked like this; his large size and proportionate weight prevented him from riding a common horse. And it was true he feared the ridicule he'd be in for at the sight of a man his size riding such a small animal.

The Day of the Owl was approaching; Bowbaq figured it would come eight nights after his departure. By the Big Bear—assuming he hadn't made a mistake in his calculations!—it would easily take him six days to reach his destination, and the possibility of arriving too late haunted him. Once in a while, the worry nagged him so much that he would break into a long run with his massive strides. He only slowed when he came across other people.

Although he made a point of taking only the smallest trails, the barely discernible paths, the trails made more by animals than by humans, Bowbaq met far too many strangers for his taste. True, he was in the Upper Kingdoms, and he should have anticipated seeing a lot more people than in Arkary, where his closest neighbor lived at least six leagues away. But more than the obvious need for discretion that made him seek solitude, Bowbaq hated crowds. For him, meeting more than five strangers in one day was an extremely trying experience. It took a lot for him to join all the gatherings of the heirs of Ji.

He had even overcome a sort of crisis. The night before, he'd come to the outskirts of Lermian, which he took a wide detour around, of course. But the mere proximity of the Lorelien city and the congregation of travelers near it were enough to unsettle him for a while. He experienced a moment of hesitation, asking himself what he was doing there. Dékades away from Ipsen and the kids, and likely running straight into danger.

Fortunately it passed as quickly as it had come, his sense of duty having won out. He had to see the heirs, to warn them. They were his only friends.

He packed up his things, checked the straps on his bags, and ran.

Yan couldn't help but feel awkward and unconfident with Léti as his passenger; after all, he had only mounted a horse twice in his whole life. Corenn noticed and gave him some advice to help him get properly situated, while Grigán, exasperated, made his horse stamp impatiently. He practically lived on horseback and was an accomplished rider. He had a hard time understanding how someone could be so clumsy.

They set off at a slow, steady trot. As they moved along, the man in black frequently rode out ahead of the group to scout the horizon from the top of any significant rise in the trail. Léti rested her cheek against her friend's back and eventually nodded off. Yan felt a pride that he knew was childish and undeserved, to be traveling with his beloved in unknown lands, like a valiant knight with his princess.

But it was far from being a pleasure ride; there was more than one shadow in the picture.

He began a conversation with Corenn, in a low voice.

"You said that Grigán saved your lives, didn't you? What happened?"

Corenn sighed and reflected before answering.

"There are men who want to kill us. Not just some isolated clan, but an organized group. They're called the Züu killers. Have you heard of them?"

"No."

"They're part of a religious sect, the Hand of Zuïa. Have you heard of Zuïa?"

Yan remembered reading something that sounded similar, in one of the few books that passed through his hands, but he hadn't been sure how to pronounce it.

"It's an island in the Sea of Fire, isn't it?"

"That's right. And it's also the name of the inhabitants' chief goddess. She's a judiciary goddess, whom you must appear before once her messengers have delivered her sentence…"

Corenn broke off, her eyes troubled. She must have recalled some very painful events. Yan was prepared to leave her to her reverie, but she continued with her explanation, making a visible effort to control herself.

"In reality, the messengers are nothing more than assassins whom anyone can hire by making an offering to the cult. But the Züu explain it by invoking predestination and divine will: if someone pays for the death of another, Zuïa is the one who condemns the second through the voice of the first. I swear, they're completely convinced."

Yan remained pensive for a moment before responding. "Why would someone want to kill Léti? And you, I mean?"

"We're unsure of the real reason. All we know is it appears that someone is trying to eliminate all of the heirs."

Yan didn't say anything.

"You know who the heirs are, don't you? Léti must have spoken to you about them?"

"To be honest, we never talk about it. The secret is sacred to her. All I know is that it has something to do with your ancestors."

"In light of the circumstances, I think it's best that you know everything."

Corenn told him the story of Nol and the emissaries, their descendants, the gatherings on the Day of the Owl, and of the lingering mystery surrounding the adventure, forgotten by almost everyone. It did her some good to share these things that she hardly ever spoke about with strangers.

Yan, fascinated by the tale, now understood Léti and her respect for tradition much better. He felt even closer to her, but at the same time more distant. He wasn't one of the famous heirs.

Corenn ended her story with the news of her friends' brutal deaths, her frantic ride to Eza, and their journey up until their encounter with Grigán and the assassins.

"Grigán is a descendant of Rafa Derkel. The three Züu who attacked us were initially after him, in Bénélia. But they didn't find him, and in the end he was the one who followed them to their next target."

Corenn went silent.

"We would have died yesterday."

It seemed that she wanted to draw the conversation to a close. Yan waited patiently at her side in silence for a moment, and then rode ahead to the warrior.

"Corenn just told me what happened. How did you manage to escape the Züu in Bénélia?"

Grigán stared at him curiously, making Yan feel awkward.

"Do you suspect me of something?"

"No, of course not!" he exclaimed. "I'm just curious."

The warrior paused to gauge the fisherman's sincerity.

"The Züu aren't the only ones who want my hide. If I didn't constantly watch my back, I would have been dead long ago."

He left Yan there, and took his horse off at a gallop toward the crest of the next hill.

He really was an odd character. They were lucky to have him, Yan thought.

Corenn caught back up to him, smiling. "I don't know what you said to him, but remember, if you annoy him, he'll hurt you!" she said, pulling a face and imitating Grigán's accent.

Yan returned her smile. Fortunately, not all of his companions were like the taciturn warrior. Otherwise their ride would seem a lot longer.

It suddenly dawned on him that he didn't even know where they were headed.

"Are we fleeing aimlessly, or do we actually have a destination?"

"No, we're not on the run. If we were, we would be going the other way," said the Mother, pointing west. "We have to try to meet up with the other heirs. Maybe one of them has some important information. And we'll go from there."

"How will we find the others?"

He guessed as soon as he asked.

"Of course. Berce. Your usual meeting spot. That's where all the survivors will go."

Corenn nodded.

Yan continued, "I suppose you've already thought of this, but if the killers are as well-informed and effective as you say, won't they also come to the same conclusion and be waiting for us there?"

"Yes, certainly. Unfortunately, it's the best solution we have. We'll make it work."

Yan's expression went grim. There was bound to be a lot of making things work over the next few days. It's not that he was against a little bit of adventure, but he was hardly thrilled at the prospect of heading straight into the lion's den.

"Do you think we'll manage to meet up with many others?"

"I hope so. I would hate to discover that we're the only three left. But looking over my list..."

She didn't finish her sentence. They just stared at each other in silence.

"How many of you are there? I mean, how many of you were there before?"

"I don't know exactly. Maybe seventy or eighty, but there must have been some births over the past three years. And not everyone came to the gatherings, far from it. I can't place a face to nearly half of them. Furthermore, I'm sure some are even ignorant of their entire history. Xan had hoped to bring everyone together this year, something that hasn't been done in a long time."

Yan made a quick mental calculation.

"There still aren't too many of you. If you estimate two children per generation, for a little more than a century, there can hardly be more than a hundred of you."

"Yes, that's true. Perhaps it's better that way, given the circumstances."

"And how many are dead?"

"According to my list, thirty-one adults and children."

Corenn swallowed painfully, then turned away.

"But it is certainly incomplete."

Yan didn't question her further. In spite of her efforts to control herself, it was obvious that the Mother was again on the verge of tears.

And he too took some time to contemplate the weight of the circumstances.

⸺⸺

They stopped for lunch at the top of a hill, where they could survey the comings and goings of riders on the road. Grigán isolated himself from the group, sitting under the trees, and spent the whole time scanning the horizon. Léti looked much better; a bit of sleep, even on horseback, had done her good. They exchanged few words and were soon back on the road, Grigán's anxiety having infected them all.

Léti rode with Corenn. Even though he could handle his horse more easily now, Yan regretted the absence of his beloved leaning against his back. But they had to alternate, in order to keep both mounts fresh.

The rest of the day was going to be monotonous; Yan was completely sure of it after they'd covered a few leagues with no trouble. Since none of his companions were speaking—all of them lost in thought—Yan decided to stifle his impatience and observe the landscape. But he quickly grew weary of the many plants covering the horizon, ones that could easily be found close to Eza. So it almost pleased him to see Grigán return somewhat agitated from one of his reconnaissance patrols.

"A horseman's catching up to us, at a swift gallop. He's wearing a priest's robe."

"A red robe?" Léti asked in an acid tone.

"No. But that doesn't mean anything."

"Do you think it's a Zü?"

"No, I don't think so. They travel in groups, most of the time. But I wouldn't bet my life on it."

"Are you certain that the three who attacked you yesterday are dead?" Yan interjected.

"Deader than the kings of Lermian," responded the warrior with a frightening grin. "Even if I'm never the first to attack, I don't leave my enemies alive. It's a basic rule of survival."

Yan had a vision of Grigán sadistically cutting the throats of dying men, as they pleaded and screamed. He banished the thought, horrified. He certainly wanted to believe that he would strike to kill in a battle.

"What do you suggest we do?" Corenn asked.

"We hide. One should always avoid combat when one can."

"So, we have to hide like this every time we see somebody?"

Three surprised faces turned toward Léti. Her tone had been almost angry.

"No, of course not," her aunt responded in a soothing tone. "But, for now, it's the best thing to do. There's no need to take any risks; our lives are at stake, after all. You understand, don't you?"

"It's just a passing horseman," Léti retorted, sulking. "Even if he is a Zü, he's alone. Grigán could kill him easily."

"Do you even know what you're saying?"

The young girl didn't answer. Perhaps she really had gone too far.

Grigán shook his head while leading the group to take cover in the trees, where they dismounted. Corenn tried to make her niece think more sensibly about the situation.

"The trail we're on is the fastest way to get from Kaul to Lorelia; actually, it's just about the only one. The Züu will inevitably patrol it, if they suspect we're headed for Berce, don't you see?"

"Yes, yes," blurted the young girl, exasperated but not convinced.

"We're not going to have to hide all the time; we're only doing so now because there's a distinct possibility that the horseman is one of the assassins hunting us. Once we've passed Bénélia, we'll be able to breath a lot easier. They can't keep a watch on all the Lorelien routes, at least not without using hundreds of men."

"Lady Corenn, you've understood the situation perfectly. Of course, I expected nothing less from you."

"Thank you, Master Grigán."

Yan kept out of the conversation, and certainly didn't allow himself to take sides. The last thing he needed was to get mixed up in an argument. Unfortunately, he was sure that one or the other was going to ask his opinion on the matter.

"Take your bow and follow me," Grigán said. "Léti, if you've finished your tantrum, try to calm this horse down, please."

"Where are you going? I want to come with you."

The warrior didn't respond as he turned toward the trail. Yan shot an apologetic and resigned glance toward Léti and followed Grigán.

Léti had never been so humiliated. She was filled with so much rage, she felt as though she could tear down a tree with her bare hands.

She went to see the rebellious horse and silenced it with just a look. The poor animal had the good sense to obey.

Léti paced about for a while, and then couldn't take it anymore, letting her anger course through her.

"Aunt Corenn! I respect Grigán, I'm happy to have him with us, and I know that we owe our lives to him. But does that give him the right to treat us like incompetent, useless fools?"

She paused for a moment before continuing.

"How can you stand him? You, a woman, a Mother of the Permanent Council?"

She regretted this final retort before even having finished it. But it was too late: Corenn, always levelheaded, the queen of diplomacy, capable of forgiving many things, fixed Léti with a stern look. Then came the sermon.

"Léti, have you ever been hunted before?"

"No," responded the young girl, embarrassed.

"Have you ever taken on the responsibility of protecting peoples' lives?"

"No. No."

"What do you know about hiding? What experience do you have with danger? Do you even know how to fight?"

"No, I don't know how to fight, I've never killed anyone, and I've never eaten raw jellyfish either. So there!"

"Grigán, unfortunately for him, has experienced and still experiences all of those horrors. Furthermore, he invariably acts in the interest of our well-being, and we must trust him."

"I'm not saying otherwise! It's just, why did he ask Yan to help him and not me?"

"That has nothing to do with you. It's due to his education, his convictions. For him, as for any native of the Lower Kingdoms, women should not fight. And if I were you, I would immediately give up any effort to change his mind."

"But that's stupid! There are women in the Matriarchy's army with the same titles as men, who do just as well as them!"

"You think so? There are some female captains, sure, maybe even a good number of female warriors. But are they really as effective?"

Léti was appalled. All of her education was based on equality between the sexes, even a certain feminine superiority. And here the Guardian of Traditions herself was telling her the opposite.

"You agree with him." Léti finally understood.

"In some ways. I have known Grigán for a long time, and I trust him. I'm happy to give him responsibility for our safety."

But Léti wasn't done yet.

"Well, I think he's wrong. A woman can certainly do just as well as a man for what amounts to stupidly swinging swords around."

Corenn preferred to drop the subject. The conversation was taking a turn that she didn't like at all. She definitely didn't need the only remaining member of her family to get it in her head that it was a good idea to face professional assassins one-on-one.

Yan and Grigán took up position at the edge of the forest, where they had an excellent view of the trail. The rider was closing in and would be galloping past them soon.

He was a middle-aged man, dressed in modest priest's clothes. Besides his haste, nothing about his behavior was particularly suspicious. Yan was sure he wasn't after them.

"Nock an arrow and be ready."

Grigán had stuck his curved blade in the ground in front of him and was straining to draw a bow that was even bigger than Yan's. The fisherman would have liked to wait and watch the warrior, but he didn't want to give himself away. He pulled an arrow from his quiver, laid flat on his stomach, and tried his best to nock it.

The man in black watched him in disbelief.

"Not on the ground! What are you doing!"

Yan quickly jumped to his feet and tried to play it off nonchalantly. He couldn't let Grigán realize that he had never used a bow before.

He studied his companion out of the corner of his eye and did his best to imitate him. Hold the arrow between two fingers, keep a straight arm...It looked easy enough.

"Only shoot if I do. Then reload immediately and wait for my orders."

Grigán followed the rider with his arrow for at least 120 yards, until he disappeared from view around a bend in the path. But it wasn't until the pounding of the hooves was nearly inaudible that he released the tension in his bow. Yan did exactly the same.

"There, to the left, shoot!" the warrior yelled, practically in his ear.

Yan pivoted while drawing the bow, searched for his target, and thinking he found it, released the arrow. The bowstring scraped the length of his inner arm while the arrow slid comically straight to the ground. He feverishly darted his gaze here and there among the bushes, not seeing anything.

On the other hand, he clearly felt a strong whack on his noggin from Grigán.

"You've never touched a bow in your life, have you? Just try to tell me otherwise!"

Yan straightened, angry and upset. He felt his face redden like a lubilee fruit, all the more upset at being so easy to read.

"You're crazy! You scared me! That was dangerous, you know. I could have killed someone!"

"It isn't dangerous if you know how to handle your weapon," argued the warrior, unruffled. "You shouldn't have lied to me."

Grigán's calm tone and logical argument melted Yan's anger like snow in the sun. But not his shame. He felt like a small child caught lying to his mother.

"I would much rather like to know where we actually stand. If we really had needed to defend ourselves, it would have been dangerous for you, for me, and the others."

"All right, all right. I admit I was wrong."

"Good. I consider the conversation finished. Now, let's see what can be done with you."

He went to retrieve the arrow and explained in a few sentences the proper archer's position and followed it up with a practical demonstration. Yan listened attentively, then shot again at the warrior's request. The result was satisfactory: the arrow flew straight, without the string burning his arm.

"Good. That's it. Now all you need to do is learn to aim, and for that, I'm of no use to you."

"I'm going to train so diligently you won't even have to worry about drawing your bow," Yan joked, displaying his eagerness.

They returned to their little makeshift camp. Yan still felt somewhat foolish and ashamed, but his trust in Grigán had grown. In the end, the aloof warrior had only one concern: to keep them out of harm's way.

Léti shouted violently at them upon their return.

"You were gone quite a while! What happened?"

"Nothing, everything's fine."

The warrior had no wish to waste time with unnecessary explanations.

"Grigán showed me how to draw a bow. It's more difficult than I thought, but it's not too bad once you've got the hang of it."

"Glad to hear it. I hope you have fun with your man's toy."

She left him standing there.

Yan was dumbfounded. He had gotten into arguments with Léti before, but up until then he always knew why. What had gotten into her?

Perhaps she was angry because he had taken an interest in a weapon? An object made to kill. That must be it; she scorned men because they only had a mind for destroying one another.

No, that didn't add up. Earlier, she was the one who suggested Grigán rid them of the rider without further ado.

He went to go after her, to talk, but decided against it. What could he tell her? When she was in this state, all attempts at reconciliation were useless. It was best to wait for things to settle down. Léti was still in emotional shock from the recent events, and she wasn't thinking clearly.

He could only hope that she would get over it as soon as possible.

———— ∞ ————

"Rey! Hey, Rey, is tha' you? Rey!"

Reyan muttered one of his vilest curses. Now that he had successfully gotten out of Lorelia without causing a stir, now that he had followed the entire length of the Gisland River all the way to Pont, now that he had almost left the kingdom with complete discretion, now some idiot screamed his name at the top of his lungs in the middle of the street.

Reyan waved discreetly and went to meet him. Since someone had already spotted him, best to avoid drawing more attention to himself by reacting strangely, like feigning deafness or running away.

It really bothered him that he was recognized so easily. He had spent a fair amount of time conceiving an inconspicuous disguise, using all his actor's talents to choose clothing that made him appear older, taller, and less Lorelien. Well, it's true he hadn't gone all the way and used makeup; no hairpiece or shading could hold for the whole trip. He would do better next time.

He was happy enough to be able to take these old rags. When he awoke Barle, three nights earlier, Reyan was scared for a moment that his troupe leader would finish the job started by the

Zü. But after a long critique on the good-for-nothing trouble-makers, the entertainers, the jokers, the revelers, whom Barle had sworn he would never allow to join his caravan, all of this in a voice much louder than usual, Barle had agreed to help the young actor. He had given him clothing, food, and without Reyan even asking—he hadn't yet been paid—a full purse filled with gold terces, under the sole condition that he return one day to perform with them and, of course, to reimburse him.

Barle and the rest of the troupe immediately began packing up and headed for Partacle, hoping to lure Reyan's potential—even likely—pursuers.

But all these efforts would be fruitless if he got himself caught thanks to some moron who kept wildly waving his arms at him. What was his name again? Tiric? Iryc? Rey hurried over to him.

"Do you really need to yell my name in the street like that? I'm not deaf," he said, trying to hide his anger.

"Ye' need to lay low, eh? I git ya."

Rey stared at him without saying anything. The man was visibly very satisfied with the impression he made. He offered Rey a mocking smile, revealing a set of yellowish, rotten teeth. His clothes were filthy, his hair dirty, and his breath suggested a weakness for cheap wine, drunk by the goblet.

How did he know him again? Rey remembered drinking with him and a few other drunkards, but couldn't remember on which occasion—meaning in which pub—he had met him the first time. If he were being honest, Rey knew hundreds of names and thousands of faces just like his. What did this one do for a living again?

The hideous man waddled back and forth, looking ridiculous but very sure of himself, hands in his pockets.

"Old chum, I don' know wha' you did, but you're definitely most sought after 'round here," he continued. "The Guild's offerin' two hundred terces for ye' head. But ye' knew tha' already, didn' ye'?"

The Guild. That meant he really was done for. If the Züu were ready to hire the services of organized crime to find him, he really had to leave the kingdom as soon as possible. He wouldn't be safe anywhere in Lorelia.

"Darlane had even said tha' if we didn' find ye' before Safrost's men, there'd be some blood between the gangs. The guys are whisperin' that Darlane's so scared to botch this contract that he's even ready to say to hell with the Grand Guild agreements. Old chum, there're some people who want ye' dead, that's for sure."

Safrost? Rey had heard of him before. Wasn't he the alleged chief of the Goranese Guild?

"But really, don' worry, we're friends, like brothers. It's not me who'll drop ye', even fer all tha' gold. Ye' know me."

Not that well, actually. I hardly know you at all, rat face. You work for the Guild.

Rey glanced around. It didn't seem as though someone were going to sneak up behind him to stab him in the back. Still, best not to try his luck much longer.

"Well, you understand I must leave you now. Thanks for the information. Maybe we'll see each other again someday," Reyan said, hoping to rid himself of Iryc.

"Wait! Maybe I can 'elp ye'. Tell me where ye're goin', I'll tell 'em you went the other way."

"I'm going to Romine. Try to send them toward Goran. And if you really want to do me a favor..."

He grabbed a dozen terces from his bag.

"It would be really helpful if you could buy me a horse and a little food. Now that I know all this, I can't allow myself to be spotted. All you have to do is bring everything to me at the Pont Inn; you know where that is? I'll be waiting for you there, tonight."

Iryc smiled from ear to ear, pocketing the money.

"I'm good for it. See ye' t'night."

"That's right, see you tonight."

They separated and Rey went down an alley, quickly split down another one, then yet another. He stopped around the corner and waited for a good while, dagger in hand, muscles tense. But no one had followed him. The terces earned the brute's trust.

There's no way he would be at that inn tonight. If Iryc pocketed the money and kept quiet, all the better. If he came through for the meeting, well, then he would have earned himself a horse. And if he were a dirty traitor, his bosses would make him pay for his stupidity in their own way.

No matter what happened, Rey needed to devise a new plan: there was no longer any point in trying to lay low, no matter where he was. The Züu and the Grand Guild combined, that made far too many enemies for him alone.

He had to find the other heirs.

He got on the road to Berce that same day.

"We must not be far from Jerval. We'll have to take some precautionary measures."

Yan regarded the warrior from the Lower Kingdoms curiously. If Grigán wanted to take precautions, that could only mean major changes to the small group's ride, which until then had been uneventful.

"What's Jerval like? A big city?"

"Not really, no. It's quite the opposite, actually, compared to the royal Lorelien cities. But we'd better not take any chances."

"We need a fourth horse," Corenn reminded them. "I think it would be a mistake to go around the village."

"I absolutely agree, especially since the detour would cause a useless delay."

"So, what do you have in mind?"

"We're going to separate. Temporarily, of course," added the warrior, noting his companions' surprised looks.

"Well, what do you have in mind?"

"You, Lady Corenn, along with your niece, will go through the village first. I will follow you, one hundred yards behind. Don't go too quickly, I don't want to lose sight of you. Pass through town without making it look as though you're in a hurry, simple as that. Answer if you are spoken to, but don't strike up any conversations."

"And me? What do I do?" asked Yan.

"You'll give your horse to Léti. Wait until we're out of sight, then follow us into town on foot and buy another horse. If things turn sour for us, clear out immediately. Otherwise, everything should be fine, since the Züu don't know who you are."

"I could be wrong, but if the goal of all this scheming is to pass by unnoticed, it won't work. When a rider goes through our village, he can act however he likes, but everyone will still stare him down regardless. He'd be the only topic of conversation that day."

"Not in Jerval. It's the first little town in Lorelia after crossing the Kaulien border. Riders go through daily, like the one we saw earlier, for example. After all, Bénélia is only a day's ride away; the villagers aren't going to raise their heads every time someone passes through."

"What should we do if we're attacked?" asked Léti, challengingly.

"Gallop on without turning back. I'll catch up to you after taking care of the suicidal maniacs who dared to put me in a bad mood. Clear?"

Léti didn't answer. Yes, it was clear, Grigán didn't allow his orders to be questioned.

The warrior gave some terces to Yan.

"You're from a farm not far away. You've only come to buy a horse for your father and you must return immediately and be back before nightfall. Barter a little, to mislead them, but don't take more than a deciday."

"How much does a horse usually sell for?"

"Seven or eight silver terces, in general. Agree to nine and your man will have no problem believing you're a stupid farm boy. You think you'll be able to play the role?" added the warrior, ironically.

Yan looked up and stared at him, a little miffed. By Eurydis! Grigán was grinning! So he could be a little human on occasion.

Yan smiled back. The joke was a bit harsh, but the warrior was making an effort for once.

"Buy something to eat too," Corenn requested. "Cheese, bread, some meat. A proper meal will do us good."

"All right."

"Try to buy everything from one place. There's no use letting the whole village memorize your face."

"Yes."

"And catch up to us quickly."

"Yes. Is that all? This all seems rather complicated for going through such a dangerous village."

"This is serious, Yan. We may all end up dead within the next centiday. Try not to forget that."

"Thanks for the encouragement."

They stopped shortly after, to let Léti mount Yan's horse. Then she and her aunt set off. Grigán was just about to leave too, when Yan stopped him.

"Hey…if all this turns out to be some plot to get rid of me, I won't think it's funny at all."

The warrior turned to him, looking honestly offended.

"I said you could come with us, so you're coming. I'm not in the habit of going back on my word."

He urged his horse to a slow trot, then turned over his shoulder with a smile and shouted, "In any case, you're the one bringing the food!"

Yan was more than reassured. Apparently, Grigán had fully accepted him as part of the group.

He set out at a quick pace toward the little village. He missed his companions already.

———⚬⚬⚬———

Despite strong motivation, it took Yan quite a while to get to Jerval. It was a little too late now, but they should have separated much closer to the little village. He could have at least avoided another forced march.

Relieved, he saw that everything looked calm; he could tell from the distant silhouettes that the others had passed through with no problem. Luckily.

For the first time in his life, Yan wasn't in the Matriarchy. Interested, his eyes searched in all directions, trying to commit this new landscape to memory. But it turned out that Jerval was a lot like Eza, and he was fairly disappointed. The inhabitants were dressed in a different way, and the architecture was different. That was all.

In fact, all the Upper Kingdom's villages must look alike, and after all, this one was only a two-day ride from his own. Bénélia, Lorelia—the big cities would be a real change.

He approached a group of children who were playing with wooden swords and asked them where he could buy a horse. They stared at him blankly. Curses, he had spoken in Kauli without realizing it. He asked the question again in Ithare, hoping that these kids had received their education from the Eurydian priests.

Their faces lit up, and they dragged him to an alley where there was a paddock. A bald, portly man came to meet him and started a conversation with him in a businesslike tone.

The deal was quick. Yan chose a horse, his only criterion being its color; unfortunately, he wasn't an expert on the subject. Then he bargained a little to agree on a price of nine terces for the animal and a basic harness. The young man didn't even have to use his prepared lies; the breeder couldn't care less what he was going to do with his horse.

Yan asked the oldest child who was still following him to go fetch the other goods he needed. He gave him three silver terces and a promise to leave him a share. The boy left running, with the rest of the group behind him.

The breeder brought out the chosen harness and let the horse out of the paddock. Yan turned the straps every which way, trying awkwardly to attach them to the animal, which shook them off each time. The merchant finally gave him a hand, shaking his head with an exasperated look.

Finally the horse was ready, and Yan stroked its neck while waiting for the kids. They were taking quite a while. He moved toward the end of the alley and looked down the main road. A little one bolted when he saw Yan.

All right. He had learned something today: Lorelien children were not necessarily honest.

He bought his own goods with the money he had left, loaded up his horse, and climbed on. He was relieved that it let him. Then he directed his new horse toward the village.

Laughter came from a side street. Yan leaned over to look down the street and saw some of the kids pointing at him, bent double with laughter. He squinted and pointed right back at them, making a snake hiss, as if he were casting some terrible curse on them. The kids' eyes grew wide and they scattered. Yan was pleasantly surprised at how effective it was.

He rejoined Grigán, Corenn, and Léti less than a half league outside the village.

"Well, apparently everything went well," Grigán commented.

"Are you kidding? I was attacked by a gang of young ogres who would have eaten me alive if I hadn't used my courage and wit to escape."

"Right, that's it."

"There were at least twenty of them, armed with knives a foot long, and drool dripped from their poisonous teeth and foul-smelling mouths."

"Sure. Come on, let's go."

"Their bloodshot eyes glared at me with murderous intent, and I really thought my time had come, when suddenly the one who must have been their leader raised his arm to the sky and broke into song. The others joined in soon after: *The crab and the lobster go two by two, the crab and the lobster never feel blue...*"

"Isn't that a nursery rhyme?"

"Yeah, I didn't get why they were singing it either."

Even Léti, who was intent on continuing her moping, laughed along with them.

─ ⌘ ─

Grigán didn't decide to stop until after the sixth deciday, almost nightfall. As usual, he guided the small caravan off the path, toward a little forest that they had happened upon. They crossed a clearing, continued on to a second, and it wasn't until they came to a third that the warrior gave the go-ahead to set up camp, only after first scouting the surroundings.

They ate before anything else, as hunger was gnawing at their stomachs. By the time they finished eating, they all felt lethargic, exhaustion from their ride and the poor sleep from the night before making themselves known.

Yan had started putting together a rudimentary bed for the night when Grigán interrupted.

"We'd better pitch a tent for tonight. I don't trust the color in the sky. I wouldn't be surprised if we get rained on."

"Cursed, I'm cursed. First ogres, and now rain."

Gathering his strength, he took it on himself to set up the two tents they had: Grigán's and Corenn's. He was going to sleep with the man in black; under normal circumstances, that might have annoyed him a little, but tonight he didn't give a margolin's ass about it, as long as he could sleep.

Soon, everyone was in bed except for Grigán, who said he wanted to keep a night watch for a while and attend to the horses. Yan wondered if he ever tired. He admitted to himself again that it was reassuring to have Grigán there. As for Yan, he fell asleep immediately.

He awoke a few decidays later, in the middle of the night. The warrior lay by his side, and silently turned over in his sleep. Yan hadn't even heard him come in.

A scattered rain was falling on the outer canvas, and a light wind fluttered the fabric, slack in areas.

Yan shifted onto his back and tried to fall back asleep. The pain in the nape of his neck, where Grigán had hit him the night before, had returned. He massaged it a bit, which didn't bring much relief. Since the pain was keeping him from dozing off, he let his thoughts wander, as he was wont to do.

At that time just the night before, he was struggling his way through the thick brush of the Kaulien shrubland. Now he was in Lorelia, sharing a tent with a stranger who had almost killed him. Where would he be tomorrow? And after that?

Although the circumstances hardly lent themselves to happiness, he was glad that these events had disrupted his routine life. But it was also true that he hadn't yet encountered any real dangers, unlike Léti, Corenn, and Grigán.

Were there really people out to kill them? Despite his companions' accounts, he had a hard time believing it. What could these Züu killers be like? Based on the description Corenn gave, he imagined them as being very tall and strong, with sadistic eyes, dressed in plain tunics stained with blood. And, of course, all of them were armed with poisoned daggers, injecting venom into their pleading victims, like a cold-hearted snake.

He could now picture a man dressed in red leather perfectly. All he could see was his back, then very slowly, he turned around. Horrified, the young man recognized his face: the Zü was none other than Grigán!

Yan awoke with a start.

He had managed to get back to sleep after all. But what a nightmare...

The back of his neck hurt more than ever and he felt a little feverish. Anxiety, due to the realistic aspects of his dream, surely.

He decided to go out for a little walk. He cautiously rose to his knees and slowly made for the tent flap.

A hand clasped his calf, and he couldn't contain a yelp of surprise.

"Where are you going?"

The warrior's voice didn't even sound sleepy. Yan tried hard to regain his calm.

"I can't sleep. I'm just going out for some fresh air."

"Don't go far," Grigán ordered as he released the boy. "And don't light a fire."

"No, no, of course not," Yan answered, annoyed.

The warrior had really startled him.

The cool night air and the drizzle calmed him down. He massaged his neck again, then paced about at random, ending up near the horses. Grigán had built a makeshift shelter for the animals out of a few branches and had also gathered some feed. Yan hadn't even thought of that. He had so much to learn: look after the horses, use a bow and arrow, develop a sense of direction, and lots of other things. He, who had always wanted to travel, was beginning to realize he'd never get very far on his own.

Even though he was anxious to learn to use a bow and arrow, he hoped he would never really have to shoot someone.

However, if someone went after Léti…

That reminded him. What day was it? Yan was far from knowing his calendar by heart, and he imagined the same went for his companions. But that was fine, after all. The name of the day didn't matter that much, so long as he didn't forget that it was the ninth day before the Day of the Promise.

Up until now, things hadn't been going so well. Léti was really shaken by recent events, and Yan hoped she would feel better soon. He was apprehensive enough before all of this, but now he'd never be able to ask her if her mood didn't improve.

The rain began to penetrate his clothes, and he quickly made his way back to the tent. He had to force himself to sleep a little: the coming days were likely to be exhausting.

Maz Lana held her breath as she pushed open the front door to the little isolated farmhouse. She knew it had been uninhabited for several dékades, but still, she was more or less expecting to come face-to-face with one of its former residents. Or the former resident's corpse.

The house belonged to the Romine branch of her family, which she had never known, descendants of the same Maz Achem as she.

She had been looking for them since the day after she arrived at the Mestèbe temple, and with patience she had discovered the place where the wise emissary had spent his final years.

She wasn't surprised to learn that her distant cousins had recently been assassinated for no apparent reason. Surprised, no. Saddened, yes. The tragedy merely confirmed her fears.

The door was blocked; locked, maybe. Lana circled the house, hoping to find another entry, but there was none, unless perhaps through the roof.

The priestess quickly rejected this idea, unable to imagine herself scaling a wall. There was only one thing to do.

She grabbed a heavy stone and began hammering away at the wood, praying to Eurydis that no one would catch her. No fool, she had been sure to keep her relationship to the victims a secret and had no wish to blow her cover by being caught breaking in.

The lock finally gave, and Lana broke the door open, splitting the stile close to the lock with a few of the strongest shoulder blows she could deliver—which wasn't much.

Breathless, she examined the house. It was all dark. Hideously, horribly dark. Under normal circumstances, she would never have entered.

But these weren't normal circumstances.

She mustered her courage and walked in with determination. She headed straight for a sealed-up skylight and set about removing the boards the same way she had opened the door. Her crashing blows echoed violently within the stone walls, and she began bashing faster and harder, allowing panic to overwhelm her.

Once the skylight was cleared, the room became sufficiently lit.

Lana gave herself some time to rest and think. What she was looking for certainly wasn't in this room, which served as both a living and dining room. But she couldn't lose hope. The few pieces of furniture still in the room were in a sorry state. The aftermath of a looting, perhaps? Or a fight between her cousins and the Züu. Or both.

Lana felt the anguish and tears returning. Ith was so far away! And more than that, she was so alone, facing events she didn't understand, facing situations too dangerous for her, facing violence...

She went back outside to collect her thoughts. The house's morbid atmosphere was getting to her. After a short prayer for strength and encouragement, she felt a little better and resumed her investigation.

She was looking for something, something very important. Something vital. It was certainly worth a bit of suffering.

So she searched the cottage inside and out, clearing the boarded-up windows in each room she entered. As she searched, she tried her best not to think of these cousins she didn't know. To avoid, for example, thinking about whom those toys belonged to, or who had bought them. She didn't want to imagine them living their daily lives, and to admit, finally, that she regretted not having known her own family.

As time went by, she felt her hopes diminishing. Reluctantly, she finally concluded that the object was not here. No longer here.

If it even existed. Which she still doubted.

There was only one way to know for sure. To know everything.

She abandoned the small cottage after she prayed to Eurydis for her cousins' rest. Then she shook most of the dust off her clothes, and mounted her horse to return to Mestèbe.

The things she planned to do to uncover the truth demanded a lot of preparation, both physical and spiritual.

After all, she could end up dead.

Yan awoke shortly before dawn. Grigán was already up. Again, the young man hadn't even heard him; it was almost irritating.

He threw on some plain clothes and left the tent. The sky was gray and overcast: it was going to be a rainy day.

The warrior was nowhere in sight, but that certainly wasn't a reason to worry. Corenn and Léti's tent was still closed up. After the emotional night before, Yan hoped they had managed to get a good night's sleep.

He usually went for a swim in the morning if it was nice out, or if not, he would just rinse himself off using the water basin in the house. Then he would join Léti for a small breakfast before tending to his daily tasks.

As for washing up, things didn't look promising. At least he would probably be able to find something for breakfast. To his delight, only a few yards into the woods, he happened upon a young lubilee tree whose fruit, though a little sparse, would be just the thing. Léti loved these sweet, nourishing oblong fruits, from which Norine used to make a delicious liqueur.

Not long after, he stumbled across an abandoned vorvan nest that still harbored three eggs. Two others had been cracked open and sucked dry, perhaps by a scavenging blackbird, which would explain the nest being deserted. Yan collected the eggs, hoping Grigán would allow him to light a small fire. Raw eggs weren't his favorite.

Finally, he found a hazelnut tree, whose branches he picked bare. No one would eat any for breakfast, but he had never been able to pass by a hazelnut tree without collecting a sackful.

As he returned to camp, he noticed the Lorelien forest's richness. A walk in Southern Kaul's brushland would have been far less fruitful.

Grigán was back as well. He was busy sealing the waterskins he had left out overnight. They were now full of rainwater.

I should have thought of that, Yan said to himself. There were two wells in Eza, which provided far more water than the two hundred or so villagers required, so it hadn't even occurred to him that they could be in need of water, despite the fact that he himself had installed a little rainwater collection system in Norine's home.

The warrior had also gone out to look for food, even though they still had some provisions left from the day before. He had collected a bunch of pitted fruits and shot a sea pheasant. Yan was a little disappointed that he wasn't the only one who thought to search for food. He placed his findings with the others and went over to Grigán.

"Good morning."

The warrior looked at him, somewhat surprised.

"Good morning to you."

"Did you sleep well?"

"Yes. Thanks."

A silence fell over them. It was clear that Grigán preferred to busy himself with the waterskins than to share in polite conversation. Yan left him alone, and then, taken by a sudden wave of inspiration, rushed over to the tent. He came out with the bow and arrow Grigán had entrusted to him.

He wandered away from the camp so he wouldn't have to endure the warrior's critical eye and his inevitable scoffing. He stopped after a hundred or so yards and chose a target: an odd marking, like a knot, in the bark of a distant tree.

It took him at least a milliday to draw the bow properly and take aim. At last he released the string, dreading pain, the immediate punishment for a poor shot.

The arrow flew straight, but missed the target by two yards, flying off into the bushes. Yan saw that he was going to lose all his arrows practicing that way. He recovered the arrow and decided on a new target: a tight cluster of young tree trunks that would stop even his worst shots.

He shot about twenty times, his greatest success being an arrow that came within a foot of the target. His arm was growing tired and he was beginning to get discouraged. This was going to be harder than he'd thought.

"Can I try?"

Léti stood several feet behind him. She must have been watching his last few shots. Yan didn't exactly feel brilliant, especially since Léti apparently didn't take to the idea of him using a bow.

But on the other hand, why then would she ask to try?

"By all means."

He handed the weapon over to Léti, whose face lit up. Of course! He'd been so stupid: she was feeling excluded by the two men. He should have seen it sooner; Léti wasn't the type to let herself be coddled.

He did his best to pass on the advice Grigán gave him, and she took position.

"What were you aiming for?"

"The slightly curved trunk, that one in front. But it won't stop moving," he added with a chuckle.

Léti smiled and slowly pulled back the string. It really was difficult. Her face tensed up, she gritted her teeth, and flexed her muscles with all her strength. But still, the bow didn't bend much. Her strength exhausted, she released the arrow, and it made a small leap to land flat on the ground, a dozen yards ahead.

"That's all right," Yan said immediately, to console her. "It's because it's too taut, that's all. We should be able to find bows that aren't so rigid."

He reached out his hand to rid her of the weapon.

"Wait. Give me another arrow, please."

Yan complied. In his opinion, it was pointless: she had already worn out her arm drawing the first arrow and could only do worse with the second.

Léti nocked the arrow, took position, and drew. Then she aimed her bow up, with the arrow practically pointing toward the treetops. Yan thought she wasn't strong enough and moved to help her, but she released the arrow before he could.

The arrow followed a curved trajectory and hit the targeted trunk dead on, sticking into the wood for a brief moment before falling to the ground.

Yan stood agape, his eyes glued to the nick made by the arrow. Léti let out a wild cry of joy and turned to him.

"Did you see that? I did it, Yan! I did it. I'm no worse than any man. I did it!"

As for him, the fisherman felt a lot worse. Léti really had all the talent and he had none.

He didn't feel jealousy, but rather genuine admiration for the woman he so often felt unworthy of. He examined her perfect face, her head of lush brown hair, her sparkling eyes that glowed with a zest for life, and her mouth that opened to reveal a joyful smile. She must always be so. Yan promised himself he would do anything so that she would be that way forever.

Léti went to get the arrow, which she handed over to him with the bow.

"Here. I don't want to start off the morning arguing with Grigán the Grump. I have my answer, let's go eat."

Yan wondered what answer she was talking about, and more importantly, to what question. But he didn't ask; he thought it best to try and keep her in a good mood. Besides, he didn't want to become another target for her nicknames.

They enjoyed the fare they had collected that morning and some leftovers from the evening before. Corenn also looked better; she, who had remained reserved all evening yesterday, was now leading the conversation and teasing the two men about their culinary talents, which according to her were limited to "picking something off a branch."

Yan protested a little as a matter of form, and even Grigán shot back one or two deliberately aggressive replies. But no one took any of it seriously, and soon they took to the road for a new day of traveling.

A drizzling but insistent rain began to fall midmorning, near the end of the second deciday. They all covered themselves as best they could, hoping the rain would stop soon. Which it did. Only to start again, and this time even harder.

Little by little, the trail became a road as other trails crossed and joined it. When they came to one of the larger forks in the road, Grigán guided his troop onto the path that turned north.

"I thought Bénélia was right in front of us," said Corenn, surprised.

"True, it is. But I'd rather take a detour and reduce the chances that the Züu will find us. If they're still looking for us. They can't possibly already know about the deaths of the three others."

"What did you do with the bodies?" Yan asked, it suddenly occurring to him.

"Left them there. If you want to live a long life, never linger over a corpse. Especially in the Upper Kingdoms," added the warrior with an enigmatic smile.

"Did you search them?"

Grigán squinted.

"Why should I have searched them?"

"I don't know, maybe you could have found a clue, or at least some items we could have used. You weren't tempted to take their purse, for example?" Yan finally dared.

Grigán stared at him sternly. Even through the curtain of rain, the young man could feel his intense gaze. Curses, he had yet again offended the warrior's strange sensibilities.

"That's what you would have done? Robbed a corpse?"

Yan only had to think for a moment.

"No, I don't think so. No. Of course not," he declared sincerely, after a moment of thought.

"Good."

Grigán looked serious. Yan promised himself he would learn to hold his tongue. He glanced over at the two Kaulien women. Corenn was wearing a slightly amused smile, and Léti seemed annoyed, by the rain perhaps.

Whatever they thought, he felt as though he had been chastised like a little boy in front of his friends. And that had happened far too often recently. So, somewhat stupidly, he continued the argument, "Still, I would have searched their corpses. You should have, in my opinion."

"Should we go back, then?"

Sensing an argument on the horizon, Corenn intervened.

"We left the path immediately afterward so we wouldn't be spotted. We couldn't have done anything either way. So it's useless to fight over it."

"Lady Corenn, I greatly appreciate your intelligence," responded the warrior. "And you know what a compliment that is, coming from a narrow-minded old bachelor like me."

"I do understand and thank you, Master Grigán. I hope you remember it later, when we have a difference of opinion," she answered with a mischievous smile.

"May such a day never come, for it would see the sacrifice of my freedom for a woman, Lady Corenn. I prefer to be wrong with you than to be right against you."

Yan couldn't believe his ears. Corenn and Grigán had completely forgotten about him. And why were they talking like that? He turned to Léti to see her reaction. The young woman was watching her aunt and "uncle" with a wide smile; he couldn't understand why. Very well, since everyone was ignoring him, he would ignore everyone.

He didn't last long. His good nature kept him from pouting for very long; his good sense warned him against such ridiculous behavior, and, of course, no one was paying him any more attention than before.

The little group passed a trio of horsemen about a league after they'd turned north. Grigán didn't give the order to take cover; in fact, he wasn't scouting ahead anymore either. Yan supposed they must be safer, now that they were on one of the many side roads.

They moved along in silence for a few leagues, passing or being passed by a number of pedestrians and riders. They even saw an ornate wagon, pulled by six horses, with two uniformed men bearing an arrogant expression copied from their passenger—apparently a Lorelien noble. Yan followed the carriage with his eyes for as long as he could. One never saw and would never see such splendor in Kaul. Could he one day travel in such a fashion?

They traveled through two villages much like Jerval or Eza. Yan didn't even ask for their names. At the end of the third deciday, which marked the apogee, and when they were passing through yet another village, Corenn stopped her mount in front of a rather large building.

"Grigán, what do you say we stop at this inn? So much water's fallen on my head this morning that I think it will take a hundred years to dry out."

"Lady Corenn, I'd love to indulge you, and I admit that I wouldn't be against a goblet of wine and a hot meal in front of a nice fire. But caution prevents me; even if we can ride safely, I fear we must wait until Bénélia before we can expose ourselves to so many strange faces."

"Of course, you're right," Corenn recognized. "Watch over us, Master Grigán, or I would quickly let my fatigue overrun my good sense."

"I doubt that could ever happen, Lady Corenn. But it will be a great pleasure to look after you."

They got themselves back on the road at a slow trot. Léti approached Yan quietly.

"Did you see that? They're courting one another."

Yan hiccupped with surprise. Suddenly, the urge to laugh came over him, but it flamed out under Léti's serious gaze.

"They aren't courting! They're just talking..."

"Of course they are. Did you see how they spoke to one another?"

Léti looked thoroughly convinced, and very pleased to boot. Yet again, Yan felt a bit stupid. What, he had to call her "Lady Léti" to make her happy? He wasn't against trying, if she didn't laugh in his face, as she probably would. Something escaped him. For a while now, a lot of things had been escaping him.

He examined the warrior and the Mother, the combatant and the diplomat, the lawless man and the Law. No, they had nothing in common, except their age. How could they get together? Did Léti think that Grigán was going to ask Corenn for her hand on the Day of the Promise, like a shy young man asking a hesitant young woman?

The idea made Yan want to laugh again. He could imagine that fateful day with slightly less apprehension. He resolved to think of the same thing every time the subject tormented him. In other words, practically all the time.

—◦◦◦◦—

They came across more and more people the closer they got to the river. Farmers, horsemen, merchants and their caravans. Yan scrutinized each one of these unique characters with an avid curiosity.

One of them was leading a pack of strange animals, a sort of cross between a dog and a sheep. Another carried a bizarre weapon, like a sword with two blades, one on either side of the handle. And there was another leading a donkey loaded with baskets of pink-colored fruits. There was a group walking in single file, their heads down, chanting a few unintelligible words—followers of some unknown cult. A man was encouraging his six wives to pick up the pace to avoid losing sight of his horse. A couple of others were arguing in a strange language. That woman over there...

"Don't stare at people like that, Yan," Corenn told him.

"I don't mean to be rude," he mumbled, "but they're all so... strange!"

"You seem just as strange to them. Everyone seems strange through the eyes of another. But courtesy demands that we overlook these details."

"It's not just a question of politeness," Grigán added. "One of those men might try to start a fight with you."

"Just because I'm looking at him? Come on!"

"Keep it up, and you'll see. I bet before dark you'll hear a few insults or get a punch thrown your way."

Yan decided not to answer. Doubting himself, he now watched a bit more discreetly.

They came to the Gisland shortly before nightfall. There, a crowd of several dozen awaited the barge that would take them to the other bank. The river was wide, and surely deep, which explained why no one was trying to ford it. They dismounted their horses and stretched their legs.

"It's a little different than the Mèche," Yan told Léti.

"Pff," Grigán condescended. "The Mèche is hardly a river at all. And even the Gisland here is nothing. You should see the Alt."

"I would love to," replied the Kaulien in a distant tone. "Someday, if I can."

Corenn called the two young ones over to her.

"Look, there, to the south. You see those little lights? That's Bénélia."

"It's a lot more beautiful from here," said Léti. "All I can remember is the stench and the filthy streets. Nothing like Kaul!"

"How would you get to Berce before?" asked Yan. "I mean, if you didn't take the barge?"

"We simply took a boat from Lorelia to Bénélia," answered the Mother. "But not everyone could afford the crossing, especially if they had baggage. You have to pay the royal tax twice on all merchandise: once in each city. And the small-scale merchants would rather go a little farther upstream and take a barge, here or even a few leagues farther. From there, you travel by land to the Vélanèse River, cross, and then take another road to Lorelia. Which is what we're going to do."

"It must be a lot longer that way."

"It's also a lot less risky," interrupted the warrior. "If I were one of the Züu, I would camp out on one of the Bénélian wharves and wait patiently for the opportunity to nab us. But they can't monitor all the comings and goings of every barge."

The boat they were waiting for was only halfway across, and it would be a while before it arrived. Yan decided to take advantage of the wait and explore the surroundings, but Grigán stopped him as soon as he turned to go.

"Where are you going?"

"Just for a walk."

"Not a chance. You're staying here."

Yan froze, undecided. He had agreed to obey the warrior, but still, the man was pushing his luck a bit.

"I'm going too," Léti announced defiantly.

"Perhaps that's not such a good idea," said Corenn. "These people here aren't your friendly Kaulien villagers. I would be happier if you stayed."

Put that way, Yan was prepared to give in. But Léti sensed that Yan was wavering and grabbed him by his arm before he could say another word.

"We're just going for a little walk! Why don't you learn to trust us a little?"

For a moment, Grigán and Corenn simply stood and watched as they walked away, unsure of what to do.

"In your opinion, would it be 'undiplomatic' for me to drag their asses back here?"

"I'm sure they would think so, Master Grigán. Perhaps it would be best to turn a blind eye on this little whim and save our authority for truly dangerous situations?"

"All right, I agree. But part of me almost hopes that something bad happens to them, just to put them in their place!"

The warrior couldn't stand still, pacing as he stroked his mustache, apparently a nervous tic.

"Would you mind if I left you here alone for a moment with the horses?" he finally said. "I'm at least going to keep an eye on our charges, just to make sure everything's all right."

"Go, my friend," she replied with a smile. "I'd expect nothing less from you."

Grigán mumbled a thank you and hurried after the young ones.

How was it that he kept losing control of the situation like this?

Except for the inn a few hundred yards from the pier, a handful of boutiques spread out along the bank were the only attractions in the area. Léti, who simply wanted to prove her own freedom, was happy simply walking aimlessly, until Yan guided her toward the little market that had caught his attention. Though hardly interested at first, the young woman eventually had a great deal of fun.

Apart from the vegetables, fruits, fish, cheeses, breads, and diverse drinks, which were already strange enough and of questionable quality, there were also esoteric or religious talismans for sale; maps of the known and unknown world; peculiar objects whose forms, origins, and uses Yan and Léti didn't recognize; diverse herbs and salves; small weapons...

Léti stopped in front of the weapons stand and examined each item with obvious desire. Yan waited silently at her side, hoping she wouldn't try to buy something here. He was already worried enough about what Grigán would do to them when they got back.

The young woman took an interest in one item in particular. Yan realized that it was a bow. Curses, he was going to get in such trouble...

An old woman dressed in rags garbled something at them.

"I don't understand," Léti answered in a clear voice.

The crone raised her arms and eyes to the sky in a gesture of thanks. She was just as dirty as Old Vosder, Yan thought. He didn't think that was possible.

"Some Kauls!" she mumbled in broken Kauli. "Some Kauls, I be sure of it."

"We say Kauliens," Léti responded dryly. "And 'I am sure of it.' Furthermore, we didn't ask you for anything."

Léti turned her back to the woman abruptly and directed her attention back to the market stall. Yan was going to do the same, but the old woman spoke to him directly, grabbing insistently at his sleeve.

"Do you want to know your future? For three tices, I give you all of tomorrow."

Yan tried to break free as best he could. This woman had quite a grip. Why did this kind of thing always happen to him?

"No, thank you. That sort of thing doesn't interest me."

"But yes, Kaulien. It interest you. Everyone care for tomorrow."

Léti curtly turned to face the pesky old woman. It seemed as though everyone was trying to order them around this evening. If it weren't for her respect for elders, thanks to her education in the Matriarchy, she would already have told this pest exactly what she thought of her.

Yan tried in vain to brush her off without being impolite.

"No, no, really. Tomorrow doesn't interest me."

He realized that what he was saying was actually nonsense.

"But yes, Kaulien. Tomorrow is important for you. Give me three tices, and I will tell you your fortunes and misfortunes. When you be rich and when you will have your Union. When you have children and how long you will live."

Yan thought about it for just an instant. He still had Grigán's money; he took it out and began sorting it in his outstretched palm, when the old woman quickly grabbed three coins. He wasn't sure, but didn't she grab one coin that was a size larger than the others?

Léti shook her head, disapprovingly. The young man knew what she was thinking. Even so, the old woman had said something that actually did interest him: "when you will have your Union."

"Good, good. Hand me object. One you carry often. One you have for long time."

Yan considered it. What could he give her? At home, he had a pile of souvenirs and keepsakes, from his parents, Léti, and Norine, or ones he acquired on his own. Like his crossbow harpoon, for example. But here?

He made a mental list of all the things he had on him. And finally remembered. Hanging around his neck underneath his tunic, Léti's seashell. The one she'd given him when they were only eight years old; the one he'd never been apart from since.

The little blue queen moon that she'd given him as a token, perhaps nothing more than a kids' game, but one he had always taken seriously.

Of course, he had changed the leather lace a few times, but since Léti gave him the shell, he had never let a day pass without it around his neck. It had become so natural he never even thought about it. Yes, if he had to pick an important object, it was that one.

He took it off from underneath his tunic, hesitant at first, but he handed it over quickly to avoid ridicule. Léti shot him a look that he couldn't decipher. Was she irritated that he took it off? Or maybe she thought it was stupid to have kept this little trinket for all these years? Or maybe she didn't even remember giving it to him? He preferred to not think about it and focused all of his attention on the old woman.

She held it tightly in her hands, after taking a moment to examine it. Her eyes closed, and almost as if possessed by spirits, her head began to turn slowly back and forth in exaggerated movements. Yan realized how ridiculous the situation was, but it was too late to turn back now. And, in spite of it all, he was curious to hear what story she would tell him, false though it might be.

The crone emitted a long quavering moan that sounded either like she was suffering deeply or its opposite, as though she were letting out a sigh of relief. Then she opened her eyes.

"You be fisherman."

Yan waited for her next revelation, before realizing that she was waiting for his confirmation. He nodded.

She smiled, all the while spinning her head around in circles like a carriage wheel.

"You want to do something. You don't want to be...only a fisherman."

Yan, not knowing what else to do, nodded again. The old woman let out a sort of strangled guffaw.

"You want woman badly, young man. Eh?"

The young Kaulien didn't move an inch. He wanted to say yes, but he was afraid of Léti's reaction.

The old fortune-teller sneered, almost mockingly.

"Now, I give you tomorrow."

She closed her eyes, sighed, and began speaking in a deep, monotone voice.

"You marry the woman you want next year. She be village chief. You never fisherman. Travel a lot. Then you have many money. Very happy. Then two sons. Very strong. You be strong. Very happy. You live long time with woman. You want to know when you die?"

"No, not at all!"

Yan didn't really want to know the possible date of his death, whether it be true or false. The old woman nodded.

"You are right. Not be good to know too strong things about tomorrow."

She handed him back his queen moon. Then she turned and walked away with small steps, leaving Yan to unravel his feelings.

What nerve, to leave like that! "Not be good to know too strong things about tomorrow." All right, then why did this old woman go around predicting people's futures?

"That went well; you're lucky."

Yan turned toward Léti. Was she mocking him? No, she looked sincere. They left the weapons stall.

"Why do you say that?"

"She could have given you bad news, misfortune, sickness, death…She could have even put a date on everything. But she only talked about the good things, while staying vague. So you are lucky."

"I didn't think you believed in that sort of thing."

"Oh, yes, I certainly do...The heirs of Ji, my aunt...You know, it all makes me wonder if the impossible may be possible. But, in my opinion, we shouldn't try to know our future. And she looked more like a beggar than a divinity."

"What does your aunt have to do with the impossible?"

"Don't worry about it. Maybe I'll tell you someday."

Yan frowned. For his part, he was largely disappointed with the fortune-teller, and he kept discovering that Léti and Corenn were hiding things from him. For now, he preferred not to dwell on it, knowing that it would only upset him.

"Do you think what she told me will come true? You think that my life will unfold like that?"

"Perhaps. It's not too bad, as far as destinies go, right?"

"I'm not sure."

"If only you could see your face right now! I was right, it's better not to know."

He kept quiet for a while. Seeing the serious look on her friend's face, Léti picked up the conversation.

"Wouldn't you be pleased with two sons? To travel? To be rich? Live a long, full life? Were you hoping she would tell you 'You will be king, you will command armies, you are the savior from some forgotten prophecy, you will live a life full of adventures, and blah, blah, blah'? We aren't living in a fairy tale."

Despite her sarcastic remarks, Yan noticed that she had omitted his predicted Union for the coming year—probably on purpose.

"Of course, that would all be very nice...But I think she made it all up. What she said about the present, anyone could guess, and the rest, it's just her imagination. And it makes me think that I would in fact be very lucky if it all turns out like that."

They both dove back into their own thoughts. Curses, and what was more, he was making Léti sad. She really didn't need that right now; he was being foolish.

They joined up with Corenn in silence, dragging their feet.

"And here we are, Aunt. See? There was no reason to worry."

"It is only after the dog bites that you know it is rabid. I'm glad that it went well, but you should realize that things could have gone otherwise."

"All right, perhaps. If you think so."

"You shouldn't use today's experience as an argument for next time. Do you understand?"

"Yes, yes," Léti admitted against her will. Her aunt always had something to add. Reasoning, giving in to secondary points, avoiding thorny subjects, but always having the last word, even if it was just to end up right back at the status quo. She could do all of this without lying, pressing, or even raising her voice. Léti knew this talent of her aunt's quite well; she had seen it used many times while accompanying the Mother on her travels throughout Kaul. But still, even she was sometimes the victim of her aunt's machinations, and her powerlessness to resist vexed her. Sometimes, she asked herself if her aunt wasn't using her magic powers to sway the minds of her listeners. But that was unlikely.

"Where's Grigán?"

"He shouldn't be long now."

Indeed, the warrior rejoined them quickly thereafter. He didn't say a word.

The ferry was close to shore now, and travelers crowded the dock, guarded by three tall, burly men. Grigán led the small group to the waiting line. The ferry docked and the passengers spilled out, pushing their way through the crowd toward the inn or the road. Finally, they began boarding.

Watching each step of the process, Yan realized that you had to pay to cross the river. To think that with his own boat he would be on the other side with a few oar strokes! Then again, they would still have the problem of the horses...

"Master Grigán?"

The warrior and Corenn couldn't help but smile at Yan's use of this title.

Yan disregarded this and continued.

"I still have the money that belongs to you. Of course I'll pay you back in full, but I'm afraid I don't have enough to pay for the crossing."

Corenn reassured him.

"Don't worry. I have enough to take us all the way to Goran, if it came to that."

"I'm pretty sure it would take me quite a while to pay back such a large amount."

"We'll work it out later."

As a member of the Permanent Council, Corenn received one of the highest salaries in the Matriarchy. She couldn't imagine herself running a young, honest fisherman into debt, especially one who would no doubt become a part of her family someday. It was simply inconceivable.

The line moved quickly, and it was soon their turn. Corenn exchanged a few words in Lorelien with one of the three dock guards, a few coins changed hands, and finally the little group could board the sizable barge.

Three crew members were bustling about carefully arranging packs, passengers, and goods, paying close attention to balance the load and guarantee stability. A fourth man was busy lighting oil lamps that hung from poles at each corner of the boat, as well as at random points along the deck.

"To my knowledge, this is the only ferry that makes night crossings," announced Grigán. "Also, I think it's one of the largest."

Léti answered the man in black in a hushed voice.

"Doesn't that make it all the more dangerous to take this one? I mean, won't that make it easier for them to spot us?"

"No, no. There are thirty or so ferries for every three- or four-league stretch of water along the Gisland. Each one makes at least five or six crossings a day, I think. It would be impossible to monitor all the arrivals and departures, unless they had an army. The Züu won't even try."

"But that's just a guess."

"Yes. Do you have a better idea?"

"Unbelievable! You're so insensitive, do you know that?"

"I don't tolerate criticism, that's all," Grigán answered calmly.

That could very well be the warrior's motto, Yan thought to himself.

Once all the travelers had boarded the barge and spread out on the deck, the ferrymen untied the mooring lines and pushed the boat away from shore by inches, using long wooden poles. A resounding "plop" brought the maneuver to a halt. A rather drunken passenger had lost his balance and gone for a swim in the cold river. Everyone roared with laughter, except for the captain, who delivered a lecture to his men and the suddenly sober victim, who was being helped back on board. Then they launched a second time.

"It's almost a tradition for the ferrymen," said Grigán. "I've even heard that now and then they organize some secret splash competition. I'll bet they made a point of putting that fellow near the edge."

"The Loreliens have some odd pastimes!" Yan exclaimed.

"Am I wrong, or don't Kauliens amuse themselves by diving off of cliffs? That doesn't seem much smarter to me."

"That's different. No one is forced to do it."

"Oh, come on, Yan, I heard you laugh too," Léti interrupted gleefully. "It wasn't all that cruel."

"You're absolutely right," Grigán went on. "There's a popular prank in Romine where you release a red pig in heat inside a friend's house. After blocking off all the exits, if possible... Needless to say, if the victim doesn't give the prankster a real thrashing, he's a true friend."

"I'll believe it. What's a red pig?"

"What! You've never seen one, Yan? And you, Léti?" asked Corenn, shocked.

"No."

"I can't believe it. They look like a mix of a boar and a pig, except they're completely red. They travel in packs of fifty or sixty, but people have seen hordes of more than three hundred. They're incredibly destructive. Romine is infested with them. A few years ago, we had to organize hunts just west of Kaul because they were beginning to spread throughout the Matriarchy."

"This is the first I've ever heard of them. Anyhow, Master Grigán, what does a red pig do when it's in heat?"

"It grunts, it squeals, it bites, it races about, it charges at anything that moves. Well, everything, for that matter. But worst of all, it stinks. They say that even with all the willpower in the world, you still couldn't stay within ten yards of a male in such a state."

"Actually," Léti guffawed, "that sounds like Yan when he comes home after fishing for vase eels!"

"Very funny. Remind me to bring some back for you next time."

"Eels are delicious," noted Corenn.

"Do you want to come along? I'll gladly take you. You'll see how much fun it is."

Yan's mood was improving. He had forgotten his worries about the future. Right now, he needed to enjoy today.

The barge glided silently along the calm river, disturbed only by the movement of the wooden poles pushing into the depths and fish jumping at swarms of insects. The soft light of the lamps and the crescent moon didn't dispel the already thick darkness, but it was soothing. Bénélia's distant lights to the south didn't shine as brightly as the fireflies fluttering in the vast darkness. Buildings on the banks lit up to signal piers and nearby inns...a promise of imminent comfort. The temperature had dropped, and Yan wrapped himself up in his tunic the best he could. It occurred to him to check on Léti's well-being, but he didn't dare break the calm spell cast by the croaking of frogs, the murmur of passengers, and the sound of the waves. She thanked him with a smile. If only things could always be that way between them.

He wrapped his arms around her, and Léti rested her head on his shoulder. They remained silent and still, hidden together in the darkness, surrendered to their feelings.

⸺◦◦◦⸺

Corenn gently pulled the two young Kauliens from their reveries; the ferry was about to dock. Yan hadn't even noticed. He released Léti regretfully and followed everyone else, guiding his horse by the bridle.

Once everyone had disembarked, Grigán steered them toward a nearby inn. In every way, this side of the river looked just like the other: the dock, the guards who collected the toll, the travelers waiting for the ferry, the small, deserted shops.

Above the entry to the inn hung a sign that seemed excessively large compared to the front door. In Ithare, the sign read *The Ferry Inn*. Clearly, the owner wasn't too original.

"Have you been here before?" Yan asked Grigán.

"Three times, I think. Or maybe four. But my last stay must have been at least six years ago. There is little chance that they'll recognize me."

"No, that's not why I was asking." Yan hesitated, hoping not to make himself look stupid once again. "It's just that...well, I've never been inside an inn before. I don't even think there are any near Eza. Is there something special I must do? Or things not to do?"

His three companions laughed heartily.

"As long as you pay for the damage, you can pretty much do anything you like," the warrior answered with a grin. "Except, maybe, kill the innkeeper, or start something with the customers. Think you'll be able to control yourself?"

"The customers might be a problem," Yan said through gritted teeth.

"Fine. I'm still going to see if they can accommodate us."

The warrior opened the little door and bent forward to avoid hitting the monstrous sign. As Grigán entered, voices, the scent of warm food, and a gentle warmth emerged to subtly caress the Kauliens' senses. He returned just as quickly as he'd gone, accompanied by a young man who led their horses to the stable after all the baggage had been unloaded.

A man ripe with age came forward to greet them when they finally entered the tavern. The entryway overlooked the main room from the top of a little three-step stairway. A dozen or so thick wooden tables surrounded by benches filled most of the room.

An enormous pile of logs—more like tree trunks cut in half—covered an entire wall. An imposing fireplace sat close by, the flames dancing four feet high. Yan could feel its heat, even from the entryway. Several doors and stairways allowed access to the kitchen, the cellar, other floors, and guesthouses. Indeed, the inn was quite large.

Thirty pairs of eyes glanced up at the new arrivals, before their attention was quickly diverted back to the food and pitchers that covered the tables. The clientele was made up mostly of men, alone or in small groups. Farmers, artisans, merchants—travelers, in short.

The host greeted them in Lorelien and led them to an open table, where they sat down. After a few brief exchanges, Corenn gave several coins to the innkeeper, who slipped away toward the kitchen.

The young man from the stable soon brought them, in several trips and out of order, fresh bread, a warm loaf of meat, a vegetable stew, a huge hunk of cheese, forks and knives, goblets, a pitcher of beer, and, per Corenn's request, a pitcher of water. They ate with relish while chatting about the differences between Lorelien and Kaulien cuisine, but without ever deciding—for lack of really trying—which was the best.

"Are all inns like this?" Yan asked.

"No, far from it," answered Grigán. "Only people passing through stop here, people who just want a hot meal and a good night's sleep. The hovels that you can find in the big cities don't really have the same clientele..."

"Actually, what I meant was, are all inns this big? You could feed the entire population of Eza at these tables!"

"If you think so, there are still plenty of surprises in store for you. I've seen dozens of places bigger than this one, in the Upper Kingdoms. Taverns and inns larger than palaces."

"It makes me wonder if you think I'm some sort of *niab* or if you're serious."

"I'm serious. In Lermian, I once spent the night in a hotel with six hundred rooms. And at least two-thirds were occupied."

Yan still wasn't convinced, but he gave Grigán the benefit of the doubt. Why not, after all?

By all counts, the warrior had spent half his life traveling, and the other half preparing for it. He had traveled across all the kingdoms, stayed in all the mighty cities, met hundreds of people, experienced thousands of things Yan couldn't begin to imagine.

Yan realized that the veteran who had been protecting them for the last few days, with his curved blade and his black garb, his mysterious past, and his strong personality, completely fascinated him.

The warrior seemed more open to discussion tonight. More relaxed, now that they had made it out of the Matriarchy. The pitcher of beer, which he practically finished himself, might have helped a little as well. If Yan wanted to get to know him, it was now or never.

"You're from the Lower Kingdoms, right? At least, that's what it sounds like, given your accent."

"What of it?"

"Nothing, just a bit curious, that's all."

"You, you aren't just curious; you're a snoop."

"That's what the Ancestress of my village always says," Yan answered, smiling. "She ended up teaching me to read so that I could find answers on my own to the questions I pestered her with all the time. But since she only owns three books in all, I kept bugging her until she finally told me one day that she didn't have the answers to all my questions. Like all children, that had never occurred to me."

"It's good you know how to read," Corenn commented.

"Only a little, and in Ithare."

Léti interrupted, a smile on her lips.

"Once, I saw him spend the whole day trying to interpret a parchment he had found at Old Vosder's house. He was so disappointed that he couldn't figure it out that I went to find the Ancestress so she could reason with him. It was hard to stop myself from laughing, seeing his face, when she explained to him that it was in Goranese."

"How was I supposed to know? They use the same marks," Yan said, pouting.

"So Yan traveled all the way to Assiora," Léti continued, "to have someone translate the parchment. A full day's walk in one direction. All of that just to look at some old words."

Yan, blushing with irritation and shame, chose not to answer.

"Do you know how to read, Léti?" Corenn asked innocently.

She knew the answer; she'd asked the question with the aim of encouraging her niece to show a little more respect for her friend's efforts to improve himself.

"No, I don't know how. But I'm convinced that it's useless," the young woman answered, not giving in.

"You're wrong," Grigán interrupted. "I've often thought the same, but I've more often regretted thinking that way."

"It's never too late, Master Grigán."

"That's what they say, Lady Corenn, that's what they say. But I don't think I can change now. The years left in my life will be like the ones behind me."

An awkward silence followed this last statement. Yan was the first to fill it.

"Where were you born exactly, then?"

The warrior let a moment drift by, as if he were sifting through distant memories, or he were hesitating to open up.

"In Griteh. Then the happiest of the Lower Kingdoms, forty-two years ago. But I haven't been back there for a long time."

Yan paused, uncertain if he should continue, but curiosity won out.

"Why?" He finally dared to ask.

Grigán let out a sigh.

"Because I'm no longer welcome there. And there's nothing left for me there anyway."

His friends could tell immediately that he wasn't being truthful. The warrior was incapable of lying about his feelings. Probably one of the reasons for his habit of silence.

"What happened to you?"

Yan pointed out that Léti was hanging on Grigán's every word, and like Yan, she was waiting for him to let his memories surface. But time passed, the silence getting longer and longer, and they finally had to concede that the warrior wasn't going to answer.

"Tell them, Grigán," Corenn said in a sweet voice. "As long as they don't know, they'll badger you with questions. And you'll either tell them or hit the roof someday."

The warrior's only reaction was to stare at Corenn, as if he were seeing her for the first time.

"Tell them and accept it, or stay silent and forget the story forever. But stop tormenting yourself," she added with an even gentler tone.

Grigán looked distraught for a brief instant, and then he made up his mind, still unsure whether he made the right decision.

"Don't think I'm complaining, and please don't take pity on me. Above all else, don't do that. Know that I'm telling you this story so you can learn from my experiences."

"Yes, yes," the young Kauliens answered in unison.

They would agree to anything to get him to talk.

"Good."

The warrior drank a final swig, perhaps to give himself some courage. It was as though he were more afraid to speak than to attack three Züu killers, Léti thought.

"Have you heard of Aleb I, Aleb the Conqueror, or, more to my taste, Aleb the Violent?"

"No," Léti replied.

Yan thought he had heard the name, but he wasn't sure. He preferred to play dumb, to get a fully detailed version of Grigán's story.

Grigán continued. "He was my leader. At the time, he was still only Prince Aleb. I fought by his side in the wars with the neighboring kingdoms of Griteh: Irzas, Quesraba, Tarul, and even Yiteh for a while. Do you understand? We were at war. Against warriors."

Yan and Léti met each other's eyes briefly, then rushed to agree. They didn't really understand, but they soon would.

"For many decades, Griteh had been a second-order kingdom whose borders any army could cross as they pleased. Thanks to our victories, peace and security had at last returned to the country. But it had lasted only a few years when Aleb called the tribes together again. And so I went to fight by his side, to defend my loved ones, as did every honorable man. But I wondered what reasons he had for rallying a defense, since no army had been spotted at our borders."

Grigán stopped. The young Kauliens waited impatiently, fidgeting for a few moments, until Léti couldn't bear it any longer.

"And then what? Then what happened?"

"I should have known from the start. Aleb spoke to us at length, and with words that went straight to the heart. Little by little, he whipped the men into a fury against Quesraba, recalling our past conflicts, Quesraba's betrayals of our rare alliances, and the lost battles that demanded revenge. At the end of his speech, he even presented Quesraba as a part of our kingdom, but occupied by enemies. He spoke of true things, things that were less true, and dreadful things—things that would even make a Rominian shepherd angry. But nothing he said can excuse what happened next."

Grigán paused.

"Go on!" Léti urged rudely.

"All the men followed his orders and launched an assault on Quesraba, and I wasn't the last one. It took us a day to reach the border, but our zeal and anger hadn't subsided, fueled by Aleb and his captains, who were now fully devoted to his cause. At last we came upon the first 'enemy' village. I ordered my riders to skirt around the village and head straight for the capital to meet the army, as was custom, but Aleb the Cursed had other plans."

Grigán downed another swig.

"He ordered us to attack the village. Hundreds of people died that night. People who weren't even armed. People who didn't care about frontier politics. People like you, people like..."

He took a short pause, and then continued the story.

"And I did nothing."

He gazed deeply into the bottom of his goblet; the warrior regretted once again his inability to get himself drunk. No matter how hard he tried, he always remained perfectly sober. He remained responsible for his actions.

"I could have tried to reason with Aleb. I could have tried to reason with the warriors. I could even have ordered my men to attack the murderers. But I didn't do any of that. I just stood there and watched the atrocities being committed right in front of me. I saw children bludgeoned by maces and elders burned alive in their homes. I saw women raped right before their dying men's eyes. I saw animals suffer the worst kinds of torture, and not just them..."

"Grigán…" said Corenn, softly.

She felt it was time to put an end to this morbid litany. The warrior stared at her for a moment, sighed, and went on.

"I know that it's difficult to hear. But that's what happened. To think that at the beginning of the 'battle,' I nearly threw myself into the madness…"

He was silent, wearing a troubled look. No tears fell from his eyes, but all the sadness and regret in the world weighed upon his shoulders.

The Kauliens respected his pain. No one wanted to ask him any more questions; in fact, they would have left it there if Grigán hadn't continued, this time in a steadier voice.

"At first, I looked for enemies. 'Where were they? Why wasn't anyone attacking? Was it a trap?' Then I began to hope that it was a trap. The Ramgriths, my brothers, couldn't really be in the midst of massacring harmless villagers. No, there had to be something else. Surely enemy warriors were hiding somewhere nearby, or among the farmers, and Aleb had given the command to attack to thwart the ruse, because he was a good leader.

"I clung to my delusion all through the night, and I willingly ignored the slaughter that was unfolding before me. At dawn, I finally admitted that I had lost my honor, even my humanity. I fled from that cursed land and retreated to my homeland. I needed to be alone, to think on how I was going to put an end to my days."

Yan and Léti looked at each other uncomfortably. Grigán took a deep breath and carried on.

"I couldn't go through with it. It seemed like yet more proof of my cowardice, but at the same time, I felt weak for not doing it. I sat, tormented by indecision, for a dékade. In the end, I chose to live to take action, rather than die for failing to.

"I went to Griteh and requested to appear before King Coromán, who was happy to receive me. My family serves... served his since Rafa the Strategist's father's father. Coromán was an unyielding man, sometimes harsh and insensitive, but he tried to be just. I couldn't believe that he had authorized the massacre in Quesraba, and the others that had immediately followed.

"I gave him my version of what happened, the only true one. His own son had dishonored the crown of Griteh, the kingdom, and all of its subjects, indulging in a bloody slaughter followed by looting, like a horde of ruthless bandits.

"Coromán's first reaction was as I had hoped. He immediately summoned his son to confront him about our exchange. Aleb flat out denied everything, and gave a detailed report of the imaginary battle against the Quesrabian troops. Then he provided proof, bringing forth his captains as witnesses and presenting the enemies' uniforms and weapons, 'war trophies' that must have dated back to a past conflict. Then the king turned to me, waiting for an answer.

"What could I say? As I had just come to understand, no one would speak out against the prince. I'm merely a warrior; plotting and treachery are not my strong suit, so I didn't see how I could contradict him.

"I suddenly felt a strong urge to have it out with Aleb the Liar. The only thing I could think about was stopping the thug from doing harm once and for all. So I challenged him publicly to a duel of honor.

"It took place the next day. I couldn't sleep at all that night, although an assassination would have confirmed my adversary's vile nature.

"We faced each other in accordance with the rules, before the king and the tribal chiefs, given the official nature of our duel. Even today, Aleb is reputed to be the best fighter in all the Lower Kingdoms. But I had truth on my side…and anger too. He cut my hand and face; I wounded his leg and took out an eye.

"Coromán called the duel to a halt, as he had the right to do. Perhaps to protect his son who had already lost an eye, or perhaps because he had seen enough.

"He granted me the honor of victory, but Aleb was still alive. The king simply rescinded Aleb's claim to the throne, which he transferred to Aleb's younger brother. And in the end, I was banished from the kingdom for disobeying my captain's orders."

The warrior uttered these last words with hate and disgust.

Yan's spirits were dampened. Indeed, everyone was now in a more serious, melancholic, and far-from-pleasant mood. He tried to change the subject.

"Is that where your scar came from?"

"No. That's another story. An *acchor* did that to me. I'll tell you about it another time, if you behave and listen to Lady Corenn," Grigán added with a grin.

Yan smiled back. He had no idea what an *acchor* was, and once again his curiosity was stirred, but he had the good sense to keep it to himself.

"You haven't returned since then?" asked Léti.

"No, never. A short while after I left, Aleb murdered his father and brother with his own hands. Then he ascended to the throne and ordered mass executions. Finally, he initiated a conquest—it would be more accurate to call it destruction—of all of the northern Lower Kingdoms. It sickens me to see how successful he was…"

"Why don't the other kings ally against him?" It seemed like a logical outcome to Yan.

"Some of them tried, but Aleb hired entire armies of mercenaries: Jez, Pledens, Ramgriths, and even Goranese. He lets them sack and pillage all of the conquered lands to their greedy hearts' content. He's not interested in making Griteh richer; he's more concerned with extending his own power. He took over The Hacque as his capital, which isn't even a Ramgrith city! Furthermore, his army is surely made up of more than twice as many Yussa as Ramgriths."

"Who are the Yussa?"

"Mercenaries. Or just men who are under Aleb's command, as one out of every three 'battles' is really just a pillage."

"Mother Eurydis, may they never get the notion to cross the sea!" said Léti.

"Oh, not to worry. Aleb despises the Upper Kingdoms. It's a pastime of his to regularly send assassins after me, to get even for his lost eye. Until one of them succeeds. Unless the Züu rob him of the pleasure. Or perhaps he's the one who's sent them, who knows?"

"You see what your poor character has gotten you into," joked Corenn.

"It's just the way I am," Grigán answered sincerely.

"How long has it been since you left?" Léti cut in.

"Fifteen years, at least…" The warrior reflected for a moment. "No. It's already been nineteen years," he said, with a hint of dread.

"And this man is still trying to kill you, twenty years later? You've been hunted for twenty years?"

"I've already met two men who have devoted their entire lives to revenge. Human will knows no limits, and neither does our folly."

"For someone who claims to not be very fond of reflection, I admire the depth of your thoughts, Master Grigán."

"Actually, those words belong to a friend of mine from the Land of Beauty. But their truth resonates with me; he was able to explain in one sentence everything I'd learned in twenty years of traveling the known world."

"I would really like to meet this perceptive man who has the honor of being called your friend."

"I hope that you'll have the chance someday, Lady Corenn. If we make it out of this terrible adventure alive."

They remained silent for a moment.

"Have you ever thought about returning to confront Aleb?"

Yan had been dying to ask the question for a while, and it took at least as long for the warrior to answer.

"I think about it all the time," he admitted, finally. "But I would no doubt end up dead. Before I even reached him." After a moment he added, "In any case, I'm banished. I don't have the right to return."

The young Kauliens spent a long moment wondering whether this remark was merely a joke or a serious objection.

Silence took hold, and seemed to last an eternity.

"I'm going to see if our rooms are ready," said Grigán finally, arising. He needed to be alone.

After a few moments had gone by, Corenn shared her thoughts with the young ones.

"I thought I knew Grigán better than anyone. But I never would have thought that you would gain his trust so quickly."

"I didn't think he was capable of doing so much talking," Léti said.

"He won't ask you, and I know that you will in any case, but please, respect his memories. He must either forget or accept them. Don't talk to him about it unless he brings it up himself. And, of course, don't speak to anyone else about it. Do you understand why?"

"Of course," they agreed together.

Yan understood that the warrior saw his confession as a weakness and already regretted it. But he had also guessed something else.

"Lady Corenn..."

"Yes?"

"Don't you get the impression that he's trying to hide something? That he didn't tell us everything?"

The Mother stared solemnly at the young, ignorant fisherman, whose mind was nevertheless astute. Then she turned her gaze to the taciturn warrior, who was returning.

"I hope that he'll tell us someday," she whispered. "When he's at peace."

BOOK II:
THE FORGOTTEN ISLAND

I t had already been four days since Yan, Grigán, Léti, and Corenn had left the banks of the Gisland River. Along with hundreds of other travelers, they crossed Kolomine County, and forded the Vélanèse River at a shallow crossing that had been used for decades. Afterward, they headed south toward Lorelia, veering east just before they reached the outskirts of the city. At last, they were less than a day's journey from Berce.

Yan hadn't really been enjoying himself these past few days. Besides the nonstop rain that followed them most of the time, slowing their pace and shortening their patience, he had to endure Grigán's growing anxiety and Corenn's apparent calm indifference, which was just as irritating. And worst of all, Léti's hot and cold remarks about the merits of his perpetual questions, his tendency to avoid taking charge, his *niab* character, and many other things that he preferred to forget.

He was smart enough to not respond to her jabs, counting them as part of the crisis of spirit his friend was going through.

The other evening was the first and only time she admitted to wondering who among her friends had been able to escape the Züu, if any at all. No one wanted to make any guesses, and the subject hadn't been brought up again.

All the same, the Day of the Promise was the day after tomorrow, and Yan would have preferred to be on the best of terms with his beloved in the final moments before proposing. Again, a feeling of apprehension tortured him. Would he have the courage?

Oh, but it wasn't a question of bravery or cowardice. If Léti asked him to jump from the highest cliff in Eza, to dive into the middle of a school of orzos, or to challenge one of the red-cloaked killers, he would do it in a heartbeat—if there were a valid reason, of course. But to go up to her and propose? No!

He acknowledged bitterly that if she were in his place, she wouldn't hesitate for an instant. When she wanted to do something, she did it, simple as that. It would be great if she wanted him too.

He shook his head, as if to chase these thoughts from his mind. The last thing he needed was to start obsessing about what Léti thought. He would know soon enough, and might regret it.

It would have been easier to propose if they had ever discussed the subject before. But no, throughout all those years of living at each other's side, all their conversations, all the time spent getting to know one another, they had never brought up the idea of a Union between them.

He regretted it bitterly.

Of course, everyone else had decided the Union for them, and they themselves had talked more than once, each in turn, about their ideal companion. Handsome, protective, and loving for Léti. Beautiful, mysterious, and joyful for Yan. But it was just a game; the young Kaulien's dream woman was, without hesitation, his lifelong friend.

Did he match up to Léti's ideal? He shook his head again, harder this time. He had to stop thinking about this.

"Are you all right, Yan?"

Corenn looked at him strangely. She must have been watching him for a while. Yan realized he must be quite the sight to see as he rattled his head around like a madman.

"Yes, I'm fine. Thank you. I'm just a little tired." Come on, Yan, that's nonsense, he thought to himself.

"We'll make a short stop," Grigán said.

"No, really, it's not worth the trouble, I'll be fine."

A bunch of nonsense.

They took a break anyway, a few hundred yards from the path as usual. While everyone stretched their legs, rubbed their backs, and tried to dry off their soaking clothes as best they could, Grigán came and went, stiffening when he heard anything suspicious nearby, stealthily approaching the apparent origin of the sound with his hand on his sword hilt.

Pretty soon he had passed his anxiety on to the others. Overcome with curiosity, Corenn tried to distract the warrior from his watch.

"Do you think we're in danger?"

"To tell you the truth, no," he answered without looking at her. "But we could be. I wouldn't bet our lives on a mere gut feeling."

"It's been rather easy going until now, hasn't it?" commented Léti.

"Yes. But the Züu had lost our trail. Whereas now, we're going directly where they'll be expecting us. And that makes me nervous."

"If they're already waiting for us there, they're not going to keep watch on the roads too, right?" she pointed out.

"Would you bet our lives on it?"

Léti kept silent. Of course she wouldn't. She was only making a comment. Mother Eurydis, the man was so touchy!

"Think about it," Grigán went on. "Why didn't the Züu just wait for the heirs to reunite in Berce on the Day of the Owl and murder us all at once?"

"Grigán!" Corenn scolded.

It would take more than that to make Léti back down.

"Do you think I haven't thought of that? Maybe they were worried about letting some of us get away, or sending a warning to those absent? Maybe they were afraid of a defeat? Or maybe they just wanted to be discreet?"

"Or maybe," responded the warrior quietly, "the Züu want to keep us from getting to the island. Perhaps they don't want the heirs to come together this year."

Grigán wanted to make this last retort an effective one, and he succeeded.

Léti silently admitted that she hadn't thought of that.

Obviously, in that case, they were still in danger. More than ever, actually.

With a black look, Corenn showed her disapproval of these revelations, which were premature for her taste. Her niece was still far too emotionally fragile for these disturbing theories about a grand conspiracy.

Everyone retreated into silence then, enjoying the simple pleasure of a well-deserved rest. Yan would have been ready to set up camp for the night, but it was obvious that Grigán, as usual, wanted everyone to put aside their tiredness and carry on a little farther.

Indeed, a moment later he asked them to get moving again. Everyone followed right behind him, accustomed as they were to obeying him now.

To their great surprise, he wasn't leading them back to the path, but deeper into the forest.

He was nice enough to grunt a few words of explanation, but they had already guessed why, once their initial shock subsided—discretion was vital as they got closer to Berce.

That didn't, however, make their walk any more enjoyable. Yan found it even more tiring than his night in the Kaulien scrubland. The ground was muddy, slippery, and spotted with puddles; the rain pooled on the leaves above and fell in droplets, which seemed to take a wicked pleasure in slipping under their clothes; and the horses' exhaustion made it difficult to tug them along.

Also, Grigán frequently commanded instant silence and stillness from his companions, with an imperious wave of his hand. He would remain motionless for a moment, listening, sometimes furtively scouting the surroundings, and then set the line back in motion again. None of it relieved the feeling of tension that had little by little taken hold of the group.

Upon returning from his fifth patrol, which was a lot longer than the others, the warrior didn't give the signal to continue on. With gestures, he ordered them to keep quiet, then led them on a large detour that took longer than a centiday. Finally, he relaxed a little and whispered a few words to Corenn. Yan didn't hear everything, but he understood that the warrior had seen three men setting up a camp, that they weren't necessarily dangerous, but he wouldn't bet his life on it.

Apparently, Grigán wasn't much of a gambler. Deep down, it was rather reassuring.

They moved onward for an entire deciday, even after the sun had gone down. Yan wondered how the warrior knew where he was going. He himself was completely disoriented and would have even had trouble saying which way was north.

"How are you able to guide us? You can't see the stars, and we don't have even the trace of a path to follow, nor the slightest landmark to help."

"Magic," he answered, without batting an eye.

"What?"

"It's magic. I focus very intently on my destination and the path appears in my mind. All Ramgrith men have this power."

Yan was dumbfounded. Was Grigán making fun of him?

"All right, fine, it's not magic. It's simply thanks to this object. You see the arrow? Once it's stopped moving, it always points north."

Yan examined in amazement the crafted ivory object Grigán held out to him. After a few moments, the little metal arrow became still, pointing more or less to his left. If it wasn't just another joke, Yan was ready to believe it was magic after all.

"Where did you get that from?" he asked, handing it back to Grigán.

"I purchased it for a fortune from a Rominian sailor. It's largely thanks to these kinds of inventions that the Old Country was able to dominate the known world for centuries. And that's also why they still jealously guard their secrets."

"How does it work? It isn't really magic, is it?"

"Honestly?"

"Yes!"

"I don't know. It works, that's it. Maybe it's magic, maybe it's divine, maybe it's mundane. I don't know," he repeated.

"It most certainly is not magic," Corenn interrupted.

"Why not?"

"I've seen plenty of needles like that before. In my opinion, there's nothing special about them. They simply fall into the same category as other natural phenomena, like the tides, for example, or the seasons, or the phases of the moon."

"In the Lower Kingdoms, and even elsewhere," Grigán commented, "I've come across cultures that consider each one of those phenomena a divine work."

"I suppose it depends on one's point of view. Why not, after all? One man's folly is another man's truth," Corenn concluded mysteriously.

Yan was far from satisfied. What Léti had said, or rather hadn't said, about her aunt and the supernatural came back to him. What could it be? What were the women hiding from him?

Thinking on it…this whole story about the wise emissaries who disappeared from an island, only to reappear two moons later…up until now, he hadn't really believed it. But as they neared the place in question and after spending a few days with the heirs, who were completely convinced of its truthfulness, he was beginning to have serious doubts.

Could it really be that this old legend was true?

His mind was buzzing with curiosity like never before. The impossible. Magic. Legends.

Yan was prepared to do anything to be at their side, even if for a short while and at a distance. When he was just a child, he eagerly listened as the Ancestress told all the stories, from the underwater kingdom of Xéfalis to the tragedy of the speaking dolphin, Quyl's endless quest, and the legend of the mage Guessardi, not to mention the religious fables about Brosda, Eurydis, and Odrel. Any confrontation with something out of these ancient tales, however minor, seemed to him some of the most valuable experiences imaginable.

All of a sudden, Yan had forgotten his tiredness and even, momentarily, his apprehension about the Day of the Promise. What were they waiting for?

Unfortunately, he had to put a damper on his enthusiasm soon after, when the group met back up with the road. Grigán made everyone turn back then to an abandoned hut they had passed, where at last he "suggested" they stop for the night.

As was his custom, Grigán made a detailed inspection of the surroundings before loosening up a bit. They had a quick bite to eat before tackling the duties they had tacitly assumed out of habit: Grigán took care of the horses, Yan was responsible for the heavy lifting required to set up camp—reduced, this time, to clearing out the hovel—and Corenn and Léti handled the general settling in.

"I think it would be best if someone kept watch tonight," said Grigán. "Yan, are you feeling up to it?"

"Of course. I'm too wound up to go to sleep right now anyway."

"Good. Just wake me when you feel tired."

"What about me?" Léti interjected. "When will it be my turn?"

"Never, so long as we can avoid it. It's more dangerous than you think."

"So what? I'm not scared, if that's what you mean. Will you let me help, or not?"

"No."

Léti rolled her eyes in frustration, feeling powerless against the warrior's will.

"I'll do it without your permission. I'll stay awake all night if I want."

"It's up to you," he said simply.

After struggling for a few moments to come up with a retort, Léti began pouting again.

"I'll miss these special, happy moments later," announced Corenn ironically.

Yan was the only one who got the joke. Once everyone was in bed, he took his post at the spot Grigán had indicated, bow and arrow in hand.

As he sat alone in the cold night, listening and watching the darkness, he experienced a strange, somewhat savage joy that he had never known before.

It was the first time the warrior had given him his complete trust.

It was also the first time he was truly watching over Léti. As if they were in Union.

———⚬⚬⚬———

The next morning Yan felt less heroic. He had struggled to keep his eyes open until the darkest of the night, then regretfully woke up Grigán. He would have liked to have let the warrior rest, but felt the fatigue slowly overtake him.

Worse, even though he did wake Grigán, and it was already late in the morning, he still felt tired enough to sleep another deciday.

Despite this, he was pleasantly surprised when he left their little shack and saw a cloudless sky. The sun was already heating the Lorelien soil, promising better weather. A light breeze rustled the leaves still hanging on the nearby trees, while hundreds of birds celebrated this welcome break from the Season of Wind with song.

Léti wasn't there, nor Grigán. Since no horses were missing, Yan didn't worry.

He walked over to Corenn, who was huddled near a small fire. She greeted him and handed him a hot, aromatic infusion.

"What is it?"

"Some cozé. It's a plant imported from Mestèbe. It has an odd taste, but it's supposed to shake off sleep for even the most tired travelers. None of the Mothers attend a full meeting without drinking a bowl or two."

Yan smiled at the reference and sipped the brew. He found it pretty tasty.

"You hide many talents from us, Lady Corenn," he said, unthinkingly.

"I wonder how I should take that," she answered, feigning vexation.

"No, no, that's not what I meant, I—"

"I know, I am kidding. Some people who know me well would say that you are entirely correct," she told him mysteriously.

Yan considered this response for a moment, but didn't know what to make of it. So he moved on.

"What will the council do? About you, I mean?"

"Since I didn't officially retire, my assistant should stand in for me until my return. But if my absence continues, the Ancestress will nominate someone else to take my place when she thinks it best. Same procedure as if I were dead, actually."

"How does that make you feel?"

"Of course I regret it, but what can we do? As long as the Züu are after us, our only chance at survival, paradoxically, is to feign death. In Kaul, only the Mother responsible for Justice knows our situation. But that's already one person too many; if our enemies capture her, she herself will be in danger. And we will be even worse off given the information that they can get out of her."

Yan nodded his head. If he hadn't yet understood the gravity of the situation, Corenn was quickly remedying that oversight.

"Why doesn't Grigán talk to us about these things? It might help Léti understand; it could make things easier between them."

"Do you think Léti needs to hear this right now?"

Yes, actually. She was already shocked enough by her friends' assassinations, and the one she had escaped.

"So, why are you sharing it with me?"

127

"Because I know you are smart. And that you will need this information if Grigán follows through with his plans."

Yan was going to ask for more information, when the missing members of their band returned to the camp. They both looked very unhappy, particularly Grigán. As soon as they arrived, they turned their backs to one another. It was shaping up to be a great day.

"What happened?" Yan asked his friend.

"It's the crank's fault. He was going to kill a standing sleeper," she said. "I kept him from shooting, and he got mad."

Yan understood. Léti had a semidomesticated standing sleeper for several years. Above all, it was important not to call the little creatures "game animals" in her presence.

"How did you do it?"

"I yelled as loud as I could. The standing sleeper woke up and ran away. You didn't hear it?"

"No, maybe I was still inside."

Yan tried to imagine Grigán's expression at the moment Léti screamed in his ears. That wasn't the sort of thing to put him in a good mood. He was always worried about their discretion.

The grumbling warrior armed himself from head to foot, and quickly left the camp, mumbling something like, "Have to go patrol, thanks to that stupid, willful little girl," to Corenn.

Yan wouldn't want to be in Léti's shoes just then.

It seemed like they were going to get a very late start today. After Yan had washed his face, packed his bags, took care of the horses, and finished other daily chores, Grigán still hadn't returned. Yan decided to get in a little shooting practice. He left the camp with his bow and arrows.

Léti quickly followed suit. They took turns practicing, the young woman getting the best results by far in terms of precision, but still having plenty of trouble putting power behind her shot.

They had a lot of fun; Yan relished the simple joy of one-on-one time with the woman he loved. Joy great enough to distract him from worrying about Grigán finding them.

When Léti started to show signs of fatigue, they headed back toward Corenn, who sat on a blanket spread out at the foot of a tree, writing in a small book. Yan was burning with questions, but stronger yet was his respect for her personal time and his fear of being rude. So he just let himself sneak a glance at her from time to time.

Finally Grigán came back. He seemed calmer, his anger mastered. He brought back some game, and no standing sleepers—thankfully—in the bunch. By chance or choice? No one asked.

The warrior set down the new rations and began to pluck the feathers from a pair of sea pheasants he had shot. Because it was so rare for Grigán to slow them down, the young Kauliens were surprised he seemed to be taking his time. After finishing with the birds, he spread out all his blades in front of him—an impressive sight—and started sharpening and oiling one after the other.

Léti approached and watched patiently for a moment.

"Are you still mad?" she asked.

The warrior didn't even look up.

"No, no, of course not; I'm just thinking, that's all."

And he went on sharpening. He seemed embarrassed, almost ashamed.

"I think I understand, you know," Yan interrupted.

Grigán stared at him, wondering.

"We can't all go to Berce and plunge into the lion's den. You don't want to go alone and leave us unprotected. The best solution is that I go, since the Züu don't know me. But you can't make up your mind."

Three pairs of eyes turned to stare at Yan, waiting for him to finish.

"You'd better get used to it, because I'm going to Berce today."

"It could be dangerous."

Yan stuck out his chest, a bit stupidly.

"I'm not planning on taking any risks. And we didn't come all this way to just give up."

"Good," the warrior concluded cheerfully.

He started to put away his weapons, while explaining to the Kaulien boy what he wanted him to do.

"Berce is less than a half day's ride to the east. You will take the trail..."

"Really? Yan is going to get himself killed!"

Léti couldn't believe that they were taking this seriously.

"Not if he's careful, and he will be; I trust him."

Yan couldn't be happier. Léti, his love, was worried about him, and Grigán the Unbending just complimented him. Where was that army of killers? Bring them on!

The warrior interrupted his daydream, "It's not like he's going off on a crusade, after all. All I want is for him to observe and report back to us. All in one Kaulien piece, if possible."

Yan answered with a twisted smile.

"There is an inn on the sea road, almost at the end of town. I forget the name..."

"The Wine Merchant," said Corenn, who had kept silent until then.

"That's it. That's where most of the heirs stay during the gatherings. Get a room there and watch."

"Am I going to sleep there?" Yan blurted out.

"You don't have much choice. Even if you left right now, you couldn't get there and back tonight. What's bothering you?"

"No, it's just that...nothing," Yan muttered.

But something still nagged at him. The Day of the Promise was tomorrow. He had to be with Léti on that day.

Grigán exchanged looks with Corenn, then continued.

"You will rejoin us tomorrow, or the next day, whenever you think it best. Just make sure you aren't being followed."

Yan nodded again. The day after tomorrow, not a chance! He already had made the firm decision to return at sunrise, if possible.

"Speak with as few people as you can. Say that you came for the Day of the Promise, that you are from a Kaulien village, anywhere but Eza, of course. That you're hoping to find someone. That will explain, at least in part, why you're nosing around everywhere."

Yan cringed at the mention of the Promise and searched for Léti's reaction. But the young woman was lost in her thoughts. Had she even heard?

"Dozens of isolated peasants from the area come to Berce for such occasions. As in your own village, I'm sure. You should pass through unnoticed. Lastly, don't trust a soul. All right?"

"Not a soul," Yan repeated in an unsteady voice.

Now all of this seemed a lot less fun.

"Good. Are you still sure?"

Yan stifled his conflicted feelings.

"Of course. It's going to be as easy as falling off a log. And I'll be back tomorrow," he said, looking at Léti.

She stepped a few feet away.

Yan could have sworn he heard her crying.

He came within sight of Berce shortly after the apogee. In a rush to complete his task and return to his loved one, he didn't give his horse a rest and was going to arrive sooner than Grigán had estimated.

After a departure marked by Corenn's encouraging words, Grigán's last bit of advice, and, more than anything, Léti's painfully tearful, "See you tomorrow," he'd led his horse to the trail they hit the night before, which he followed until he got to a wider road.

The apprehension he felt for the first couple of leagues had slowly subsided, mainly because he didn't see anyone. But it was coming back even stronger now and taking hold of his body, tying knots in his stomach, stiffening his arms and legs, and shortening his breath. Yan knew the cause well enough: fear.

In spite of his slightly *niab* character and the occasional verbal floggings he endured, he was far from being an idiot. If even a fraction of what his companions told him were true, which had to be the case, Berce was going to be a genuine snake's nest, a hunting trap the size of an entire village, set by a powerful organization of fanatical assassins.

Upon reflection, he didn't really see how he could discover anything important, besides confirming it was best for his companions to avoid the place. He couldn't recognize any of the other heirs if he saw them and couldn't even trust anyone claiming to be one.

Oh, well, he was just going to do the best he could, and return straight back to Léti the next day. Best to hold on to that thought.

Berce was a citadel, or more accurately, a town surrounded by a wall about nine feet tall. It was much larger than Eza. In fact, Berce was already a small city. The front gate was open, but Yan counted four men near the opening, lounging about carelessly, sitting against the wall or sprawled out on the grass, nevertheless vigilant enough to keep Yan from passing by unnoticed.

He studied them closely as he came near. They hardly seemed like standard city guards. In addition to their most unmilitary attitude, they weren't wearing uniforms or anything close to them, and didn't demonstrate the slightest care for hygiene.

All four of them were even dirtier than Old Vosder: unkempt beards, grimy faces, black hands, clothes that hadn't been changed for several dékades...

One of them rose to his feet at Yan's arrival. Yan preferred to bring his mount to a halt and wait patiently for the "soldier" to come over to him, thinking it better to keep a distance from the other three.

The filthy man spoke a few interrogative words to him, meanwhile grabbing hold of his horse's reins. Yan took note of the gesture but didn't understand a word of what he said. Was it a Lorelien slang?

"I don't understand," he said in Ithare.

One of the other soldiers came over to them. Yan fought the impulse to tear the reins away and gallop at full speed back to his friends. The new arrival addressed him in Ithare.

"Yer not Lorelien?"

"Nope," he answered in a defiant tone. He continued, more calmly, "No. I'm from Assiora, a village in the center of the Matriarchy."

The two hideous men stared at him in silence.

"Kaul!" Yan added. "The Kaul Matriarchy! It's not even a dékade's ride away!"

The second man's face finally lit up with recognition. He smiled, then burst out laughing before translating for his counterpart, who caught on and laughed in turn.

"So ye come from wom'n country?"

"Women country?"

"Yeah! There's jist women o'er there: women-men and men-women!" he laughed even harder.

Yan didn't quite get the joke but was sure that he didn't like it. He really wanted to respond in kind, attacking the apparently liberal Lorelien standards of hygiene, but he was able to control himself and grit his teeth as he waited for the degenerates, who were now all gathered around him, to stop laughing idiotically.

It was a long wait, but they finally showed an interest in him again.

"So, wha' cha here for?"

"For the Day of the Promise."

The guard translated for his pals, and the brutes' potbellies shook with another explosion of laughter. Yan suddenly realized the potential benefit of having clothes like Grigán's. He would have been treated differently had he come dressed in leather armor, with a four-foot-long blade at his waist. Instead he wore a stupid beige tunic belonging to Léti and a headband Corenn had tied around his forehead—"A finishing touch for your bachelor look." Ridiculous!

"So can I enter or not?" he asked, annoyed.

"Yeah, yeah," the soldier answered, wiping away tears of laughter. "Good luck, friend!"

Yan ignored the new tempest of hilarity that broke out behind him as he passed through the outer wall. Danger, heroism—yeah right! He was sure he was going to hear more of the same over the next couple of days.

He swallowed his anger and shame, and observed his surroundings. That's what he had come for, so the sooner it was done, the sooner he could return to Léti.

The little city was in quite a stir, surely due in large part to the preparations and excitement surrounding tomorrow's festival.

Berce looked like a nice city. The houses, stables, artisan's workshops, and other buildings appeared to be somewhat old, but that gave them a certain charm. He noted that a lot of them were several stories tall, in contrast to the traditional Kaulien architecture.

He walked up what must have been the main street. He passed many busy people on his way, the majority of whom barely glanced at him. Good, at least he would pass through unnoticed. The only exceptions were those who stopped and stared at him in amusement. At first Yan tried to remain indifferent, but then he couldn't stop himself from responding with dirty looks. He ended up ripping off his headband and undoing his tunic altogether.

Children of all ages scampered about in groups around the streets. Bitter, he promised himself he would keep a close eye on the purse Corenn gave him. He wasn't about to be fooled twice; he had learned his lesson in Jerval.

He passed another horseman traveling in the opposite direction. Yan noticed he was leading his horse by the bridle. He figured he might draw fewer looks if he did the same. He dismounted and continued on foot.

He came upon what must have been the central square. As it was Lorelien custom to avoid work as much as possible on festival days, preparations for the following day were already well under way.

Citizens had set up various tables, collected from the community, and an equally dissimilar assortment of benches, chairs, and stools. An impressive pile of wood and a fireplace built specifically for the occasion sat a short distance from all the furniture.

But what struck and alarmed Yan the most was the platform. Were the promised couples expected to go up there together, in front of everyone? Or worse, was it that the men had to stand up there alone and propose? It was possible, after all, that the procedure for the ceremony in Lorelia was very different than in Kaul.

Yan was standing there as if hypnotized by the whole scene, his imagination painting the most terrible scenarios, when a face sprung up right in front of his own.

He had neither seen nor heard the man approaching. The man had slithered his way in front of Yan like a snake, and now stared at him insistently.

Yan briefly returned his fierce stare. The man was shorter than him and wore a common priest's cloak with the hood pulled up. He must have been in his thirties, but his clean-shaven face and bald head made him look younger. He kept his hands hidden, but that wasn't what was most alarming.

A shark. His eyes reminded one of a shark. Yan had only seen one once, at the end of a long fishing expedition with a group of fellow villagers. But he would never forget those cold eyes, devoid of all feeling.

Of course, then it had only been a child's simple interpretation, made at the sight of a dead animal. Now the shark was alive and seemed to be relishing its prey's fear.

"Excuse me."

Yan turned around as calmly as possible to avoid starting something he'd have to finish, even though he had only one desire: run away at top speed.

He met another shark behind him.

The second man was less than a yard behind him. He hadn't made any more noise than the first, and was dressed the same, and had the same hungry look.

Yan froze in terror. For just an instant, he thought he saw a flash of metal in one of the man's hands. Then the hand disappeared in the folds of the cloak.

Yan continued forward, calmly, without turning back around. He expected to take a dagger in the back at any moment. He led his horse in such a way as to situate it diagonally behind him. Even then, he could feel their eyes burning into the back of his neck.

He stopped at the other side of the square, where a pub offered patio seating, calmly tied up his horse next to another, and chose a seat from where he could observe the frightening men.

They were no longer there. Yan looked over the whole square, but in vain. He couldn't stop himself from whipping around to make sure they weren't sitting behind him. But the sharks had fled these waters.

A high-pitched nasal voice made him jump in his seat. He tried as best he could to slow the beating of his heart, and realized that a woman in her fifties had been questioning him since he sat down.

"Wine!" he answered shakily in Ithare.

For a moment he was afraid he'd mistaken the sense of the question, but the woman nodded her head and shortly after brought him a full goblet, which Yan paid for, letting out a sigh of relief. He hated wine and had answered impulsively. However, given the recent rush of emotions, he found the drink had a particularly cheering flavor and mildness.

He turned around again, falsely relaxed. He thought of Grigán. Did the warrior always live that way? Always watching his back?

Would his personal experience be enough to get them out of this mess?

He thought back to the fleeting flash of metal he saw. Beyond a doubt, it was the Züu. Had they planned to kill him?

No, he would already be dead if that were the case…

In his place, an heir wouldn't have had the slightest chance.

Yan didn't give a margolin's ass how they were able to distinguish between heirs and nonheirs. The important thing now was to avoid making a blunder that would cause them to change their mind.

As his eyes scanned the crowd, he noticed that, on the whole, Loreliens weren't any dirtier than Kauliens. So what were those four hairy apes doing guarding the gates to the city? Were they even from here?

He had to be constantly on alert.

He finished his goblet, stood up, and started walking toward The Wine Merchant, which the matron had indicated.

He crossed the entire southern end of the little city, almost as far as the gate that opened onto the sea road, before arriving at his destination. He almost passed it by without noticing. Unlike The Ferry Inn, this one had only a tiny little sign.

A beggar sat not far from the door, holding out a small cup with a few sad coins in the bottom. Yan opted not to abandon his horse in the street and, hollering through the open door, asked the innkeeper to point him toward the stable. The round, ruddy, pleasant-looking man in the door did him one better, taking charge of the horse himself and inviting Yan inside the inn so he could be taken care of.

Yan agreed, but followed the innkeeper with his eyes until the man reached a building close by. It was possible that he would need to fetch his horse on short notice, and he wanted to know where it was stabled.

"A small coin t'eat, sir," the beggar asked with difficulty, in a quavering voice.

He looked just like any other old beggar that he had come across up until now: dirty, hairy, grimy, dressed in clothes washed only by the rain.

It was possible that this guy was working for the Züu. Or simply unfortunate…He looked more like a sickly fellow than he did a drunkard. Yan reached into his purse and tossed a coin into the little cup. Curses, the man stunk! Undoubtedly, he must have rolled in his own filth. The beggar backed away as soon as possible.

"Thank you, sir. Thank you, thank you," he said, effusively.

He had hardly even glanced at the coin. Yan shrugged his shoulders and entered the inn.

The hall was empty this early in the evening. The innkeeper rejoined him inside soon.

"You don't have anyone to look after horses for you?" Yan began.

"Yes, yes I do, my older son. But it's the Day of the Promise for him tomorrow too. It would really be cruel of me to make him work today."

Yan took an immediate liking to the man. It wasn't surprising that the heirs had stayed here. Provided that the cuisine was as good as Corenn had said.

Yan told him he wanted to stay two nights, and paid in advance, even though he wasn't asked. He then took advantage of the man's obvious thirst for conversation to get some information.

"The men at the gates? No, they're not from here. Well, except for Nuguel, and Bertan's son. No one knows where the others are from; perhaps the city. One thing's for certain: they're not the kind of people you want to associate with. They haven't harmed anyone, for the moment at least. So no one says anything. If you want my opinion, they're looking for someone. And I wouldn't want to be in that someone's place if he decided to show his face around here. Mind you, he's probably just another good-for-nothing thief or cutthroat, the kind who wouldn't think twice about ransacking my place. What do you think? For that matter, why do you ask? Did they give you trouble?"

Yan took a moment to digest the whole speech. His throat felt sore just listening to the innkeeper.

"No, no, they just made fun of me a little, that's all. Are there a lot more of them waiting for this someone?"

"Now, that I couldn't say. With all the young people like yourself and their families coming in from the countryside for the Promise, there are twice as many people in the village as usual. And there's also a sort of large family that organizes a festival here every three years, and it falls on this year. Some of them might also be part of the crowd."

Yan wondered if it would be suspicious to ask, but the opportunity was simply too perfect and the answer too important.

"Have you seen any of them?"

"You mean people from the big family?"

"Yes, uh…"

He desperately searched for a reason why he might be asking. He didn't find one, and was going to change the subject when the innkeeper answered him.

"No. Not yet. But it's still early. Perhaps in a couple of days. They always come here, you know. They nearly take up the entire inn. At the moment, the only people here are you, a couple from Lermian, and a group of five priests who only took two rooms! Can you believe it? Two rooms for five! I'm very respectful of priests, I am, so I told them, 'If it's a question of money, go ahead and take one room each for the same price, since they're available.' But they refused. Don't you find that a little odd?"

"Yes, very."

Very strange. Frightening, even. He was going to spend the night next to five Züu.

And if he made one false move, he wouldn't see daybreak.

It took Yan some time before he got back to the city center. Mostly thanks to the garrulous innkeeper, who had kept him a long time by trapping him in an endless chat. Then it was the beggar's turn, who had the nerve to demand alms from Yan again. He looked a lot less sick this time. Some people have a very strange sense of humor.

Without his bow to defend himself, and without his horse to flee, Yan felt very vulnerable. All he had on him was Grigán's borrowed dagger, to replace the knife he had given to Léti. Not the most helpful thing, but on the other hand, even with a giant sword, he didn't see how he could get the upper hand on those seasoned assassins.

So it was with fear in his stomach and his mind racing that Yan arrived at the location where they were preparing the festival. A detailed examination revealed that not a single Zü was there, or more accurately, none were visible. Yan wondered which was better.

The workday coming to an end, more and more people gathered around the plaza. Apparently, the Loreliens celebrated the Promise on its eve as well. He noticed that a good number of young people—his exact age, actually—waited around excitedly, in any places their elders left to them. They were all grouped together, but always of the same gender: boys with boys, girls with girls. Yan casually leaned against a wall, next to two young Loreliens who completely ignored him, captivated as they were by the fairer sex adorned in their finest regalia.

As for Yan, he scrutinized the foreigners. Maybe some of them were heirs? Others working on the Züu's dark plans? Who was who?

Léti, Corenn, and Grigán had done their best to describe some of their friends, but the list grew rapidly, and it didn't take long for Yan to jumble up all of their descriptions. Besides, his companions had warned him about the reliability of their own memories. Even more so because all the details came from three-year-old memories, so they couldn't rely on them, anyway.

He realized with dread that the beggar from the inn was watching him, and must have been for a while. Did he just avoid making eye contact? Was he following him?

Yan told himself he had better steer clear of the squalid character during his stay in Berce. To protect his purse, if nothing else.

"Hello."

Two young blonde girls, standing quietly in front of him with their hands on their hips, were smiling insistently at him. He blushed up to his ears when he saw them. They wore skirts that were much shorter than was permitted in Kaul.

"Uhh, hello," he answered lamely.

"Is it true you come from Kaul?" the taller one asked innocently, a smile still plastered on her face.

Yan frowned. Could they see it on his face or what? If he couldn't even pass through unnoticed by two village girls, it was useless to try to trick his enemies!

"How did you know, miladies?" he couldn't keep from sounding formal.

"My uncle told me. He hangs out with Nuguel's cousins and they saw you at the Lorelien gate today. Nuguel told all of his friends about you coming for the Promise, to give them a laugh."

Seeing Yan's face turn pale, she quickly added, "But I don't think it's funny. I think it's charming."

Yan turned an even brighter shade of red. Completely stupid, he was completely stupid.

"Oh. Really?" was his only answer.

She persisted, "Kauliens are so romantic. Is it true you don't let your wives work? That you prefer to give them everything?"

Yan gave a strangled hiccup. Was she messing with him? Or did the rest of the world actually say such things about Kauliens?

"That's a bit exaggerated..." Yan began.

"Any way you look at it, it must be better than here. All the men I know are just fishermen without any real future, who only want to marry so they can make babies. As for me, I want to experience a real love story. I would really, I mean really, like to be promised to a Kaulien..."

The minx winked at him, making her desires even more obvious, before she turned her back and walked away with her silent friend. Yan watched them walk away like they were dancing on an imaginary tightrope.

He didn't have any worries about the enterprising Lorelien girl's future. How would Léti have taken this? He didn't have the slightest idea. He'd like to imagine that she would be jealous. But that would have ended with a fight, either verbal or physical, between the two women. Léti wasn't the type to just let things like that go.

A clamor pulled him out of his musings. A few members of the crowd were pointing in one direction, where Yan turned his gaze. Two or three leagues outside town, from a very distinct spot in the surrounding hills, something was sending up flashes of light.

A group of ten horsemen pushed themselves through the crowd toward the gates. Fear rising in his chest, Yan recognized at least three Züu in the party; the others were only scoundrels like those guarding the gates.

The assassins had reacted very quickly. If the man who had made the signals was an heir, he didn't have much chance of escaping, unless he fled immediately.

Maybe Yan could warn him, if he hopped in the saddle. But he would have to pass the others without being seen. He wasn't a good enough horseman for that. Also, he would have to first make it back to the inn, which would slow him down even more.

But surely there was something he could do. He had to do something. He knew it was important.

He grabbed a clump of dirt and vigorously rubbed it on his cheeks. Now dirtied up, he ran across a good number of streets before stumbling upon the type of vendor he needed. Feigning anger, Yan cursed himself for his clumsiness at getting himself so grimy on such an important day. The merchant laughed at the poor young man's misfortune, and sold him a glass mirror so that he could clean himself up.

As soon as he left, Yan began looking for a suitable location for his plan. He soon found it in the form of an abandoned house, which he entered through a window after first assuring himself that no one was watching—looking out specifically for the beggar from the inn.

His heart threatened to beat through his chest. He was really in danger now. Even if the least dangerous of his enemies saw him, that would be the end.

He climbed along the banister of an unsteady and fractured stairway, trying to avoid the steps, which were in an even worse state than the handrails. Then he cautiously climbed a rotten ladder before opening a trapdoor covered in dust.

He finally was on top of the house, panting and breathless, his temples pounding. Someone was still making light signals, ignorant of the danger galloping toward him. Yan lifted the mirror as high as possible and twisted it around in every direction. Would that be enough to send the rays of the sun so far?

Would he get himself caught and die today?

On the hillside, the flashes disappeared. Then there were three short ones, like three knocks at a door. They were the last ones.

Yan stopped moving his mirror. That must have been a response. He had succeeded!

A huge smile bloomed on his face. He had succeeded at something, maybe saved a life, maybe only given a little bit of hope to the man at the other end of the signals. An heir...definitely an heir.

Hopefully this idiot wouldn't get the idea to come all the way to Berce now.

He chased this dark idea out of his head; he needed to worry about his own well-being. After cleaning his face, he wrapped the mirror in a piece of fabric he found in the house and threw the whole package onto a roof two houses over. He proceeded with an acrobatic descent along the exterior wall, worried about exposing himself by passing through the house again.

He who makes himself a sheep will be eaten by the wolf...He never would have believed himself capable of such things!

Did Grigán really live like this all the time? Yan asked himself again, jumping to the ground.

By the time the horsemen returned it was late in the evening and the festival was already well under way. To Yan's relief, he noticed they didn't bring back any bodies or prisoners with them. Nor did they have the proud and arrogant look of victors. Fortunately, the stranger had gotten away.

He shot only a fleeting glance at the three "priests," afraid that a longer look would draw their attention. But it was long enough for one of them to meet his eyes. Again, Yan was frozen in terror at seeing those predatory eyes. Luckily, the Zü continued on his way, observing everyone indifferently.

Was he the only one who was scared? The others must not have noticed. He wondered how the locals would react if they found out a group of murderous Züu had taken root in their own village. Surely the town would be deserted the following deciday.

The horsemen separated, the three assassins heading for The Wine Merchant. Yan made up his mind to follow them, desperate to gather any additional information for the night. There was little chance that the people reveling in drink, those dancing to airs played on vigolas and moon lutes, and especially those who were courting would be of any interest to Grigán. On top of that, the young Lorelienne who had approached him earlier wouldn't stop signaling to him; it was obvious that before long she would come up to talk to him again. Maybe even suggest a dance! It was best to avoid another embarrassment.

He gave a limp wave in response to one of her gestures, and then took advantage of a surge in the crowd to slip away unnoticed. It was hardly civilized, sure, but he couldn't find a better solution. And since others might have had their eyes on him...

He briskly walked back to the inn. Away from the large fireplace in the square, the night became bitterly cold.

No meal had been served at the festival. Tortured by hunger, Yan had eaten bread and forcemeat at the inn. He now congratulated himself. If he had to dine alone with the Züu as tablemates at the inn, he wouldn't have been able to swallow a bite.

He soon reached his destination. The beggar was no longer sitting across from the entrance. Several times throughout the evening, Yan had thought he'd caught a glimpse of him in various places around the festivities. He was happy not to run into him again.

With a quick glance in through the window, Yan made sure the inn was empty. He pushed open the door, which had the immediate effect of summoning the innkeeper, who without delay tried unsuccessfully to strike up a conversation. Yan simply took the candleholder he handed to him, politely wished him a good night, and fled upstairs. He couldn't handle another deciday of ceaseless babble.

He silently walked past the two rooms where the Züu were staying, the two rooms closest to the staircase, situated across from one another. The tireless host had pointed them out earlier in the day, after showing him his room. The priests had insisted on staying in these rooms: a most strategic placement, Yan noticed. No one could go up or down without them knowing.

The door on the left was cracked open. One of them was on watch, or at least keeping an open ear. Yan continued forward calmly. The last thing he wanted was to arouse suspicion. An idea came to him just before he reached his room, and he pretended to drunkenly stumble as he neared the end of the hall. That might throw them off.

Yan clumsily slipped the key into the lock of the door to his room, struggling with it for a moment. He didn't even have to pretend: it truly was difficult. He finally managed to turn the lock, enter, and close the door behind him with a sigh. He felt like he was in a snake pit, or rather, a pool of sharks.

One night, he only had to hold on for one night, and he could return to Léti. The news he would bring wasn't good—the entire village was under surveillance by their enemies, and the hope of finding other heirs hung from a few flashes of light from a stranger, who might have had nothing to do with their business.

The only thing he had left to do was wait. He resigned himself to his fate and thought about how he would get through the night.

His room had a roof hatch, rather small, but big enough for a slender man, or more simply, a crossbow bolt, to slip through. He made sure that it was closed tight and even reinforced the latch with a thin rope. It wouldn't make a big difference for a determined individual, but it was better than doing nothing at all.

He wasn't going to fall asleep tonight. Not right away, at least. Despite the lateness, he didn't feel tired in the slightest; the cold and the anticipation kept him wide awake.

He resolved to get his clothes together for the next day. He refused to put on that stupid tunic meant for girls.

That's when he noticed that someone had gone through his things.

He took a quick inventory—they hadn't stolen anything. Furthermore, he didn't see that he owned anything attractive enough to justify a robbery.

Of course, the aim wasn't robbery. For that matter, they'd made a conscious and careful effort to put everything back as they found it, and it was mere coincidence Yan noticed at all.

He checked his lock. It appeared to be in good condition, stiffness aside. Unless that had actually been caused by the break-in.

Now he definitely wasn't going to get any sleep that night. He even felt ready to start the return trip immediately...but that would have been too dangerous, too suspect.

He sat down resolutely on a stool in front of the door, dagger in hand. All right, the first person to come through this door was going to get it. As for the second...he didn't know how he would hold him off.

To think that a few days before he had found it all so exciting! Given his current situation, he far preferred his life from before— monotonous and uneventful.

In the end, he managed to nod off—for a short while at a time, anyway—despite his uncomfortable position. Hardly a deciday went by, but he felt like it lasted two.

Voices in the hall.

It took him a few moments to realize that they were in fact real, not just something from his troubled sleep. Then they became all too concrete.

Two or three men, maybe more, were talking among themselves, or with the assassins, at the top of the stairs. Yan glued his ear to the door, but he still couldn't hear the conversation. All he understood was, "I...fifty, no less." The rest, said in a lower tone, was unintelligible.

He decided to risk it and open the door, since a discussion so late in the night could only be truly important. He hid his candle under the stool covered by a blanket, and then turned the key in the door ever so slowly. Finally, he gently cracked the door open.

The hinges creaked, very faintly, but to Yan's ears it sounded louder than a vorvan's cry. He waited motionless a few moments, his hand gripping his dagger, but no one came. The men were still talking and seemed not to have heard anything.

"No, no," proclaimed the loudest voice. "I want fifty silver terces, no less. And furthermore, I want them before I leave."

"Fifty, that's quite a sum," said a calm voice. "Do you truly believe your knowledge to be worth that much? That a half day of your time deserves two gold terces?"

"If you find someone else, go ahead, hire them. But I'm telling you, it's just me. And without me, you'll never find the guy with the mirror. You have to read the signs, and despite your holiness and all that, you don't know how to do that. So, I want fifty."

"Are you very familiar with the goddess Zuïa?" asked the smooth voice.

Silence.

"Zuïa is the Goddess of Justice. Take careful note of how I didn't say *a* goddess but *the* Goddess of Justice. Other gods are just weaklings; they only judge humans after their deaths. Zuïa is the only one who carries out her sentences immediately. She's the only one who wields a real power, the only true goddess."

Another silence. Yan could easily imagine the loud voice losing its confidence.

"My brothers and I are Zuïa's messengers. If you refuse to help us, you will be siding with those already condemned. And Zuïa will judge you for that."

At least it was unequivocal, thought Yan.

"So," the smooth voice resumed, "are you going to lead us to them?"

The loudmouth apologized profusely, mumbling that it didn't occur to him that they were dealing with a sacred mission and that, of course, he was completely at their disposal. For free! The smooth voice concluded with a simple, "Good," and they set a meeting for the following day at the square when the third deciday sounded. They then turned and left down the stairs.

Yan waited for all to go quiet again before closing the door with infinite care, placing a piece of clothing on one of the hinges. The noise was muffled enough to be unnoticeable.

Locked safely in his room again, his mind was racing. What to do? What could he do? What would Grigán do in his position?

If he stayed put, the man with the mirror was going to die the next morning. If he moved, he too would perish that very night, unless he thought of something. But what?

He had no means by which to warn the stranger. He believed he could find the place in the hills by memory, but only in broad daylight. By night, it was impossible. Not to mention this talk about "reading the signs"...What would Grigán do in his position? He would need to ask him.

Even if it was going to be risky to slip away from Berce and ride at night, he figured it was best to rejoin his friends. Perhaps the warrior would have a better solution?

His decision made, Yan began addressing the practical concerns. One glance out the opened roof hatch confirmed that he couldn't plan on making his exit that way. The slope of the roof was far too steep and looked right over a busy street. Not the most discreet exit.

So the door remained the only solution. What if he were to just walk out forthright, without acting like he was trying to hide something?

Either way, he should wait a bit. It would be too obvious to leave right now, just after that conversation.

He rubbed his face as he sat pondering. Here he was, forced to think like a fugitive, an outlaw, a convict, while he was the victim. His life really had changed.

It was better to leave his belongings in the room, he decided. To abandon them, actually, since he didn't see how he could come back for them afterward. If the Züu on watch saw him walk by with his whole pack, no doubt they would be suspicious.

So he quickly sorted what he absolutely had to take from the rest. To his eyes, Léti's beige tunic was the only thing of value, because it didn't belong to him. He resigned himself to leaving the rest behind.

When he judged that enough time had gone by, he left the room without locking it, carrying only the candleholder.

He consciously made little effort to be secretive, sure that he was being spied on anyway. To his great relief, he managed to make it to the other end of the hall, pass in front of the killers' rooms, and descend the staircase without being bothered.

On the ground floor, a boy his age slept soundly with his folded arms resting on the counter. Yan went around the boy without waking him, set the candleholder on a table, and went out.

Step one, accomplished. The next one was going to be a lot trickier: how was he going to exit the city on horseback, this late at night, with guards at the gates? Because they most certainly were still there.

He made his way to the stable, still hashing it out. He couldn't see any solution other than just charging through. He lacked the energy to invent some sort of story believable enough for the uncouth soldiers who'd made a laughingstock of him.

Curses! The door to the stable was fitted with a lock. That was unexpected. After a few unsuccessful attempts with his dagger to break it open, he resolved to smash it with the blows of a rock. Luckily, the lock quickly gave way.

He wanted to close the door behind him while he readied his horse, but it was so dark inside, he left it ajar. He more or less groped his way forward, using the animals' breathing and the sound of their hooves to guide him. Finally, he found his horse. A bad feeling had been niggling at him since he left the inn, and he had almost expected to find the stable emptied of horses but filled with enemies.

He rapidly saddled the horse and made for the door.

A man was blocking the way.

Due to the poor lighting, Yan couldn't see his face, but his stature and clothing were telling enough. He wasn't a Zü, Yan saw with relief. His features more closely resembled one of those crass soldiers who seemed to be working for the Züu. He wondered if the man had followed him, or if he had already been in the stable.

"Who are you?" Yan asked.

He wondered if it wouldn't be too aggressive to stab the man with his dagger immediately. But that could start what he wanted to avoid at all costs: a fight.

"A friend," answered the stranger. "I'm one of the heirs, and so are you, no?"

Yan remained uncertain for a few instants. Grigán had ordered him to not trust a soul, and he took the advice to heart. If this man was a friend, why was he blocking the way? Why didn't he close the door? Unless he wasn't being careful himself.

"And what is this friend's name?"

Yan never would have thought himself capable of such impoliteness.

"Reyan. Reyan Kercyan. I'm from Lorelia. You're one of the heirs, aren't you?"

This friend's tone of voice wasn't friendly. But that could also be explained by this so-called Reyan's own distrust. Should he believe him? Yan remembered hearing Corenn cite his name at least once. Was he one of those dead or alive?

"I'm not one of the heirs," he answered, decisively. "But some of them are my friends."

"Are they here? In the city?" he asked eagerly.

Yan had no desire to provide the Lorelien with that kind of information. He didn't move away from the door. Yan noticed that one of the man's hands was hidden from view. He didn't like that at all. Could he hop in the saddle and trample the man before he had time to react?

"Well? Are they in the city, or not? You're slow to answer. Don't you trust me?"

Yan suddenly became convinced that he should not, in fact, trust this man. He was getting ready to jump onto his horse, when he saw, with horror, another man appear in the doorway. This one he recognized right away—he was the beggar from the inn. Certainly the other man's accomplice. The situation was going from bad to worse.

"Don't be so difficult, it's no use," the first man continued. "You'll end up telling anyway, whether it's me or those nutcases in red. It's simply a matter of time and pain."

Yan was frozen with fear. Was this guy threatening him with torture? Did he not just admit loud and clear his involvement with the Züu? Yan clenched his dagger and held it in front of him, his thumb on the blade, like Grigán had shown him. It must not have had as impressive an effect as intended, because the first man burst out laughing. As for the beggar, he just continued inching his way toward his companion.

Why so slowly?

"All right, you want to play?" said the other, as he pulled a curved blade out from underneath his cloak. "With pleasu—"

The beggar, who was now right behind the louse, violently raised the other man's chin with one hand. With a dagger held in his other hand, he traced a dark groove across his throat, which quickly gushed forth blood as it widened. The wounded man let out a few sickening gurgles and collapsed.

The murderer leaned down and wiped his blade with his victim's clothes.

"Even when they're dying, they're revolting. These fellows really have no style. Except for pretending to be me, of course."

Yan kept hold of his dagger. What was going on here?

"Oh! I hope you aren't too upset with me, depriving you the pleasure of ridding us of this fat heap. An opportunity presented itself, so…"

Yan stared blankly at the beggar, who had by now put away his dagger and stared back at him with his hands on his hips.

"I mean, I hope you aren't too upset with me for saving your life and all."

"Um…thanks," mumbled Yan.

He couldn't dispel the image of this man coldly killing the other. It was going to be just as hard to grant his trust to this newcomer.

"Who are you?" he asked, with a feeling of déjà vu.

"Rey Kercyan, the original. And it's just Rey, not Reyan. This guy should have known that I don't let anyone call me Reyan. That's way too fourteenth eon. And you, Mr. Horse Thief?"

"Yan. And this horse belongs to me!"

"The door too? As well as the lock?"

The Kaulien remained silent.

"Come on, I'm kidding. Let's not hang around."

The so-called Rey leaned over the body again, from which he pulled out a dirty purse that he weighed in his hand, a disdainful look on his face. Shocked, Yan didn't want anything to do with this immoral man. This reeking man had to be aiming for some sort of reward he didn't want to share with anyone, which is why he killed his accomplice. He certainly wasn't an heir!

"I must leave you," attempted Yan. "Thanks again."

"Wait!"

It wasn't an order, and no sudden movement was made to stop him, so Yan decided to hear him out, for a few moments at least.

"I heard what you said earlier. Everything you said. Since I got here a dékade ago, it's the first bit of good news I've received. You don't have to believe me, of course, but I'm also part of the family. To my misfortune," he added, in a low voice.

Yan didn't know what to think. His tone seemed sincere, but the stakes were too high. It could merely have been part of some scheme to locate Yan's friends.

"I can't take you to them. I don't even know you."

"I know, I wouldn't have thought otherwise. So, go find them and tell them I'm alive. I've grown up a little since they last saw me, but surely they'll remember this: tell them I'm the boy who lit the tent on fire a few years ago. They can't have forgotten that," he added with a smile.

Yan nodded. He didn't understand everything, but he did know that Rey didn't have any immediate ill intentions toward him. That was enough for him.

"Then what? If that's enough to convince them?"

"Come find me. Oh, not here," he added, noticing the fear in Yan's eyes. "I don't plan on sticking around here either. Let's say tomorrow at the apogee, on the beach where we held the old gatherings."

"I guarantee it's being patrolled," objected Yan.

"It's not. I checked. At least it isn't yet. By the time the Day of the Owl comes, it will be."

Yan accepted. He would have liked to suggest another meeting point, but he wasn't familiar with the region. Grigán would decide the best course of action later.

"One last thing. Warn them that the Grand Guild is also after us."

"The Grand Guild?"

"Do you not know what it is, or do you not believe me?" asked Rey in surprise.

"I don't know what it is," admitted Yan in all seriousness.

"Great. Good thing I've found some help," he said to himself, ironically.

"I'm going to share your criticisms with someone I know," Yan retorted. "I bet he'll have a lot to say on the subject."

They let a moment of silence go by.

"Touchy, huh?" Rey continued, breaking the silence.

"Less touchy than you are cynical," Yan answered, with the same frankness.

They faced each other for a few moments, with knowing smiles. Then Rey calmly took Yan by the arm and led him outside.

"Let's get going! The sun will soon be up and we'll still be pestering one another, sitting over this dead body. Can you imagine how that'd look? Tell me, how did you plan on making it out of here with your horse?"

—⊛—

A whistle rose up in the night.

Nuguel, the only man posted by the Züu at the Leem gateway, wasn't in the mood for games. All his friends, or at least most of them, had been sleeping for a while, or were out carousing with girls, and on girls. Whereas he had to stand guard all night at a gate that no one ever used anyway.

So that little moron who was whistling like an idiot was going to feel real pain if he didn't quit it soon.

Nuguel would have already solved the problem, if he could only figure out where the whistles were coming from. But that high-pitched sound traveled far in the silent night, and the imbecile could be in any of the alleyways he faced.

It wasn't just some simpleton happily passing by. Someone was really messing with his head. The whistler stopped and started, over and over, as he moved between the alleys in front of the gate. Nuguel would have given anything to work out his frustration on him. Or on one of those people they were looking for. Or on anyone, so long as he could hurt him.

"When I've caugh' ya, I'll make ya eat yer tongue," he mumbled under his breath.

"If you can catch me, I'll eat it myself," someone answered loudly.

Nuguel ran toward the alley he heard the voice coming from, thrilling with fierce joy at the prospect of finding the whistler.

The only thing he saw—but from too close—was a thick beam that brutally smashed into his forehead.

Rey wondered if he should kill the now unconscious guard. But as he hadn't, after all, raised the alarm, had fallen for the trap, let Yan pass right behind him, and, finally, collapsed without a sound, Rey decided that he had played his role perfectly and Rey would spare his life. Plus a nice bump on his head and minus a purse.

He didn't wait around by the body lying on the ground, which he simply dragged a little farther into the shadows. Then he exited the Leem gateway himself.

The young Kaulien was no longer visible, but Rey could still hear his horse's gallop. It was best that he make a quick getaway as well, so he hastened his step.

The first thing he thought of, after putting some distance between himself and Berce, was to wash up. Even after more than a dékade, he wasn't accustomed to the distinctly strong odor that was part of his disguise. And it hadn't improved over time. From time to time, the stench would overwhelm him, as if the rot he had rolled in was still fresh. He had struggled to not be sick. But the idea was a good one: no one had spoken to him in a very long time.

Well, at least until the young Kaulien arrived.

He suddenly realized that he hadn't even thought to ask how many heirs were left, and who they were. The young man wouldn't have given him an answer, anyway, but he still must have come off as pretty self-absorbed.

He'd worry about that later; he had done his best. If they didn't show up, well, he would just figure it out on his own, as always.

In the meantime, he would gather his things, hidden a half league away, and above all else, wash up.

After all, he was going to meet his family.

Time was of the essence. Thanks to the beggar, Yan was able to leave the city without difficulty, but he had to exit through the east gate and he needed to go west.

So he traced a long detour to skirt around Berce without being spotted by the guards posted at the other gates, and to avoid sowing curiosity among any potential onlookers. And, of course, he got lost for a moment. On foot, he believed he could maintain his bearings anywhere, even in unfamiliar places. But on a horse...did this animal understand the simple concept of going straight? He had his doubts. Fortunately, he ended up finding the road again and he sensed he was getting close now.

Ultimately, a lot of things had happened in Berce, and he was anxious to tell all about it, especially those parts that concerned the stranger in the hills and the beggar. Of course, he no longer believed he was a genuine beggar.

Yan had also been granted the opportunity to taste the real danger they faced. He had now become a target as well. It only scared him a little; he'd expected to be implicated sooner or later. Strangely enough, he was even happy about it, because he could share it with Léti.

What worried him the most was the apparent lack of solutions to their problem. The Züu seemed more than determined and appeared to have significant resources at their disposal. He had started to realize that it would be difficult for him and his friends to resume a normal life someday, if they ever could.

So he might as well take advantage of the present. Not much longer and he would see his dear Léti. In a few decidays, the sun would come up to greet the Day of the Promise. The moment he had been awaiting for so long. He thought it better to keep his mind on that.

He finally reached the fork in the road where he had to penetrate the thick shrubbery. He uttered a short prayer to Brosda in which he pleaded not to get lost, as he kept doing. The god must have heard him, because he quickly came upon the small, ramshackle house they had established as their camp the evening before last.

Something wasn't right.

The place seemed deserted.

Upon inspection, he was completely certain: the place was empty. There was no remaining trace of his friends: no horses, no bags, not even warm ashes. Nor a message, or any sign at all.

Yan sat down on a moist stump and listened to the sounds of the night. He felt very tired.

———⚬⚬⚬———

Léti felt as if she had abandoned her friend. Shortly after Yan left for Berce, Grigán had ordered them to pack up camp. Infuriated, she had protested, hurling insults and menacing remarks, prepared to force them to come around to her point of view, until she finally listened to the warrior's explanations.

Grigán simply wanted to move the camp just in case someone followed Yan on the way back, or made him talk. It still took a lot of argument and promises from Corenn and Grigán before she finally gave in.

So they left the abandoned hut and moved a bit closer to Berce, and set up a new camp at a spot chosen by Grigán.

Léti, calmer now, was a bit ashamed about the things she had said to the warrior under the sway of her anger. Thinking that they were abandoning Yan, she had called him a liar, a callous old man, a traitor, and other names, many of which Léti regretted. If her aunt had not intervened, they would have surely come to blows; that was how much her fury had deafened her to the warrior's explanations.

Still, he sure had a way of putting things. And this habit of never asking anybody anything, giving orders as if it were only natural. Just because he had a bow and a scimitar? Perhaps that impressed the others, but not her.

She had had enough, more than enough actually, of simply submitting to what happened to them. All those people she loved, dead. Herself, Yan, Corenn, threatened. Worse, hunted. And they expected her to do nothing, to serenely await Grigán's good favor? Didn't she have a say in this?

And the first thing to do was to arm herself. She wouldn't let herself be caught powerless in front of a determined assassin as she had been on the road from Eza. She could still remember the supreme calm of the three men, their simultaneously cruel and detached expressions, and the way they surrounded her and Corenn, slowly tightening like a vise.

Never again. Never again would she put herself at the mercy of someone else. Never again would she stand there paralyzed, waiting for the fatal blow.

She wanted to fight.

She pulled out the fishing knife that Yan gave her and began diligently training herself by throwing it at a dead tree.

Corenn and Grigán, who were talking some distance away, stopped to watch her.

"Cursed Züu," the warrior said under his breath. "The poor girl is in an utter state of shock. It will take some time for her to get over it; and I know of what I speak."

Corenn responded solemnly, "It's sadder than just that, do you see? She has lost her innocence, her peace, her youthful ignorance. She has lost her childhood dreams. She has lost her self-respect. Cursed Züu, she's an adult now."

They contemplated it for a moment.

"You knew it would happen someday," Grigán said in a consoling tone.

"Of course, but not so brutally. She has changed dramatically in just a few days. I have lost my Léti."

The warrior felt uneasy. He hated to see Corenn so sad, and would have preferred taking a physical blow. He looked for something to distract her.

"You know, she isn't doing too bad."

Corenn couldn't hold back a smile.

"Now I have really seen it all," she concluded, a little mysteriously to a disconcerted Grigán.

—∞∞∞—

Yan settled into the abandoned house for the rest of the night, but couldn't get to sleep. His thoughts invaded his dreams, flashing a frightening jumble of images in his mind: Léti, Grigán, the beggar, the murdered man, the flirty Lorelienne, Léti again, the Züu, the innkeeper, the flashes on the hill…

He was awake more often than asleep, mulling over, as best he could in this dreamy state, what he might do. He figured the best thing to do was to stay put for a day or two, hoping to see his companions return. But pessimism was winning out, and he began to imagine them taken by the Züu, dead. He slipped into a brief moment of drowsiness, which quickly threw him into a nightmare where his fears became reality. He jerked awake and pondered it over again, still indecisive.

Which is why when he heard Grigán's voice calling him from outside, at first he believed it was another phantom emerging from his sleep. All the more so because it was dark. But the call repeated, again and again, and Yan awoke completely. He leaped from his bed, and noisily threw the door open.

There was the warrior, a few yards away, a drawn bow in his hands, which he lowered at the sight of the young Kaulien.

"What happened? Where's Léti?" Yan asked, approaching him.

"All is well. All is well. They're not far from here."

Yan closed his eyes as he let out a great sigh of relief. My, was it good to be alive!

He opened his eyes to the warrior standing before him, busy scrutinizing the surroundings.

"For your sake, I hope you have a good explanation," Yan said, in a voice full of implication.

"We moved the camp for safety reasons. I came here this morning to wait for you."

"Uh-huh."

Yan wanted to argue a little bit with the warrior to make him pay for the torturous night that he had just endured, but he was too good-hearted for that. Furthermore, he was far too relieved by the happy ending to provoke a quarrel.

"What happened? You aren't supposed to be here for at least another deciday or so. What if I hadn't come earlier?"

So now Grigán was the one getting angry all on his own.

"I came looking for you. I have a lot to tell you, but we need to hurry."

"Did you see any other heirs?"

"Yes. Well, maybe. But I'll tell you about it when everyone's listening."

Needless to say, it was with great haste that the warrior led Yan to their new camp. Léti and Corenn rose and came to greet them as soon as they finished tying up the horses.

"Yan, oh, you look awful!"

It was the first thing Léti could find to say. She had worried so much about him that to see the bags under his eyes and the exhaustion on his face was like a confirmation of her fears. She realized her insensitivity afterward, and came over to him to plant a kiss on his cheek, adding, "But we're still very happy to see you."

The kiss dispelled all of Yan's fatigue; he now felt ready to face an entire army of Züu killers. Soon, the sun would rise on the Day of the Promise. Soon, Léti...

"So?"

Grigán was pacing around impatiently. It was understandable. Yan cleared his throat and began, "For the moment, the most important thing I have to say is that someone was sending signals from the hills behind Berce. I'm sure it was one of your own, because a group of Züu rushed off in search of him immediately afterward."

"There are Züu in the village?" interrupted Léti.

"Several. At least five, maybe more."

"They didn't catch him?"

"No. I'm nearly sure of it, after seeing the Züu come back with such disappointed looks on their faces."

"What were these signals like?"

"Uh...not natural. Steady. There were two kinds: a strong one, and a weaker one."

Grigán and Corenn exchanged a look.

"A cyclops," said the warrior.

"A what?"

"A cyclops. It's a sort of complex instrument, about a foot long, fitted with two mirrors and a lens. It's used during large hunts in Arkary."

"Bowbaq?" suggested Léti, hopefully.

"It's definitely him," answered Corenn, smiling. "Mother Eurydis, may it please be him!"

"Who is he?" Yan inquired.

"A very, very good friend. The nicest man in the known world," answered Corenn. "And the rest, I'm sure."

"You know, he's the one who knows how to talk to animals!" added Léti.

Of course. Several times, she had told him the story of this tall, bearded man who charmed a standing sleeper during one of the heirs' meetings.

Yan had always thought it was just a prank pulled on a gullible little girl, but he had never said anything. Either way, everyone seemed to like him, so he had to be a nice person.

"Whoever it is, he's going to be in serious danger if we don't act extremely quickly."

He told them about how he responded to the signals, and then about the conversation he overheard from his bedroom. He was quite pleased with the admiring looks Léti gave him when he got to the most dangerous parts.

"Bowbaq certainly isn't waiting right next to the spot where he made the signs," Grigán said, having given it some thought. "Knowing him, he must have left a trail leading to him."

"A trail? Just an ordinary trail, that's all?"

"A trail of Arque signs. They form a genuine language. For the most part, they're composed of combinations of about ten elements: rocks, pebbles, branches, bark, bones, fabric, nuts, and I can't remember what else. You can, for example, indicate the direction and distance to a given village, as well as whose clan it belongs to, the size of its population—everything with one single sign."

"What should we do? We're already too late if we can't outpace the Züu!"

"I know the main signs," Grigán replied casually, as he stood. "All right, we'd better get going quickly."

"Where did you learn the signs?"

Yan knew that the warrior hated questions, but he couldn't help it.

"I spent two years traveling across Arkary," he answered simply. "Bowbaq himself took me in for several dékades. If it's him on that hill, the Züu won't take him without getting a taste of my steel."

The warrior never ceased to surprise him. How many things had he done and seen over the course of his existence?

Everyone was bustling about now, packing up camp. Yan still had plenty of things to recount, but it would have to wait.

They set off, deciding to risk the road in order to move swiftly. Grigán gave them a formal order to remain silent, since voices carried farther than the muffled sound of horse hooves on wet ground. So for a long time they were quiet. However, not long after sunrise, Léti couldn't refrain from questioning Yan.

"Why are you looking at me so strangely?"

Yan blushed all the way to the roots of his hair. Here they were, finally, on the Day of the Promise, and the first thing he did was embarrass them both.

"No, no, I'm just thinking, staring off into space, that's all."

He spent a good part of their ride trying to decide if, when, and how he was going to propose to Léti, causing him to break into a cold sweat. He didn't even dare look at her anymore.

One moment, he would decide the circumstances hardly lent themselves to that sort of thing. Then a moment later, he could recall the demonic look in the Züu's eyes and decide to make the most of his life, and to live it to the fullest.

When Grigán asked him to take the lead and guide them to the spot where the flashes came from, he obeyed with relief. He absolutely had to focus on something other than the proposal.

In no time, their enemies would be following this same trail, stronger, more numerous, and more determined. Somewhere ahead of them, their ally didn't suspect a thing. They were his only hope, and they had to act quickly.

He devoted all his attention to locating the spot, racking his memory, which, fortunately, was very good. It was harder than he thought it would be. The landscape wasn't the same as seen from

Berce, and he had few reference points, since all the wooded hills resembled one another.

Wooded hills...of course! This Bowbaq must have made the signs from the top of a tree, he was almost sure of it! All they needed to do was locate the tallest tree in the area. Obviously, Bowbaq would have thought to mark the beginning of his trail with a sign that was easy to find.

Yan explained his idea to Grigán in a few words; the warrior recognized its merits. Galvanized by the support of the warrior, Yan hopped off his horse and began scaling a tree whose weakest branches were collapsing under the weight of its sweet fruits. He reached the top in a few moments.

The landscape was magnificent from this vantage point. Beyond Berce to the south sprawled the immense and peaceful Median Sea.

In all other directions, the landscape was covered with trees shaded by the magic of the Season of Wind in a palette of green, brown, and ocher.

It had been almost a dékade since Yan had seen the sea. He, who had practically spent his whole life on the shore, didn't realize how much he'd missed it.

Grigán "asked" him to hurry up. With a sigh, Yan finally began the search for his tree. It didn't take long to find it; in fact, it was less than three hundred yards distant.

But something else he saw prevented him from declaring victory.

He let himself slide down the length of the trunk. Léti and Corenn observed him with a surprised expression. Grigán gripped his blade and shot sweeping glances around them.

"The Züu," whispered Yan, pointing. "They're over there."

Grigán dismounted his horse and came over next to the boy, without taking his eyes away from where Yan had pointed.

"How many are there?"

"I don't know, at least seven or eight. Well, they're not all Züu, actually, but the others work for them."

"Are they far? Did they see you?"

"No, I don't think so. They've all got their eyes glued to the ground. They must be looking for Bowbaq's trail. They're about four hundred yards out. Fortunately, they're moving away from us."

Grigán paced back and forth, stroking his mustache, a sure sign of agitation. Then he took his turn scaling the fruit tree.

"They must have changed their plans following my escape last night," Yan murmured, saying aloud what everyone else had concluded.

But he hadn't told them everything. He went on. "One of theirs was killed when I went to retrieve my horse."

"Was it you who killed him?" asked Corenn, worried, while Grigán descended the tree as quickly as the boy had.

"No, someone else, a beggar, perhaps one of yours. He said his name was Rey Kerfian, or something like that."

"He said Rey? Not Mess?"

"No, no, Rey. It even seemed particularly important to him."

"Do you think it's possible?" Corenn asked Grigán.

"We'll see later," he grumbled. "So, Yan, are there still a lot of things we don't know?"

"I was going to tell you afterward," he answered, a little annoyed. "I think the most urgent matter is to save your Arque friend, right?"

"It's not looking good," Léti pointed out.

They went quiet for a few moments, during which Grigán began pacing again, juggling his blade in the air. He didn't even seem to be aware of his own skill.

"Well," he simply said, stopping.

Then he immediately launched back into pacing back and forth. Yan noticed they were all waiting on the warrior's decision, as if they couldn't act on their own. He decided to relieve him of some of his exhausting burden.

"Master Grigán, what would you do if you were alone?"

The warrior finally halted, staring at Yan with a glimmer of hope in his eyes.

"I would follow the trail. There might be some way to overtake the Züu."

"So, go on then. Do it."

"Three chances out of four that I'll end up dead. But you're the ones I'm worried about. I hate the idea of leaving you alone, just as I hate the idea of leaving them to massacre Bowbaq without doing anything about it. You can understand."

"And if I come with you? Would that even the odds?"

Grigán stared at him for a few moments, undecided. The warrior wasn't used to asking for help, he, who constantly offered his own.

"You make more racket than a red pig in heat."

"I've come a long way," Yan replied through gritted teeth. "If you want to know the truth, last night I heard you coming before you even started calling."

He was lying, of course.

The warrior stroked his mustache again, with an absent expression. He was uncomfortable. Then he let out a loud sigh, having finally made his decision.

"All right, let's go," he said, as he retrieved his bow and quiver from his horse.

Yan did the same without a word, fearing that Grigán would change his mind. His heart beat wildly. This time, it really was dangerous. There was no guarantee he would return. He turned to Léti to forever etch her image into his mind.

He was horrified. Léti had dismounted her horse and was intently examining the fishing knife he'd given her.

"What are you doing?" he asked with difficulty.

She faced him with an expression of resolve.

"Can't you tell? I'm coming with you."

Yan's thoughts whirled and smashed together like giant waves in a monstrous squall. He was prepared to die himself, but not to see Léti die. She had to live. She had to because he loved her. He loved her more than anything in the world. He had seen enough death up close since yesterday to become fully aware of how valuable life was. Léti had to live.

"No," he heard himself saying, as if in a dream. "No, you're not coming with us."

"Yes, I am."

It was the first time Yan had disagreed with her. She was saddened all the more, but too bad. It would pass. What counted now was to go and fight. To no longer be powerless in the face of danger; to avenge her friends. That's what she'd said: avenge. Make those murderers pay with their own blood. Even if it meant dying to kill only one of them.

"No, you're not."

Yan noticed he'd just raised his voice, which was out of character for him. Oh, well, it might help Léti come to reason. Why did she talk back to him like a stupid child? Didn't she understand he was doing it for her?

"I say I'm coming with you. It's not up to you to decide," she continued, on the verge of tears. "No one can decide for me," she finished, nearly shouting.

"You're staying here, that's it! Understood? End of discussion!"

Yan was seeing red now. Curses, she had to realize it, didn't she? And, by Eurydis, did it infuriate him to watch her fidget with that stupid fishing knife! He had the urge to rip it away from her, but that would have only made things worse.

She was truly crying now. Ashamed and furious with himself as much as he was with her, Yan searched for something comforting to say. The words didn't come, and it annoyed him even more. Ugh! As long as she stayed there, out of harm's way, all was well.

He adjusted the laces of his boots and turned away from her toward Grigán, who was waiting impatiently.

Corenn dismounted and wrapped her niece in her arms. She was very careful not to intervene in the discussion, but would have done so had the outcome been different.

It seemed like all the children in the group were becoming adults.

It didn't take them very long to find the giant tree, a Lirel tree that was hundreds of years old. Despite the precautions they needed to take, they had tacitly decided to move quickly in an attempt to pass the Züu.

Grigán soon found a use for Yan; he sent him thirty or so yards out ahead, but still within sight. This way they could cover each other with their bows if they needed to.

Yan feared that the Züu left someone close to the Lirel tree, but luckily there was no one nearby. He was also relieved when he passed in front of the tree and saw that he was right: sure enough, there was a sign in between the roots. He continued to advance until he was almost out of Grigán's field of vision, and concentrated his efforts on keeping a lookout, while Grigán deciphered the man-made pile of rocks and plants.

Time passed and Grigán, standing in front of the sign, still hadn't moved. Yan started to worry. Curses, did he not understand it, or what? If that were the case, their only solution would be to follow the Züu all the way to Bowbaq, hoping to bend the circumstances in their favor at the last second. In other words, they would have much less than a one-in-four chance of making it out alive.

The warrior finally emerged from his contemplation and signaled Yan to join him, which Yan hastened to do, filled with curiosity.

"You see the stick with the three notches? Grouped with those four rocks, on the left side, they indicate a point somewhere to the east, three thousand yards away. Three for the notches, a thousand, a four-digit number: as many as there are rocks."

"And?"

Yan wondered where the warrior was going with this. It wasn't his usual habit to provide explanations; there must be some other reason.

"The knotted branch in the form of a triangle represents a human. The stone placed outside the triangle, in front of the point, indicates a man in a temporary camp. If the stone had been on the inside, it would indicate a full household; if there were many stones, a community: family, village, city, depending on the case."

Yan nodded. This all made sense with Bowbaq. He still didn't get where Grigán was going with this.

"What's more interesting is the little coriole's skull. This bird's beak is the symbol of Bowbaq's native clan; why would he provide proof of his family's clan here?"

Yan shrugged his shoulders. Maybe there was nothing to it? If they were ever going to find out, they should hurry up...

"I might have an idea," the warrior continued. "Have a look at this."

He removed the little skull from the pile. Beneath it was a plain black stone.

"I once heard, in Crévasse, the story of a clan that modified their signs to trick their enemies. I would have never guessed that it could have been Bowbaq's clan. Or that the big, timid fellow would be bold enough to use the trick himself."

Yan still didn't have all the information he needed, but the faint smile creeping over Grigán's face was encouraging.

"Ah yes: if I am not mistaken, we have to interpret all the directions of these signs in reverse."

The two men smiled broadly. If Grigán were right, they could avoid a whole lot of trouble.

"We should hurry anyway. The Züu will turn around when they realize their mistake."

The warrior carefully replaced the small skull. Not before, however, chucking the little black rock behind them.

Yan remarked, "Seriously, he might have been a little too cautious. If you didn't already know about the cyclops signals, if you hadn't made it all the way here, and finally, if you hadn't thought of…of this trickery, he could have waited a long time!"

"It isn't over yet," Grigán cautioned. "I could be wrong. These signs are so complicated…I've always hated puzzles."

Yan quieted himself. It was the first time he had seen the warrior doubt himself. He shifted his focus to the little Rominian compass and the approximate count of their strides.

They walked quickly for a while, anxious to arrive at the sign's destination. After a while, Yan succumbed to his worries.

"Does it make sense that we haven't seen another sign yet? The ones I know are usually repeated regularly."

"If I'm right, yes, it makes sense. No need to lie about a sign just so you can reveal yourself with another one a few dozen yards away. If not, then I'm wrong, and Bowbaq is in the other direction. With the Züu."

Yan didn't add anything. For him, an entire trail filled with false signs didn't seem impossible. But the warrior was already worried enough.

So they continued, compromising between the compass's directions and the natural contours of the terrain. Yan thought that they should have warned Léti and her aunt, maybe even have brought them. After all, what they were doing now wasn't that dangerous.

He brooded about all the things he had said to Léti. How could he get her to forgive him?

He stopped suddenly, as if struck by lightning.

How could he propose today?

Grigán shot him an inquisitive glance. Yan signaled that all was well and started walking again.

How could he even propose, ever? Right now, she was probably cursing his name for being so disrespectful. Worse, he had humiliated her. He had humiliated the woman he loved.

In the best case, she would ignore him for a couple of days. Worst case...despise him? Avoid his company, yell at him, and just quarrel with him? Forever?

Flooded in the cold rain of his thoughts, he took at least ten strides before noticing that Grigán had stopped. Dragging his feet, the boy rejoined him. The warrior was examining a new assemblage of rocks, stones, and branches that must have been another sign from Bowbaq.

"Apparently, you were right," Yan commented listlessly.

"Maybe, maybe not. To tell you the truth, I don't understand anything about this sign."

He went quiet for a moment to think on it.

"If I translate it as is, it means 'temporary camp of a man no yards away.' But there is a less complicated sign that marks a camp, so that can't be it. Maybe there's something missing."

Yan was going to make a suggestion, but something happened that prevented him.

There was a frightful clamor as branches were forcefully smashed against each other in the tree above them, followed by the loud sounds of someone falling behind them.

Yan turned around, trying feverishly to grab an arrow from his quiver. Despite his quick reflex, he had enough time to curse himself for not keeping one nocked and ready.

Grigán had been faster and was already aiming at the new arrival. He didn't fire.

The first time Yan had seen the warrior, he was impressed. The man in black seemed—and was—formidable, seasoned, experienced, pitiless.

He was just as impressed standing in front of Bowbaq.

This man was gigantic.

He was at least two heads taller than Yan. But one saw people of this height every once in a while; Yan had already seen some in Kaul. No, it was the proportions of his body that were most striking.

Two men could fit inside the vest that hardly stretched around Bowbaq's chest. His arms looked stronger than a bear's, his legs more powerful than the tides. His excessively large hands seemed to have their own lives, for such fists couldn't simply, stupidly, depend on just one being.

The man was wearing immense boots laced up to his knees, various skins and furs, an enormous metal bracelet, and he carried a frighteningly large bag in one single hand. Given how the sac was full to bursting, and its metallic reinforcement, Yan knew he couldn't even lift such a mass off the ground.

The man had a head of thick, dark hair and a beard just as thick; his face, hidden underneath a hat, didn't show much emotion. So this was Bowbaq? the boy asked himself.

The giant dropped his sack and rushed toward Grigán, who lowered his bow with amused resignation. Bowbaq hugged him almost brutally, even lifting him up and spinning him around.

Yan was only slightly reassured. Next to the Arque, Grigán seemed so small, so vulnerable. The giant only had to squeeze his arms a little harder to permanently smother the warrior to death in a bear hug.

Luckily, that didn't seem to be his intention. He finally let his "victim" go while continuing to laugh warmly.

"My friend! My friend!" he managed to get out between two thunderous roars of laughter, his eyes locked with Grigán's. Then he couldn't help himself, and dragged him about again in a very physical, circular dance.

The warrior made a halfhearted effort to reason with his admirer, but without much hope. Grigán shared in the giant's joy, although much more moderately.

"If you only knew! If you knew! It's been more than a moon since I've spoken to anyone! My friend, my friend!"

Yan patiently waited for them to remember he was there, which they did shortly thereafter, when Bowbaq finally put Grigán down and let him regain his balance.

"I'm pleased as well, Bowbaq. Very pleased."

"Who's this young man?"

"This is Yan. Léti's promised one."

The giant's face lit up again, while Yan recovered from the shock. Is that what Grigán thought? How? When?

He didn't have much time to think about it. Bowbaq had bounded toward him, and Yan took his turn being twirled around in an embrace. Curses, the man was strong! The giant lifted him two feet in the air as if it were nothing.

"My friend! Léti's promised one," Bowbaq repeated, laughing, twirling the poor Kaulien around to get a good look at him.

His good mood was contagious, and Yan couldn't help but find this giant very nice, simple, and good-natured. His presence in the group might restore a bit of joy.

The Northerner finally put down his new friend and turned toward Grigán, who took a step back, scared of a fresh display of affection.

"There's only two of you?" he asked in a more serious tone.

"There's also Léti and Corenn. They're waiting for us a few leagues from here."

"Léti and Corenn! Good! All my friends! And the others?"

"The others, we don't know. Actually…for some, we know," Grigán concluded gravely, gripping the Northerner's shoulder.

They only exchanged a glance, but it was long enough. Bowbaq lost his smile.

"Etólon? Jasporan? Humeline?"

"We don't know about Humeline."

After a few moments, the giant asked with hope "And Xan?"

Grigán shook his head sadly. Bowbaq's face darkened.

"We are unsure about many."

The warrior was about to add something else. It wasn't like him to lie and give false hope. Then he asked, "Is Ipsen all right? And Prad, and Iulane?"

Bowbaq lifted his head a little. He still had his family.

"Yes, as far as I know. Ipsen is in Rowk, with her clan and the kids. Mir is with them. They should be safe for a few moons."

"That's good." Grigán didn't know what else to add.

Yan filled the silence; he also was worried about his loved ones.

"Well...what do you say we go meet up with the others now?" Bowbaq's smile returned.

"Yes! I need to embrace my little Kauliennes!"

They were immediately on their way.

Even though Yan was filled with apprehension at the thought of a gathering with his beloved, he couldn't help but laugh in advance at the idea of the giant noisily twirling a pouting and rebellious Léti.

Léti was bored to death. It had been over a deciday since Yan and Grigán left, and she didn't know how to keep herself busy. Sitting stupidly against a tree made her crazy, and when she stood up and made as if to walk off, however short a distance away, Corenn was the one who went crazy, only with worry.

She admitted, only to herself, though, that she had acted without thinking. Of course she couldn't have gone with the men—she used the word as a slur—and left her aunt alone. It was also out of the question that all four of them should go and abandon the horses, or to impose such a march on Corenn, who wasn't used to that.

Yet all that didn't excuse Yan's behavior. He, who was supposed to know her better than anyone, from whom she expected help and support, treated her like a mere capricious child. And no, she didn't think she deserved that.

If that was the kind of influence Grigán had over them, well, then it was harmful. Despite everything they owed him, certain things couldn't be ignored or forgiven. His arrogance and contempt, for example.

Before, she would have confided in her aunt about her feelings. But Master Grigán had become a taboo subject of conversation for them: Corenn, so at ease with the art of diplomacy, admitted she felt completely overwhelmed by problems relating to war, and joyfully left this responsibility to her old friend. She would undoubtedly side with him.

Furthermore, Léti knew there was no possibility of getting the last word in a discussion with her aunt. Not for her or for anyone else, for that matter. She preferred to avoid diving headfirst into certain defeat.

There was no solution to her problem. All she wanted was to be useful. And all she needed to do was convince Grigán, since whether she liked it or not, everything depended on him. But the grump was as thickheaded as a block of wood, hidebound and stubborn, with a mind no wider than a fishing line.

She stood up again to take a few steps. Following the warrior's directions, they had put several leagues between them and their point of departure. But Corenn had overdone it, and they'd gone farther than expected. Maybe the men had gotten lost?

She began hoping that was all it was.

Corenn also showed signs of worry. She, who was usually so patient, was constantly on the lookout for their companions' return and startled at every suspicious sound. She was now pacing as well.

Léti felt her anger subside bit by bit as time went by, and now she was left feeling frustrated, with a hint of anxiety.

What if something had happened to them? Something serious?

———∞———

"No, no, and no! Really, it's not a good idea. I mean, Bowbaq, you should understand how dangerous it is."

"I know," the giant apologized, embarrassed. "But it's wrong to leave behind useless signs. You should always do your best to erase them."

"It's wrong? And getting yourself stabbed over and over with a dagger, that sounds right to you? You could have dated your signs, if it bothers you so much!"

"I didn't find enough fangs. And it's not the same. A sign, even an old one, even with a date, should be trustworthy. That's why it's wrong."

"No. Please humor me and forget it. If you want, I can come by here and pick them up someday. I promise you."

"Thank you, my friend," the giant said simply, giving the warrior a thump.

Yan noticed that the warrior took his time giving explanations to Bowbaq. Doubtless because they knew each other well. Maybe there was hope of softening the warrior up yet.

Finally, after a long walk through the Lorelien forest, they found Léti and Corenn, whose worries were instantly swept away.

Léti ran to the giant and threw her arms around his neck, to Yan's disappointment. He had hoped for something for himself, without knowing exactly what.

The gathering between Corenn, Léti, and Bowbaq was just as acrobatic as the one with Grigán. The young woman didn't protest against this somewhat violent form of greeting, but actually seemed to enjoy it.

When Léti was back on the ground, Yan gathered his courage to attempt a reconciliation.

"Everything go all right?" he said in his kindest voice.

She responded sharply, "Obviously. What did you think would happen?"

She had stopped smiling when she turned toward him. That hurt him even more than her acid tone. Curses, curses, curses! It would be dékades before Léti would forgive him.

The idea crossed his mind, only for an instant, to stand up to her and argue about it. Frightened, he shoved the thought out of his head. Once was enough. He had done enough damage already.

The compliments and polite exchanges continued. Bowbaq raved about Léti's beauty, and teased her at the same time, regretting that she had grown up so fast. Corenn inquired about the Northerner's family, and rejoiced at the good news.

Grigán politely waited until everyone had calmed down a little before he asked them to pack up camp. They headed out on foot, since Bowbaq didn't have a horse. It would only be a slight exaggeration to say that it would have been easier for Bowbaq to carry the horse than vice versa.

Bowbaq told them all about his trek, from the frozen plains of Arkary to the Lorelien scrubland, making sure to include his last few days of waiting.

"Someone responded to my cyclops in Berce. Was it you?"

"It was me," Yan told him proudly.

"Alone?"

"Of course, alone. Do I really seem that incompetent?" Yan joked.

"No, what I meant was that two people responded. From two different places."

They all thought about this second sign for a moment, then Grigán suggested, "That could have been a trap from the Züu."

"The what?"

"The Züu, the people who are hunting us! Clearly we have a lot to tell you."

"It could have been Yan's beggar," Léti suggested.

Yan smacked his hand on his forehead and looked at the sun's position. Caught up in his problems with Léti, he had forgotten about everything else.

"We're supposed to meet him at the apogee. Today!"

They all looked at the sun's position.

Grigán remarked, "So you mean right about now. Where is he?"

"He told me to meet him on the beach where the gatherings used to take place. I guess he means the beach behind Berce."

"Well, at least it's not that far away. What happened exactly?"

And Yan told them about their dangerous first encounter in the stable, Rey's decisive intervention, and how the young man had helped Yan get out of town without a hitch.

Grigán didn't know what to think.

"I don't know that particular Kercyan. Zatelle, yes, and her grandson, Mess. But not Rey."

Corenn interrupted, "Yes you do. Zatelle had another grandson that she brought one or two times."

"That's true, I remember," Bowbaq added.

"But no one knows him as an adult. Anybody could be trying to impersonate him, without us knowing the difference."

"He said that he set the tent on fire," Yan interjected curiously.

His friends exchanged knowing looks.

"It's true, he's definitely the one who pulled that stupid prank."

Grigán confirmed Corenn's memory. "I remember it too. And the well-deserved punishment Zatelle gave him. I also remember that I was the one who dragged him out of his hiding place, while everyone else was wondering if he hadn't been burned up."

"I feel sorry for the poor fellow," Léti said half-jokingly. "That must have been enough to turn him off to life as an heir."

Grigán didn't respond to her comment.

"So, you think it's him?" Yan asked Corenn.

"I can't see why not. Zatelle told me once that he had become an actor. Sounds like he would be the type to disguise himself as a beggar."

Yan agreed. He figured the jokester, with his cynicism and taste for drama, must be an artistic type. Or a depraved thief.

"One last thing. He wanted to warn you that the Grand Guild is also in on the hunt. What is that anyway?"

Grigán stopped as if frozen.

"Are you sure?"

"That's what he said. So what does it mean?"

The warrior and Corenn exchanged a dark, foreboding look. No one else understood.

"The Grand Guild," Corenn began joylessly, "is the organized consolidation of virtually all the largest criminal bands. Simply put, it means that the Züu have an army at their disposal. Several hundreds of men, even thousands."

Yan understood better. Grigán could congratulate himself for having been so extraordinarily cautious on their trip to Berce. All the roads, all the towns, must have been watched by the same type of crooks that he had met at the gates.

"How does he know?" the warrior asked, stroking his mustache.

"I'm not sure. That's all he said."

Grigán and Corenn seemed deeply affected by this news. The Züu really weren't taking any chances.

The warrior drew the discussion to a close. "We have to go. This Rey might be one of ours. Yan?"

The boy cringed. He didn't realize that Grigán would need his help again, but he was the only one who could recognize last night's savior. A shame. He would have really liked to spend some more time with Léti, in hopes of making up with her before the end of the day.

Léti! Hopefully she wouldn't try and join them again. He would oppose her once again anyhow, but didn't relish the idea of a new fight.

PIERRE GRIMBERT

Grigán told the others to meet at the little abandoned house where they had stayed two nights before. Apparently, Léti didn't have any objection. Shocked, Yan saw that Bowbaq wasn't coming with them.

He watched the three of them as they grew distant in the woods. Bowbaq's presence was definitely one of the reasons for Léti's new docility, but all the same, someone of such strength could be a valuable asset.

Grigán jumped into the saddle and Yan followed suit, still surprised.

"Why don't we bring Bowbaq?"

"He doesn't like to fight. Let's go."

"Neither do I! And he's so strong."

"He has sworn to never kill anyone."

"What? But why?"

Yan was going from surprise to surprise. It was the first time he had heard of such a thing.

Grigán responded a little brusquely, "I've never asked him, so he's never told me. That's the whole story. Now let's go, or we'll never make it on time."

Rey was starting to get nervous. Not only did he feel the minor apprehension he experienced before every performance, it was genuine worry: he wondered if he would remember his lines, if his performance would be good, if the audience would like him.

That was the main question today: would his audience like him?

Not that he absolutely needed to make the heirs like him. In fact, he more or less didn't give a margolin's ass what they thought, and even scoffed at these ridiculous traditionalists and

184

their stories from the last century. But he needed their help, and their information.

He'd seen the Züu. He'd witnessed the Grand Guild's omnipresence. And he'd come to this conclusion: if there were any chance of salvation, it wasn't in fleeing, but in direct confrontation.

The surviving heirs had to join forces in order to find out who had commissioned the assassins. And take care of the problem, one way or another.

His only hope was to find attentive ears and minds not too sluggish. If not, well, then he would make do on his own, as usual.

He stood up from the comfortable bank of fine sand he was lying on and walked around a bit, keeping his eyes on the edge of the forest. The apogee had already passed, and it wouldn't be long before he had visitors. At least, he might.

He came back to the sand dune and sat down, patiently accepting his situation. He was awarded for his patience shortly thereafter, when the young Kaulien from the night before finally emerged from the forest.

Rey breathed a sigh of relief, waving to him. Despite his own resourcefulness, he didn't want to keep fighting alone for much longer.

Yan stopped his horse a few dozen feet away. Rey didn't move.

"You're not alone, I imagine? Tell them to come here; this isn't a trap."

"You must first lay down your arms," Yan announced in an apologetic tone.

Rey expected nothing less. He detached the sword hanging on his back, then the knife he wore at his waist. For good measure, he pulled out the dagger he had concealed on his ankle.

"There. Go on now, tell them to come; I feel naked like this. I could catch a cold."

Yan smiled at the joke and signaled toward the forest, where Grigán appeared on foot with his bow drawn.

"My! He looks like an intimidating fellow," Rey laughed. "Ha! I know him: he's the guy who doesn't like pyromaniac children. That's just my luck!"

Yan smiled again. With both the actor and Bowbaq, the group would soon be a lot more lively.

"There aren't just two of you, are there?" Rey continued. "All right, he has a bow, but that just might prove to be a bit insufficient for taking on Zuïa and the Grand Guild."

"There are three others, and one of them has a knife," Yan replied, laughing loudly.

"Oh, good, we'll be fine. For a moment there, I was worried."

Grigán finally joined them. He wasn't at all in the same joking mood as the other two.

"Is it him?" the warrior asked Yan.

"It's him. Suffice it to say, I really had to look at him up close to be sure, but it's him. Speaking of that, these clothes suit you much better than the others—they were in dire need of a good washing."

"Thank you," Rey answered, with a slight bow.

"I don't recognize you," Grigán interjected with a serious tone. "Who are you?"

"You know, you don't have to threaten me with an arrow to get an answer."

"Well?"

Rey gave his real name, and convinced Grigán by giving him a plethora of details about his grandmother, Zatelle, and his cousin, Mess, and a few snippets of memories from the gatherings. The warrior finally lowered his bow.

"Do you still have the urge to light fires?" he asked, in a tone he meant to be jocular.

"No one ever understood that it was an accident. That's the story of my life," Rey pretended to complain. "All right, so we're good, you believe me now?"

"I believe you."

"Good. I'll warn you, no sudden moves please; I have to pick something up."

Rey didn't move toward his weapons, as could be expected, but leaned over and cautiously lifted up a loaded crossbow, just barely hidden underneath a layer of sand.

"You can never be too careful, don't you agree?"

Grigán didn't answer. Yan, who was getting to know Grigán quite well, knew that the warrior was going to consider it a defeat. Too bad, Rey seemed like a resourceful guy.

"You only could have shot one of us," Grigán said finally.

"You're right. Who, do you think?"

The warrior stared the actor down for a moment. Rey didn't even notice, busy as he was rearming himself from head to toe. Then Grigán turned to go back to the forest.

Yan waited for Rey to get ready to leave, letting his eyes wander over the horizon. Only an eight-day journey away, and the sea was a different one from Eza's. The same water, the same waves, but a different sea.

"Is that Ji out there?" he asked Rey.

"That's it. Say, you wouldn't happen to know a god who wouldn't charge too much to sink it into the depths of the sea, along with its curse, would you?"

"Its curse?"

"It's a hunch that I have. That I've had for twenty-six years," he added. "Ji is a jinx, you know."

Yan watched the small patch of darkness amid the blue-gray water. It looked like nothing more than a rocky island.

"Have you been there before?"

Rey, now equipped with his weapons and the bags he'd retrieved from nearby, shot him one last look.

"No. But something tells me this dreadful shortcoming will soon be rectified."

Despite his lack of respect for the actor, Grigán decided to strike up a conversation. He needed some answers.

"What's your story?"

He didn't want to sound so confrontational, but too late now, it was done. A hint of a smile spread across Rey's face, and he let some time pass before he responded.

"I don't mean to offend you, Grigán, but I would just as well like to wait until everyone is here. We need to talk about a lot of things, and despite my taste for telling stories, I would rather not have to tell mine twice in the same day."

Grigán let out a solitary "All right," that sounded more like a crotchety growl than any human language. Yan hurried to interrupt a potential argument.

"Have you been in Berce for a long time?"

"For more than a dékade. I was starting to wonder if I were the last one alive."

"You didn't see a single heir?"

"No, I mean, I didn't recognize anyone, but that doesn't mean anything. Someone on the hills signaled Berce with flashes from a mirror, for a couple of days. But he kept moving around, and neither I nor the Züu could find him."

"So we're more clever than you," Grigán interrupted in a cynical tone.

"You found him?" Rey said, unsurprised. "Did you run into him by accident or something?"

Yan answered smiling, "Running into him would be an accident. Maybe you remember him? His name is Bowbaq."

"That name must mean something to you, I guess, but for me it means about as much as my tenth harlot."

Yan explained, "Since everyone else seemed to know who he is, I figured...he's an Arque, a giant. They say he can talk to animals, maybe that will help you remember?"

"Oh, I see now. He must be very popular with some of you."

"With that kind of attitude, you certainly won't be," said Grigán, who had understood the allusion and didn't much appreciate it.

Then he stood directly in front of the actor and continued.

"Our group is currently stable, and made up of only good company. I will personally hunt down the first who decides to sow discord in our group, or who puts us in danger. Heir or not. You understand?"

"If you're thinking of me, have no fear," Rey responded just as seriously. "I won't mix myself up with you any longer than required to fix our little problem, maybe even just the time it takes to talk about it."

"Excellent."

Grigán finished the conversation the same way he always did, by turning his back and storming off. He moved so fast his horse could barely keep up.

"Do you think he would get mad if I tell him that his accent is thicker than a Mestèbe sailor's?"

The Kaulien, frozen with fear at the mere thought, responded, "If I were you, I would hold off on that...He isn't kidding, you know."

"Oh, I'm sure of it. That's why it's so funny."

Yan figured these next few days were going to be full of emotions. Between his own dispute with Léti and the obvious antipathy between the actor and the warrior, Corenn was going to have to deploy all of her diplomatic talents to keep the peace.

"Master Rey, was it you who responded to Bowbaq's signs?"

"By the gods! Stop being so formal with me! Do I look old or uptight enough to deserve that?"

"No, no…"

"Anyway, to answer your question, yes, it was me who responded to his signals. For three days. But I could never find this Bowbaq. I'm curious to see what the fellow looks like."

"Master Rey…uh, I mean, Rey, you might be surprised."

"All right, you're getting better! Now say the same thing but with a curse word thrown in for good measure."

Yan looked at him, not getting the joke.

"I'm just kidding. You're too gullible, you know? I have a feeling we're going to get along. Actually, which one of our ancestors has the honor of having you as a descendant? Is it possible we're cousins?"

"No, I'm not one of yours. Just two dékades ago I hardly knew a thing about the whole story."

"Lucky man! So are you here just out of curiosity?"

"I wanted to accompany my friends. It was going pretty well until a certain corpse was abandoned in a certain stable in Berce…"

"That's funny! The same thing happened to me just last night. That means we already have something in common!"

Yan smiled. It was a bit hard for him to follow the Lorelien's conversation, but once he understood his sense of humor, he enjoyed it.

Hopefully the others would agree.

Corenn filled Bowbaq in on everything he needed to know about the Züu. The giant's good mood progressively faded as she spoke, and completely vanished when the Mother listed the victims' names. It wasn't her intention to hurt him, but it was her duty to tell him the truth.

After a few comforting words, Corenn left the giant alone to reflect in silence, dragging Léti along to give him space. Poor man. He had abandoned his family, traveled for several dékades, endured loneliness, hoping to warn a few friends of the danger that threatened them, even though it was already too late.

Léti's morale also took a hit. Listening to the tragic recital of their lost friends' names affected them all. But it was no time for mourning.

Corenn forced herself to remain composed. She was a Mother, and it was her duty to represent safety, tranquility, and authority in every Kaulien's mind.

"I'm going to need you, Léti. We're going to prepare a feast so delectable that all these men will wonder what they're good for on this journey."

The young woman agreed, happy to fix her mind on other things. Plus, Corenn had carefully chosen just the right words.

"After all," she continued, "this is sort of the heir's reunion, isn't it? We're going to celebrate accordingly."

The women first took an inventory of their provisions before choosing a menu. Next, Corenn sent Bowbaq off in search of certain vegetables, roots, herbs, mushrooms, and whatever else they were missing, and even some things they weren't. The important thing was to keep the giant from mulling over his dark thoughts, sitting with his back against a tree and his head between his hands.

It was a good thing that Grigán had shot a decent amount of game during his reconnaissance excursions the night before. Corenn knew the Northerner was incapable, for moral reasons, of killing anything other than fish.

Everyone got to work. When Grigán, Yan, and Rey arrived at the camp at nightfall, they were welcomed by the pleasant aroma of roasted meat.

With great delicacy, Corenn, Bowbaq, and Léti had prepared three roasted sea pheasants and several corioles. They had also roasted various mushrooms and wild vegetables, whose smells were just as mouthwatering. Finally, using a few planks salvaged from the abandoned house, Bowbaq had managed to set up a very satisfactory table equipped with benches. Léti took care of decorating it all with a few candles and a small bouquet. She was in the middle of arranging a basket of freshly picked fruit when Yan, Grigán, and the stranger showed up.

"Welcome, heirs!" Corenn exclaimed, a lot more cheerfully than she ordinarily would.

She wanted to prevent any potential objection from Grigán about the numerous fires they'd started. The warrior wouldn't dare be a killjoy.

"Thank you for your hospitality, but I'm afraid I've come alone," Rey joked, making his entrance.

"Well, I hope you're hungry, Mr. Alone. So this is Zatelle's grandson?"

"And you must be Corenn. My grandmother had a lot of respect for you, and if I trust my nose, I can bet it was deserved," he concluded, with a little bow.

"Why, thank you. I must say, I pictured Lorelien beggars a bit differently," she said, laughing.

"Let's hope you won't change your mind after seeing me eat, my lady. Well, well, who's this young woman, whose existence has been kept secret from me until now? May you be so kind as to introduce us?" Corenn complied with a smile.

"I have the pleasure of introducing you to Léti, the only daughter of my late cousin Norine. Léti, this is Reyan Kercyan the Younger, the apparent descendant of the wise man whose name he bears."

"I have the weakness of preferring Rey over Reyan," he interrupted. "By all the gods, if I had known about the presence of such charming individuals among the heirs, I would have never missed a single gathering. Please, tell me you haven't already taken someone in Union?"

Yan experienced something like a strangled hiccup. While he had been struggling for years to win over Léti, while his greatest anxiety was to bring up the subject of the Promise before Eurydis, this newcomer Rey the Bold was making advances at their very first meeting. Yan awaited her response with bated breath.

Léti was spellbound. She had taken notice of the actor's good looks from the very start: the unsettling gaze of his deep blue eyes, his rebellious mane of long sandy blond hair, his confident movements, and his unique clothing, which looked as luxurious as it did comfortable. Like his immaculate shirt, for example, made of unquestionably rich fabric, but which he wore as if it were a simple work tunic. Or his finely crafted boots that seemed custom-made. Maybe they were.

The character also had a strange, or eccentric, side to him as well. The band in his hair, his cape made of fine hide, and an unassuming ring, for example, all lent him a mysterious air. The sword he wore on his back and the daggers at his waist made him look like a protector. And last, but not least, his graceful manners, his education, and his humor made him very charming.

Léti was spellbound indeed.

"I'm not in Union with anyone, my lord. In fact, my Promise has yet to be requested."

She was only telling the truth, but for some reason she had the odd feeling she was lying. Except for Rey, her response seemed to bother everyone else too.

"I can't believe it!" the actor said. "Unless men are too struck by your beauty to even dare speak to you. Ah, that must be it."

Léti thanked him with a smile but didn't add anything more. It was certainly the first time in her life she'd received so many compliments, and what compliments they were! Rey had succeeded in putting the young woman off balance.

As for Yan, he wondered if the actor was always so perceptive. How could he have guessed that Léti intimidated her suitors? Or rather, intimidated him?

Corenn finished the introductions with Bowbaq, who, not going so far as to twirl him in the air, greeted the Lorelien with a clumsy hug.

"I don't know if you remember," the giant said with a smile, "but we were close friends when you were younger."

"I hope we still are. I would hate for you to be angry with me," the actor added, evaluating the Northerner's imposing muscular mass.

"I have a hard time imagining our Bowbaq angry," Grigán teased.

"Actually, I do remember you now. You didn't have a beard back then, and you spent the whole time at the gatherings playing with the kids, didn't you?"

"Of course. And you couldn't keep yourself from cheating. There must have been at least a few times that I didn't catch you!"

"A few? Dozens!"

They laughed heartily. Rey was pleasantly surprised. He was afraid he would end up in the middle of a gang of imbeciles who almost religiously worshipped people who, although a part of their family, weren't any less dead than they were a century ago. And now he found himself among good people, all of them readily welcoming him with open arms. Well, almost all of them, he thought, thinking back on Grigán's sermon.

"I suggest we take a seat at the table right away. The meal is nearly finished, and I'm sure you're dying of hunger," Corenn announced.

"With pleasure," answered Rey. "I haven't eaten anything since dawn, and I intend to do right by each one of your dishes." He got rid of his bags and hastily offered to help Léti remove the various game and other food from the flames.

Yan and Grigán, exchanging a grim look ripe with undertones, tied up their horses and dragged their feet as they came to join the others at the table.

The warrior was afraid of losing his authority over the group, and as a result, putting its members in danger. The fisherman was afraid of losing Léti, and as a result, everything he had built his life around until now.

He wasn't angry with anyone. Léti wasn't tied down in any way, and so was free to respond to the advances of whomever she pleased. And Rey, who quite naturally found her pleasing, was only wrong in his audacity.

Yan only had himself to blame. He should have declared his love a long time ago. Now it was too late. He couldn't possibly imagine defeating the actor in a competition for Léti's affection.

The only thing he could do was pray that such a thing wouldn't come to pass.

The meal prepared by Corenn, Léti, and Bowbaq was unanimously declared a delicious success. Rey was full of praise for the corioles stuffed with plons, while Grigán raved about the mushrooms grilled over the embers.

Bowbaq pulled a canteen practically full of liquor out of his pouch, offering everyone a generous swig. Then it was Rey's turn, who shared a rich bottle of green wine from Junine. He didn't explain how or why he had it in his possession.

Only Yan, though he hadn't eaten a thing all day, didn't share in his companions' enthusiasm. He couldn't help but watch Léti and Rey, and that took away all of his appetite. It was obvious that she was swayed by the actor's charm. And he, poor fisherman, didn't know what to do.

The needling, cruel voice of his conscience whispered to him: if you had proposed earlier…if you had spoken to her…And he couldn't shut the voice up. Everything he ate tasted like regret. He finally gave up eating and was tempted to drink instead, but quickly abandoned the idea. Normally, alcohol didn't suit him very well, and it certainly wouldn't help him right now. He really didn't feel like celebrating, so he listened to his friends' conversation, without really paying any attention.

"For me, after being alone for so long," Bowbaq was saying, "I swear, it sure feels good to talk to someone."

Corenn agreed, "Of course, and now there are six of us."

"Do you think there any other heirs in Berce?"

"I do not think so. If any show up now, it will be on the Day of the Owl. The others are in hiding, like Ipsen and your children, if not…"

Grigán finished for her, "If not, they're dead. There's no use in denying it. And if we're here, it's only because we were lucky."

"Lucky to be hunted by the Züu," Rey interrupted. "Lucky to have lost my cousin. I'd gladly give up that kind of luck."

"Be thankful, first. Think what would have happened if you had come in through the front door, instead of the window. Or if Bowbaq hadn't woken up before they got to his house. Or if Corenn hadn't guessed the true danger when she learned about Xan's death."

"All said and done, Master Derkel, you are the only one who has just yourself to thank for your own survival."

"Maybe, Kercyan. And it will stay that way as long as you don't stick any spokes in our wheels."

"Well," Corenn said firmly to cut short the conversation, which was heating up, "I think the problem that concerns us is elsewhere. We should all concentrate our thinking on the future more than the past. Am I right?"

"I share your opinion entirely," Rey responded.

"Sure," Grigán simply said.

"We should take advantage of being reunited to share our ideas. We're faced with three main questions: who is the one who started all this, why do they care about the heirs, and finally—and most importantly—how will we put an end to it? I am convinced we only need to know one of these things in order to deduce the other two. Everyone in agreement?"

Of course, everyone nodded. If, up until now, Corenn had let herself fade behind Grigán, she was clearly determined to control the debates, which was perfectly within her capabilities. It seemed like the group would have two leaders, one a warrior, the other a diplomat.

"Before we propose any theories, we should gather and compare our information. Everyone has briefly told their story, but I want you to really search your memory. Did any of the Züu whom you met say, do, or even suggest anything that might point us in the right direction?"

The interrogation was mostly directed at Rey and Bowbaq, and just as much at Yan, who still hadn't had much time to process everything he saw in Berce.

"Mine shot me a good series of insults," the actor joked. "I would like to repeat them to you, but I doubt that would be very useful!"

"The ones who attacked me didn't say much, and I didn't understand their language. I might have been able to interrogate one of them, but Mir killed him too quickly..."

Rey chimed in, "Mir, that's your snow lion, right? Isn't that what you said earlier? You sticking with that?"

"Of course," the Northerner responded innocently. "I mean, he's not my lion, but a lion. No one owns Mir."

"He's sticking with it. Either you are more susceptible to wine than you look, or you will have to show me how to train animals one day."

"It's not training. It's a dialogue. From mind to mind."

"You'll have to show me, then."

"We are getting off topic," Corenn reminded them.

Yan rummaged through his memory, but couldn't find anything to add. All that he had to say about the Züu, the others knew already. He preferred to keep quiet and to let himself wallow in the pain of his thwarted love.

"I found a piece of parchment on one of them," Bowbaq announced, after thinking about it for a while. "But it was all tattered and unreadable, so I destroyed it. Maybe I shouldn't have," he finished, lowering his head.

"Too bad," commented Grigán.

"I also found one. And it's in perfect condition."

Rey went over to his bags, from which he pulled out a paper and something rolled up in a piece of fabric.

"What's that?" Léti asked him, while Corenn leaned toward the parchment.

Rey, smiling, handed over the object. He couldn't look at her without smiling, Yan noticed with a pang of jealousy.

"Be careful not to hurt yourself. The smallest scratch would be fatal."

Léti delicately pulled out the item. A dagger. A long, thin, horrible dagger, whose point was stuck in a piece of wood.

"A Züu dagger?" she asked, disgusted.

"Indeed. As genuine as they come. But its old owner is no longer with us to verify that."

"So much the better," Léti noted in a dark tone.

She firmly gripped the weapon's handle and observed it in the fire's dancing light. It was just such a blade that had killed her friends. It was such a blade that these men were trying to plunge into her heart. Almost as thin as a needle.

"I would just as well that you put that down," Grigán asked.

Léti acted like she didn't hear anything, even daring to remove the piece of wood that covered the point. Ignoring the warrior's repeated request, she took a salted apple from a basket and carefully stabbed the steel into it. The fruit's peel withered and blackened, as if it had been burned.

"Léti, put that horrible thing down," Corenn ordered in a harsh tone Yan didn't expect from her.

Rey held out his hand, and Léti put down the dagger and the fabric with resignation. The actor then passed on the object to Bowbaq, who just gave it a nauseated look, then to Yan, who set it down in front of himself to examine in detail.

Bowbaq said, "I wonder how they manage to avoid injuring themselves."

"Oh, I'm sure it happens, just as with anyone. But the Züu have a big advantage over their victims. An antidote."

Rey pulled a little box out of his pocket. Inside was a slightly damp, dark-colored paste, which he showed to his companions.

"Careful, I'm not sure about it. I also found a little vial, which apparently contains the poison, judging from the odor on the dagger. But it could very easily be the reverse; just as this paste could have nothing to do with the dagger."

"I found the same things," Bowbaq said. "I was stupid to not keep them. I beg your forgiveness—"

"Stop torturing yourself!" Grigán exclaimed. "You're alive, your wife and your kids are safe, that's all you can ask for."

"Thank you, my friend."

"It looks like there are some sort of notches on the handle," Yan pointed out.

"I saw them as well. They're some sort of eye-shaped carvings."

"How many are there?" Grigán asked without batting an eye.

Yan leaned in again to get a close look.

"Seventeen."

"Reyan, in killing this Zü, you have avenged the deaths of seventeen of his victims. At least. They only tally their 'official' murders. Their contracts, if you prefer."

Revolted, Yan pushed away the dagger.

The dagger no longer fascinated him at all. It was simply repulsive.

"Aunt Corenn, are you all right?"

The Mother hadn't said anything for a while, immersed as she was in reading the parchment.

"I'm all right," she responded with a sigh. "I was lost in my thoughts. Apparently, this piece of paper is just a list. An appalling list: all the heirs living in or near Lorelia. A dozen or so people. And there is a cross next to each name, except for Rey's."

They all understood what that meant.

"It's tragic, but at least we will know the fate of some of our friends," declared Grigán. "Lady Corenn, would you mind reading them to us?"

She gathered up her courage and began, pronouncing each name with gravity, despite the fact that she desperately wanted to finish the reading.

"Jalandre, Rébastide, Mess, Humeline, Tomah, Braquin, Nécéandre, Tido, Rydell, Lonic, Salandra, Darie, and Effene…"

"Poor Humeline," Bowbaq murmured after a long moment of silence. "Poor all of them."

His pain was sincere, as was the pain of Corenn, Grigán, and Léti. But at the same time, they were freed from the painful uncertainty that had gnawed at them until now. They weren't any less tortured than before; all had sensed the terrible news for some time.

"The parchment that you found must have been the same type of list," Grigán remarked. "But you and your children are the only Arque heirs, right?"

"Yes. The family had another branch, but they died out with my grandfather's brother."

"How did the Züu make these lists?" Léti asked.

"Excellent question. That brings us back to one of the three we brought up earlier. Who started all of this?"

"Corenn, I'm sure you have an answer you want to suggest," said Rey.

"Maybe. But I would like to hear your opinions first. If I tell you now, that might influence your judgment."

"All right. I suggest we immediately eliminate the idea that the Züu are solely responsible. They never act on their own."

"That's not true," objected Grigán. "History is full of exceptions. The Züu have always used their…influence to preserve and expand their territory."

"Yes, I've heard of the Kurdalène story too. Don't forget that I'm Lorelien. But the heirs never planned on annihilating Zuïa's cult, at least not that I know of. Nor invading their island!"

"That's true. I didn't even know that they existed two moons ago," Bowbaq added.

"You, no," Corenn said in a serious tone. "But another heir? Or several?"

"Do you think it could be one of our own?" Léti said, surprised.

"I don't know. It's possible. That would explain the precise lists, at least."

"The Guild might have found the names and addresses," Rey proposed. "Just a little bit of research, two or three 'hands-on' interrogations, and the Züu would have all the necessary information."

"That's a possible explanation. The other, more frightful one requires the culpability, or at least the complicity, of an heir."

Léti observed seriously, "Unless it really is their goddess who is judging us."

A silence spread over the group, no one wanting to react to the idea, too fantastic and horrifying.

"Well," Corenn began again, "*think*. What could bring someone to unleash all this?"

"I want to say greed, because that's often the right answer," Rey said. "But I don't see how that could be true in our case."

"Vengeance," Grigán said with confidence. "I know you don't agree with me, Corenn, but I am almost sure I'm right. Only revenge could bring someone to carry out such horrors."

"Who would want vengeance upon us?" Bowbaq asked.

"And why?" Léti asked, incredulous.

"Lots of people, maybe. The nobles who still grieve their emissaries, like in Goran or Jezeba. A descendant of Nol the Strange. An heir, unhappy with his lot in life."

"None of these reasons seem to justify the assassinations of eighty or a hundred people," Rey objected.

"You really think so? I will give you an example: your own, actually. We all know that Reyan the Elder carried the enviable title of Duke Kercyan. A title that should have been passed on to you, as well as the land, the castle, and the family's wealth. On returning from the island, everything was taken from him. And you received nothing. Is it really inconceivable to think that you, or any one of the heirs whose ancestors were disgraced, could develop over the years an unrelenting blind hatred, tinged with madness?"

"That sounds so real coming out of your mouth, I'm starting to wonder how I haven't considered it before," Rey jested, wincing. "All right, fine, a point for you. Your explanation still has one flaw. Since I have nothing, how could I have hired and paid the Züu?"

"Someone as mad and determined as I described could very easily hide away his riches for years. And I wasn't accusing you, either."

"Oh, really? I was starting to doubt my own innocence."

"Grigán, according to your theory, why wouldn't this man, thirsty for vengeance, just wait until we were all reunited on the island? Why would the Züu instead do everything they could to prevent us from meeting up?"

"Precisely to prevent us from doing what we're doing right now: finding the one responsible. I'm sure we must know him. We just have to search among those who are still alive."

"The culprit could easily fake his own death," objected Yan, who was forcing himself to forget his own worries to participate in the communal reflection.

"We will never find him," Bowbaq said in despair. "We don't know who it is, we don't know what he wants—"

"We will find him," Corenn declared firmly. "Our only chance of getting out of this mess is to have a conversation with him. A candid conversation."

Rey threw in, "I'm pleased to see that everyone here realizes how futile fleeing would be. Beyond living on the summit of some inaccessible mountain, or in the middle of some desert, sooner or later we'd be flushed out one by one by the Züu and the Grand Guild."

"Thanks, Rey, I really needed something to cheer me up," Yan said.

"Aunt Corenn, we aren't getting anywhere. Tell us what you think."

Five attentive faces turned toward the Mother, who took her time collecting her thoughts.

"Well, I don't think that the Züu started this either. That would mean they are acting solely out of religious fanaticism, and nothing, to our knowledge, has pushed them to do that. So they were hired."

No one interrupted her, waiting impatiently for her to continue.

"Maybe it is a bit naive on my part, but I do not think that vengeance could make someone, even someone who had gone mad, assassinate children they did not know and never could know. Especially since the victims more or less share his misfortune, and certainly aren't responsible for it."

Grigán couldn't help but add, "You know what I think about vengeance and madness."

"Yes, I know. But in my opinion, someone as deranged as you have described could not organize something that requires so much preparation. And it seems to me that his behavior would have given us reason to begin suspecting something years ago."

"Maybe. But not all the heirs came to the gatherings."

"Logically, those who did not come were either uninterested or completely ignorant about Ji and of their ancestor's past. So they would not have much reason to hate us so vehemently."

Grigán didn't offer any more objections. He remained unconvinced, but had no more arguments left.

"I think, in spite of everything, and as horrible as it sounds, it is one of our own. The Züu are too well-informed about our history and our traditions. How many people in the world know about the Day of the Bear? One hundred? One hundred fifty? Not much more. And how many have been to the island?"

"You think it has something to do with the island?" Bowbaq asked.

"I am sure of it. There's only one interesting thing about the heirs—what's on that island."

"I don't see how that would make us targets. We don't even know what it is," Grigán disagreed.

"Sorry to interrupt you," Rey said, "but could someone tell me what there is on the island?"

Corenn and Grigán exchanged a look, but their decision had already been made.

"I am sorry, but we cannot speak of it," Corenn declared. "We have already gone too far…"

"Wait, wait—I am, myself, an heir. I would appreciate it if you kept that in mind, so I can get something out of it for once."

"I've never been to Ji either, you know," Bowbaq said to the actor. "It's not so important; it's not an obligation."

"We made a solemn oath," grumbled Grigán, "as did our ancestors before us. No one has ever broken it. We aren't going to start for you."

"That's a shame; I thought I'd found some open-minded people—"

Corenn cut him off. "Your curiosity will soon be satisfied anyway. We are going to the island on the Day of the Owl. As we have always done."

Yan, Bowbaq, and Léti froze. This statement was heavy with meaning.

"That's only a few days away. A little earlier, a little later, what's the difference?"

Grigán responded clearly. "We aren't allowed to talk about it, except when we're on Ji. That's all there is to it."

Rey gave up on trying to change their minds, and signaled to Corenn to continue.

"Right. As I was saying, in my opinion the only thing that could interest anyone in the heirs is the secret on the island."

"Well, now I'm going to have trouble following!" the actor complained.

"That's why," Corenn continued, "I am almost sure that it must be one of the heirs. Only the heirs know about it."

"And so?" Rey interrupted.

"Corenn, I'm curious to hear how you're going to explain the connection between the assassins and Ji," said Grigán.

"Only two things can be the cause. Only two things, since we have already dismissed vengeance as a motive, can drive a man to such acts. Ideology and self-interest."

"Now I'm the one who's completely lost," Léti said. "What's ideology?"

"The convictions and beliefs, moral, political, philosophical, religious, or otherwise, that an individual or a group hold to be true. Simply put, their opinions on a subject."

"I don't see how the heirs' gatherings could go against someone's beliefs," Grigán said. "Or we'd be talking about madness again."

"I do not think it is about ideology either. I am more inclined toward self-interest."

"I should have stuck with my answer from earlier," Rey joked. "Is there treasure there?"

"I wish. At least that would make everything clear," Grigán answered. "What kind of self-interest? Wanting to keep anyone from finding out about the secret?"

"Something like that. I think the man behind all of this knows a lot more than us about the island's mysteries."

Corenn let some time pass, enough for her words to sink in.

"Maybe he has always known about it, or maybe he recently discovered it. But it's obvious that there is something fabulous on that island. Riches, limitless power, supreme knowledge. You know, it could be any number of things like that."

Grigán nodded. Corenn's theory was very reasonable.

"Whatever it is, he doesn't want us to discover it. Something very peculiar has happened, or will happen, on Ji. That's why our enemy did everything he could to keep us from getting there. And that's why we need to go."

They stayed silent, impressed by Corenn's ability to reason, and more than that, by her conclusions, so weighted with implications.

"Who do you think it is?" Bowbaq finally asked.

"Unfortunately, I don't have any names to propose. Given the evidence, it must be someone who has considerable wealth…"

"But the only rich heirs are the descendants of Arkane of Junine," Grigán said. "Who never came to the gatherings, Thomé excepted."

"And the Arkane lineage is coming to an end," Corenn added. "The queen Séhane will die without children; the barons are already arguing over the throne."

"Remember when I said that Ji was nothing more than a curse?" Rey commented. "But this queen has to be our main suspect?"

"In theory, yes," Corenn responded, "but I already had the chance to meet her, and she didn't seem all that devious. She is an elderly woman who cultivates kindness and politeness, while the barons display only condescension. Moreover, she doesn't know the secret."

"Since I'm missing a piece, you could say a very significant one at that, you will have to excuse me for not understanding right away," Rey complained again. "Do we at least know if she's still alive?"

"She is not on my list, which leaves us some hope."

"Maybe we could ask her for help?" Yan suggested. "She would do it, for your ancestors."

"And what kind of help do you want from her? We won't be any safer in the Baronies than here," Grigán answered.

"Actually, I was thinking, since she's a queen, she could more easily find traces of the other heirs."

"That's a good idea," Corenn announced, upon consideration. "Maybe that is what we will do, if we do not learn anything on the island."

"I have something else to propose," Rey responded. "The Small Palace Market."

"In Lorelia?" Grigán asked. "What do you want us to do there?"

"Meet the Züu. And buy information from them. That's what I was planning to do before I met up with you."

"Refresh my memory," Corenn asked. "I know I have already heard about it, but the details escape me."

"Once a dékade, in the old Royal Commerce Commissioner's palace, they host a market that is a bit special. There, anyone can sell any type of merchandise, even illegal. Especially illegal, actually, as that is what is exchanged there most often. And the Züu are there…how should I put it? Permanently."

"You want us to bargain with them?" Grigán protested.

"Why not? If they gave me the option to buy back my life, you better believe I wouldn't hesitate."

"Just walking up to the Züu doesn't seem safe," Corenn objected.

"The Small Palace is a truce zone. The Crown uses it as a method to keep an eye on all the traffic, and the place is overflowing with spies. The officers watch the entryways and guarantee safety. To my knowledge, everything's always gone smoothly."

"I'm warning you, Corenn, I refuse to haggle for my life with assassins."

"The idea repulses me too, but maybe we should try that avenue, if Ji doesn't deliver a solution."

The warrior didn't add anything. He figured he would make himself heard when it mattered.

"Well, either way, the best we can do for now is wait for the Bear. That leaves us two days to think it over," he concluded, standing up from the table.

His companions soon did the same, then they all attended to their nightly chores, except for Léti, who approached the warrior. "There are three days left, right?"

"Two. You've counted wrong."

Léti froze.

"That's impossible! That means that today was…"

She couldn't finish her thought, which died in a sob.

Feeling awkward, Grigán waited hopelessly for someone to come help him, but no one had paid any attention to their conversation.

"It was the Day of the Promise, yes," he finally said. "I thought you knew; everyone thought you knew…"

She turned around and observed each of her friends. Yan seemed to be sulking.

"I'm going to go for a walk," she said to Corenn, tearfully, before running off.

Four inquisitive faces turned toward Grigán, who mumbled, "I didn't do anything. I can't fix all our problems."

209

He refused to offer any other explanation. Yan wanted to go and comfort Léti, but he couldn't bring himself to.

Surely, she would prefer it if Rey were the one to go.

For everyone, it was an extremely long wait for that fateful day. Curiosity gnawed at each of them, as did anxiety at the thought of exploring Ji and its mysteries. Needless to say, the prevailing tension in the group didn't improve the atmosphere.

Rey and Grigán stuck to haughtily ignoring one another, except when the actor made a joke behind the warrior's back, which happened often enough, and consistently triggered a more acerbic verbal spat.

Léti didn't know how to act toward Yan, and he didn't know what to think or how to react. From time to time, the young woman would make an attempt at reconciliation, but was it out of pity? She also spent a lot of time with Rey. In the end, Yan decided he wouldn't make any decisive moves until things became clearer. Léti soon made the same decision, and so things between them remained unchanged.

Grigán spent most of his time patrolling the area surrounding their camp and keeping a close watch on the island. He didn't come back to camp until nightfall, when it became impossible to discern a boat landing on the small island. His biggest fear was that they would fall right into a trap set by the Züu on Ji, and even if they didn't talk about it, everyone else feared the same thing.

From the start they considered the question of how they would cross the sea to the island, but the problem was soon resolved. The fishermen of Berce, like plenty of other fishermen, simply left their boats on the beach. So all they needed to do was "borrow" one.

Grigán had already picked out a craft, equipped with a sail, whose owner lived outside the village. The skiff, separated from the rest by a few hundred yards, might escape the Züu's likely surveillance. The rest of their preparations didn't amount to much. The warrior asked them to make a few torches and suggested that they take advantage of their forced inactivity by gathering provisions of all varieties. As usual, Grigán took charge of hunting and brought back plenty of game.

But, at the end of the day, they were still left with a lot of free time, which they filled as best they could. Rey tried to give his companions lessons in different Ithare dice games, but none among them was a very good player, whereas the actor was very experienced and won almost every round.

They thought for a moment to be entertained by a demonstration of Bowbaq's powers; he could not say no to Léti's urgings. But the results were far from spectacular. The horse that served as a guinea pig simply charged and whinnied, as if it had gone crazy. Worried about maintaining their low profile, Grigán asked that they stop the experiment, to the great disappointment of Léti, Yan, and Rey.

The young woman, now carried away by the idea of seeing a spectacle, then begged her aunt to provide them with a demonstration of her own mysterious talents. She quickly abandoned the idea after getting a scolding look from her aunt as her sole response. No one dared to ask questions.

Corenn took advantage of the free time by studying the lists of heirs, which she updated. Based on their collective memory, she drew and completed, as best she could, the genealogical trees of the seven Sages who survived the journey. She counted seventy-one individuals over three generations.

Of the seventy-one, she knew the fate of at least forty-nine: herself, Léti, Grigán, Bowbaq, and Rey were—by the grace of

Eurydis—still alive. Forty-four others, according to Rey's list and her own, had been assassinated by the Züu.

That left the fate of only twenty-two heirs uncertain, a number that grew slightly after accounting for a few individuals overlooked by her initial census. It certainly didn't leave them with much hope for growth.

Logic told her that their enemy was one of those twenty-two or so names, but her intuition told her otherwise. Corenn was more anxious than any of her companions to land on the forgotten island.

❈

"How can you navigate? It's a crescent moon and there isn't even a star in the sky!"

Even though Bowbaq spoke in a whisper, they could hear the anxiety in his voice. Yan, on the other hand, felt perfectly at ease: the sea was calm, the night still, and soon enough his curiosity would be satisfied, finally putting an end to these three long days spent waiting.

"It's magic," Grigán answered for the young man, who was at the helm. "I think of a place, and the path simply appears in my mind."

"What?"

"All right, it isn't magic. I owe it to this object: a Rominian compass. I haven't shown it to you already?"

The warrior explained the principle of the instrument briefly; Bowbaq wasn't reassured in the slightest.

"Are you sure it works? We've been on the water for a while now, and we still can't see the island!"

"That's good. That means the Züu can't see us either."

"Don't worry," Rey added. "We aren't going to get lost at sea. Look at those distant lights over there. You see them?"

"Zélanos and his children. Lorelia's lighthouses, in other words. As long as we can see them, we know where the coast is."

"That's at least a day's sail away," Yan commented.

"A day!" wailed the Northerner, terrified. "A day! We're so far!"

"Is it your first time on a boat or something?" jibed the actor. "One might think it's the first time you've seen the sea your whole life."

"That's not far from the truth, in fact," Bowbaq explained. "You're going to think it's silly, but I have a dreadful fear of water. Especially now. You can't see a thing!"

"Is that why you've never been to Ji before? And here I thought you just wanted to stay with the kids," Corenn gently teased.

"Yes, that was part of it," he mumbled.

"Then how do you explain the hundreds of pounds of fish you catch every year? Don't they come from the water?"

"That's not the same, my friend. You can trust a creek, a stream, or even a river. You're never more than a few yards from shore, a few oar strokes and you're there. Here, there's no land in sight."

"Mind you, you might be able to touch the bottom," joked Rey. "Thirty feet, forty feet, what's that to a big guy like you?"

"Forty feet! Forty feet deep!" the giant exclaimed, before resolutely sitting down on the floor of the boat.

Léti sat down next to him. She couldn't find the right words to reassure him, but she didn't like seeing her kind friend in such a state.

They floated onward in silence for some time. Finally, Grigán pointed toward a point in the darkness.

"There," he said simply.

As they had planned, Léti silently lowered the sail while Yan, Rey, and Grigán took position with their bows; the others lay on the floor of the boat. They slowly drifted across the remaining distance.

The island emerged out of the darkness, at first a mass just a bit darker than the water; as they got closer, its contours became progressively more defined. The silence was complete, disturbed only by a playful colony of marine frogs.

"It looks quiet," murmured the actor.

"Maybe," Grigán answered tersely.

Yan couldn't help adding, "But he wouldn't bet his life on in it."

He had long waited to pull that joke out of his comedic reserve. The warrior responded with nothing more than an impassive look out of the corner of his eye, whereas Léti, squeezed between Corenn and Bowbaq, burst out laughing, joined by Bowbaq and Corenn.

The boat scraped the sandy bottom before coming to a complete halt. Grigán waited a moment before giving Yan the signal. The boy responded by crawling overboard and wading toward the beach, covered by his friends' bows. Rey followed and took position opposite Yan on the beach.

Finally, it was Grigán's turn; he slipped right past them, penetrating farther into the rocky landscape. He came back soon after, reassured, at least for the moment.

"All clear," he instructed. "You can come ashore. Light the torches."

Not a moment later, Bowbaq hopped into the water and dragged the massive boat to the beach, pulling Léti and Corenn along with it. He didn't even seem to notice the incredible feat he had accomplished.

"Ground! At last, solid ground!" he exclaimed, relieved. "Are you sure we can't wait until dawn to make the return trip?"

"Positive. We would be too visible from the coast."

"Too bad."

The giant walked off and placed his palms on a rock, as if to reassure himself of its solidity. He preferred even this dreary landscape to the sea.

Yan had been told that the island was somewhat austere, but he didn't expect this. Apart from the small, bare beach they stood on, the landscape was nothing more than enormous blocks of rock. It was as if a somewhat lazy god had simply piled them on top of one another to create a new land.

It was quite small. A walk all the way around wouldn't take more than four or five decidays. Assuming the entire coastline was passable, of course, which wasn't the case.

"No one has touched the torches we left here on our last visit," Grigán said, leaning to look behind a pile of rocks. "Do you think that's a good sign, Lady Corenn?"

"Unfortunately, we can't conclude a whole lot from it. Aside from those present, it appears that nothing has changed for three years."

"Say, that's the entrance to the famous labyrinth, isn't it?" Rey pointed to a sandy passage between two large boulders.

"How did you guess?" asked Corenn.

"Grigán's footprints. He scouted ahead before coming back to join us on the beach."

"Good deduction," grunted the warrior. "And according to you, which way should we go next?"

"You're the guide. Guide us. I suggest we get this over with as quickly as possible. I'm anxious to finally know this stupid secret that ruined my family."

"You mustn't say that," scolded Léti.

More than the others, she found a certain charm in the actor. She thought his cheerful disposition and his character made him very likable. Except when he spoke like that about the Sages and the ancestors. In her eyes, they were sacred, especially now that the majority of them were dead. To disrespect their legacy was like...like insulting and forswearing Eurydis. It was wrong.

"All right," began Corenn. "I think it's time."

Everyone gathered before her and Grigán, attentive and impatient.

"First of all, although I trust each and every one of you, you are going to have to swear an oath."

"Come on now," moaned Rey. "Is this whole ceremony really necessary? Can't we just go see what's going on instead? We might miss it."

"We still have time," Grigán grunted. "And anyone who doesn't accept the oath won't come. Period."

"All right, then. I promise to respect and assume all obligations, restraints, duties, and responsibilities you wish," he muttered insolently. "Can we go now?"

Corenn answered calmly for Grigán, "Reyan, that's not what we're asking of you. The oath doesn't have any value in and of itself, since we'll have no means to guarantee that it will be upheld. It's just a brief moment of seriousness before the coming excitement, a moment of reflection to help you realize the gravity of the situation, and the importance of your silence. Do you understand?"

The actor reflected in silence for a moment.

"Corenn, my grandmother didn't lie to me about you," he declared. "You have a gift for getting what you want from people, which would make a Lorelien jeweler green with envy. You've got me. I'll listen."

Corenn nodded with a smile. Then she began her "oath," in a serious and didactic tone.

"The things we're going to show you are unknown to most people, and it must remain that way, as ordained by the will of our ancestors. Since them, for over a century, each generation has kept the secret, and it will be up to you to do the same in the years to come."

"Excuse me for interrupting, Corenn," Bowbaq said, "but there's something I've never understood and I think now's the time to ask. If it's a secret, why didn't it die with our ancestors? Why are you, in turn, passing it on to us?"

She reflected for a moment before answering.

"Because it's too heavy for our shoulders. As it was for our ancestors. They judged it advisable to share part of it with their family members, as I am now doing with Léti. Personally, I also believe that, in some respect, we've become the guardians of the secret of Ji, even if we don't fully grasp all of its implications. Do you understand?"

"I have an objection," Rey chimed in. "Though it's far, very far, from my intention to exclude our friend Yan, he isn't one of us. Does that mean you're breaking your oath?"

"I trust him more than I do some others here," said Grigán, acidly.

"Yan is, or will someday be, part of the family," appended Corenn. "This isn't a problem. But we can take a vote—"

"It isn't worth the trouble," Rey interrupted. "It was just a theoretical question."

Yan intentionally kept himself out of it. He was dying to satisfy his curiosity, and therefore was very happy to hear the various statements his friends made on his behalf. Especially Corenn's. Was she thinking of a Union between him and Léti? Or was he imagining things again?

Corenn continued. "You must promise to keep silent about what you're about to see. Even in the face of suffering, dishonor, loneliness. Death. You will only talk of it with very close family members or other heirs. Take the time to consider, and if you agree, simply say so."

"I agree to everything," Rey said immediately.

Yan did as he was asked, closing his eyes, and reflecting in silence on Corenn's words and their implications.

"I agree," he said finally.

Everyone turned to Léti, who remained silent.

The young woman was terrified. She had been waiting impatiently for this moment since she was a young girl. All her life, she had wanted to share in the secret of her ancestors and become a full member of the group. But now that the day had come, she hesitated.

Everyone who went there came back sad.

And she had already endured her share of suffering.

Was the secret more beautiful as it was—unknown?

"Léti?"

The young woman opened her eyes to her aunt's call.

She decided impulsively. "I agree," she said, wishing she had said it with more conviction.

"Good," concluded Grigán. "Let's go. I ask that you all make as little noise as possible, and of course that goes for certain loudmouths too."

"Can I let out a cry of pain if I fall?" Rey asked sourly.

"Only if you really, really hurt yourself," shot back Grigán in the same tone. "That would be delightful."

With Grigán at the front of the column, they disappeared through the narrow passage, just as Nol the Strange had done more than a century before. Rey walked behind Grigán, followed by Léti, and then Corenn and Bowbaq. Yan brought up the rear.

His heart was hammering in his chest. It was all very exciting. Much more so than his adventure in Berce—this time he wasn't alone. His mind was galvanized as never before.

Even the most insignificant things seemed strange. The dancing torchlight on the rocks. The distorted echoes of every sound. The odd arrangement of gigantic blocks that made the whole landscape feel like a real labyrinth.

After about a centiday of this silent walking, Grigán led the group inside a cave. Yan held his breath, certain they were nearing their destination.

"Are we here?" whispered Rey.

"No. Be quiet."

After a short time underground, they emerged from the natural shelter through a small opening where they had to crouch to pass through—practically a crawl for Bowbaq.

Once through, the warrior made them wait for a moment as he watched the small exit, his bow drawn. This must have been some sort of standard procedure for him, a precaution to foil anyone's attempts at following them, because Grigán quickly gave the order to carry forward again as if nothing had happened.

More focused on watching the landscape than memorizing their path, Yan was already lost. They had changed directions at least twenty times, ignoring passages on the right and left that nevertheless seemed to be going in the same direction. If he had to, he might be able to find his way back to the beach, but definitely not using the same path.

An encounter with a large, slavering turtle forced them to make a further detour. They had disturbed the reptile right as it was laying eggs, and it showed them just how menacing a vulture turtle can be. Though it was slow just like its brethren, its powerful jaws were infamous, and Grigán preferred to turn the group around rather than risk a perilous crossing.

"Maybe Bowbaq could have negotiated our passage?" Rey muttered. "Maybe we could have even asked for directions?"

"It wouldn't have worked," the giant objected seriously. "It only works with mammals."

"Too bad. Maybe we'll come across some stray goat or cow and have a chat with it."

"That's enough, you two!" Grigán said. "A bit of silence, please!"

"You know," Rey continued brazenly, "these discretionary measures are completely useless so long as we keep these torches lit."

"That's for me to judge. So long as you're with us, you will do as we do."

"You're the boss, boss. Let's hope that if some guy's hiding over there he's blind rather than deaf."

Grigán chose not to respond. He had already given up discussing anything with the actor, who was obviously bent on provoking him.

If he were alone, of course he would have gone without the torch. But the whole lot of them groping their way forward—clearly they'd make more noise than a red pig in heat. It seemed childish. Sometimes he got the feeling that no one made any effort to understand him.

"Wait for me here. Silently, if possible," he added, giving Rey a gimlet eye.

They watched as he crept forward. Bowbaq thought to himself that Grigán must have an excellent reason for such caution. The warrior didn't even bring his torch.

He came back presently, via another path that adjoined theirs right behind Yan, who jumped at his arrival.

"I didn't see anything," he said to Corenn. "Everything looks normal."

"I'm tempted to say that's a shame," she responded. "It could have been our first step toward finding an answer."

"There's still hope. Perhaps later. Once it's occurred, which shouldn't be long, for that matter. Let's make haste."

They all trekked onward after the tireless warrior, their curiosity freshly fueled. He led them straight toward another cave, which wasn't marked in any particular way to distinguish it from the one they had already passed through or the others they had spotted.

The entryway looked like a natural arch, which opened up into a small room. It was only after they had covered almost the entire length of the room that a sort of gradually descending hall-way appeared off to the right.

"This must be it," Rey declared. "There are traces of soot on the rocks. The torches..."

"Good catch, Reyan. I had never thought of that. We'll have to remember to clean that up."

"If we still get the chance," Grigán muttered.

He had definitively given up trying to keep the undisciplined members of his little group quiet. It was beyond his control.

Everyone's excitement level was at its peak. Yan wondered which was louder: the sound of his steps or his heartbeat. Léti feared a morbid discovery, and the descent had hardly reassured her. Bowbaq felt very uneasy, having a difficult time being confined underground. The sound of water below and the drops streaming down the walls heightened his anxiety. Rey let his imagination wander about what they were going to find...this one thing that was so important to every one of their lives, but that they didn't know.

"I hope we won't have to swim," Bowbaq grumbled. "If we do, don't count on me. I'll turn right around."

"Nothing to fear. There's a chance you might get your feet a little wet, that's all."

The long slope ended at the edge of an underground lake, which was large enough that the opposite bank disappeared in the darkness. Grigán waited until everyone was together.

"It's beautiful," Léti said baldly, relieved to find nothing more frightening.

Yan squatted, cupped some water in his hands, and wet his lips.

"It's salty," he said, grimacing. "It's seawater."

"It's freshwater, actually," said Corenn, "but the banks of the lake are covered in salt."

"Grigán, my friend," Bowbaq pleaded, "don't ask me to cross."

"I told you, you have nothing to worry about. We're going to go around."

And that's what they did, one behind the other, on a narrow, uneven ledge that ran the length of the wall. They soon lost sight of the path behind them.

The room with the lake had to be 120 yards in diameter, Yan thought to himself. Maybe more. It was impossible to know, short of making a full circle or lighting the whole room, which was also impossible at the moment. They already had enough trouble focusing on their feet, trying not to make a false step and slip into the dark water.

But they overcame the obstacle without difficulty. The only spot that was somewhat perilous being a yard-long section of the ledge that had crumbled away long ago, which they had to jump over. Corenn, lacking confidence in her physical abilities, was the only one who really had trouble, before Bowbaq carried her across the gap.

"It's a shame we can't leave any trace of our passing," the Mother commented, her feet back on the ground. "I've been wanting to put a little bridge at that spot for years."

"We could always hide a plank somewhere," Yan suggested. "And remove it each time."

"There's an idea worth considering."

This unsteady walk finally came to an end soon after. The ledge butted up against a wall pierced by a thin, three-foot-tall opening. Grigán asked for a torch, clasped his scimitar, and slipped through the narrow opening, followed by Rey, armed with his crossbow, then the rest.

Bowbaq thought he was going to die here in the depths of the earth. In order to move forward through the small space carved in the rock, he was forced to turn himself sideways, which restricted his movements. He felt like he was squeezing himself deeper and deeper into a huge trap, and that he was going to be squashed or imprisoned at any moment. Briefly, he wondered whether he preferred being on the water.

Then, little by little, the crack widened, becoming a wide hallway, and soon even wider. At last, they emerged into another room.

"Stop," Grigán ordered.

The warrior swept his piercing gaze over the darkness. Léti found it a little ridiculous; he couldn't see a thing. Unless he was listening? She listened closely, but all she could hear, like everyone else, was the distant sounds of the sea.

Grigán paced around, inspecting the room before coming back. There was something uncanny about the sight of a man dressed all in black wandering about in the darkness, with nothing but the faint flickering light of his torch.

"Nothing, Corenn. No one."

"That would mean that I was wrong…"

"Maybe, maybe not. We'll see when it happens."

"Speaking of that," interrupted Rey, "now that we've fulfilled the conditions, would it be possible to finally get some explanations?"

"It's better to be surprised," Grigán answered. "But I'm going to show you something anyway. Follow me, and be careful where you step."

They complied, all except for Corenn, who wedged her torch into a crack in the wall and sat down. Yan figured that everything was going to happen here. However, there was nothing extraordinary about the place. It seemed like any other cave, perhaps smaller than the one with the lake, but again, it was hard to tell in the dim light.

They came to the edge of a pond, which Grigán waded into without hesitation, followed immediately by Léti, Yan, and Rey. Bowbaq sufficiently mastered his fears to not be left behind. But the water stretched a good fifteen yards. The warrior stopped on the other side, waiting for the others to catch up. They could hear the sound of the sea much better from here.

They covered the remaining distance cautiously. Grigán finally came to a halt at the edge of a dark pit that spanned the whole floor of the cavern.

"There. I wanted to tell you to watch out for that."

"And here I was thinking you didn't like me," Rey needled him. "Now you're mothering me."

"Fall in if you want, it doesn't matter to me. But I wanted to warn the others."

"How deep is it?" Bowbaq asked, almost shyly.

"Sixty or eighty feet, depending on the tide; the sea comes up right underneath. The entire underground of the island has been hollowed out by water."

"Don't tell me this is where our ancestors began their journey?" Léti asked incredulously.

"Oh, no. In fact, they never went any farther than here. But I challenge you to find any clues."

Nothing could have galvanized the young woman more than Grigán putting a challenge to her. She immediately set about searching every dark corner of the room, helped by Yan, who was recruited by default, but was no less curious for it. Bowbaq went back to keep Corenn company, while Rey proceeded with his own search, all the while trying his best to hide it.

They soon gave up, admitting defeat. An absolute scouring of the entire room—the ground and the walls—didn't turn up any clues. Léti felt more and more frustrated. Corenn noticed and decided to step in before it degenerated into another nervous breakdown.

"Bowbaq, would you join me, please?"

The giant docilely agreed and they walked over to Léti, who was examining a fault in the rock. They all gathered around her. "Here, I am going to help you a little. Climb onto Bowbaq's shoulders. As long as he doesn't mind, of course."

"Absolutely not. It's just like when she was younger."

He simply picked her up and lifted her over his head, before setting her down on his shoulders. Grigán aside, they were all curious where this was going.

"Now, go look at the rock face near the little lake," Corenn finished with a mysterious smile.

Bowbaq immediately trudged over to the wall, hurried by an encouraging Léti, whose mood had suddenly improved. Even with his feet in the water, the giant brought the young woman to a height that was unreachable before.

They began to understand. The cavern ceiling, and the highest walls, escaped the faint torchlight. But they still needed more light to fully see.

Rey took a step back from the others and threw his torch up in the air. It began its spinning arc up; before it fell back to the floor they could see, just for an instant, the highest wall. It was at least seventy feet high.

"I found it!" Léti exclaimed.

She found it right away. It was there, right in front of her eyes. Even though she didn't know exactly what it was, she was sure she was right.

Yan and Rey approached the wall, hoping to see something.

"I don't see anything," Rey declared. "Point it out for us."

"There! And over there! And here too—oh, and it continues on up, really high," she concluded, pointing all over the wall in front of her.

"From here, all we see is the rock," Yan objected timidly.

"I see it," said Bowbaq, who wasn't much lower than the young woman. "It looks like the rock has been sculpted."

"That's right," Corenn said simply.

"Yan!" Rey called, motioning to Yan that he wanted to give him a leg up.

Using Rey as a ladder, the boy could see the higher walls for himself. Indeed, it couldn't be a natural phenomenon. Various curving geometric forms had been carved into the rock wall, in a foot-wide ribbon that ascended vertically until it disappeared into the shadows.

The lowest patterns were also the crudest, and their lines almost completely erased. But the ones higher up seemed surprisingly intricate and well-defined.

Yan dropped down and took his turn hoisting the actor, who was just as curious.

"What is it?" he asked, after examining the rock. "Some sort of writing? Or is it simply decorative?"

"Unfortunately, we don't know," Corenn answered. "In his time, the wise Maz Achem thought there was a resemblance between these signs and those of the Ethèque language."

"Which no one speaks anymore, of course," the actor complained as he jumped to the ground. "I mean, since he was Maz, we could expect this kind of quasi-religious delirium."

Léti frowned. She still didn't appreciate his lack of respect for the Sages.

"Does the pattern go all the way to the top?" Bowbaq asked.

"And even higher," Grigán answered with a knowing chuckle.

Yan and Rey simply looked at each other before heading straight for the wall on the other side. Without a word, the actor locked his fingers together as a step for Yan, who hoisted himself up.

He found the same signs.

"Personally, I prefer the left-hand side. The marks are more intricate," Corenn declared, joking.

Bowbaq carried Léti over to the other side, so she could see for herself.

"It would take years to do all this," she declared admiringly.

"I can guess that the patterns also cover the ceiling?"

"Exactly."

"What is all this, Aunt Corenn? Magical symbols, or something like that?"

"Exactly," Corenn responded seriously. "These designs have a power, but we don't know how they work."

This final answer was met with a long silence, as they all tried to put their thoughts into some sensible order.

Arque tradition taught that one should respect and fear that which is beyond human intellect, which was clearly the case here. Therefore, Bowbaq was anxious for all of this to end, for them to leave this hole and cross that cursed stretch of sea, so they could return to normal things.

For a long time, Léti had accepted the existence of magic, gods, and other unexplained realities and legends, such as her aunt's powers and the mysteries surrounding her ancestors. But for the first time, she was finally getting to the bottom of things. For the first time, she was really going to see it happen. And she was as excited as she was apprehensive.

Yan felt changed. Two dékades earlier, he wouldn't have believed—even if he had been warned—that he would soon be hunted by and fleeing a large band of assassins.

Yet that's what had happened. He wouldn't have believed himself capable of risking his life in a little Lorelien town he had never heard of, and yet that had happened too. He wouldn't have believed he would travel with strangers, or argue with Léti.

He never would have believed he would do all of these unusual things. But he had indeed braved them all.

Now they were telling him about magic. And he was ready to believe anything to satisfy his thirst for experience, which kept growing day after day. Yan was easily the happiest among them.

Only Rey still doubted. His run-ins with magicians consisted of the sleight-of-hand tricks of fakes, which took place in all the big cities' marketplaces. Completely rigged tricks. On top of that, he felt like the others were messing with him, and furthermore, he had waited long enough for them to tell him more.

"All right," he declared seriously, "that's enough riddles for now. Corenn, I beg of you to explain something clearly, anything."

She paused in thought.

"What do you think it is? Even if you feel stupid saying it?"

"In my opinion? I would say really strange symbols, carved we don't know when, how, or why, at the bottom of a remote cave, underneath a tiny Lorelien island no one gives a margolin's ass about."

"A door," Yan suggested, quietly.

"What?"

"In my opinion, it's a door. The designs come together to form an archway along the walls of the cavern…"

"And where's the knob?" the actor said mockingly.

"Yan's right," Grigán interrupted, happy at the chance to contradict Rey.

"You will have to really work hard, I mean really work, to get me to swallow that load of nonsense."

"We won't need to. It shouldn't be long now. All of you come over to this side," Corenn said, leading them to her side.

"We shouldn't be in the doorway when it opens, is that it?" Yan asked.

"No, that doesn't matter. But my feet are cold!"

The boy realized that they had all been wading in the little pond for a while now. He had completely forgotten about everything else.

"How do you know that it's almost time?" Léti asked, once Bowbaq put her back on solid ground.

"It always happens around this time of night, that's all. For a while now, I have wanted to bring a clepsydra, which would give us a more accurate time, but there was always some reason I couldn't."

"Tell me, friend Corenn..." Bowbaq began timidly. "This... this thing that we are waiting for, it's not dangerous, is it? I mean, not sacrilegious, or something like that?"

"We wouldn't have asked you to come if it were," Grigán responded for her. "Don't you trust us?"

"No, of course I do!" the giant apologized fervently, but a part of him continued to agonize.

The conversation died. One by one, they quieted down to simply wait, staring into the dark void where something was supposed to happen.

Even Rey stopped trying to interrogate his companions. After a few moments of waiting, Bowbaq sat down. The sensation of the cold, damp stone had the strange effect of calming him. It reminded him a bit of Arkary's frozen plains.

Corenn soon followed suit, fatigue overcoming her. The others stayed standing. For Grigán, who didn't easily give up his vigilance, caution kept him on his feet. For Yan, Léti, and Rey, it was simple excitement.

They didn't really know what they were waiting for. Yan's imagination ran wild. Léti simply waited, more and more nervous. And Rey meditated on his beliefs and whether or not they were well-founded.

He frequently approached the archway, all his senses alive, looking for the smallest sign of change. But each time he returned more unsatisfied and frustrated.

After his eighth trip, he walked straight toward Grigán.

"We can't wait here all night! You can see for yourself that there's nothing here!" he yelled, pointing to the shadows.

As if in response, a faint buzzing sound sprang up from the walls, and it grew louder and louder, quickly becoming a piercing hiss.

"What's happening?" Bowbaq asked, raising his voice over the sound.

"It's nothing; it's normal," Corenn reassured him.

In the time it took for her to say those words, the noise stopped in a sort of sputter. Then, absolute silence.

They all remained still, because they were awestruck, but also because it was happening so quickly.

The center of the archway was still dark. Then the shadows began moving, brightening. A light appeared: first only a little dot, but it quickly grew as large as the cavern, illuminating it completely.

It was a stunning sight. They saw before them a luminous form, as if the sun itself were trying to enter the cavern by the new gateway.

A sixty-foot-tall gateway.

The light slowly waned, no longer blinding, and was replaced by a hazy vision, as if hidden by smoke. Then the fog cleared little by little, allowing Yan, Léti, Rey, Bowbaq, Corenn, and Grigán to penetrate its secrets.

It was like they were looking across a thin veil of water. It all seemed so close, but at the same time, as if beyond reach, a simple image, a cloudy trick of the eye.

Yan rubbed his eyes, then gaped at the scene. He couldn't deny it; before him, he saw a garden.

Under his feet, the cavern's rocky soil spread to the edge of the pond. From there, water, of course. And, three feet beyond the bank, he saw there was grass. The rest of the cave had disappeared. All of it.

The gateway was a perplexing frontier between the space where they were and another, a living painting wherein dawn rose over a magnificent landscape, a verdant valley set in a mountainous backdrop.

Yan focused all of his attention on the barrier between the two worlds. It was something…unexplainable.

Bowbaq didn't dare move. He too was under the enchanting vision's spell. He had the impression that if he were to move, the spectacle would stop…or take a much darker turn.

Rey searched for the trick, the trick that made such a thing possible, but he couldn't find it. He decided to get closer and see, and dipped a foot into the pond.

"Listen!" said Léti, with a smile on her lips as she placed a finger over her mouth.

She heard something. Hidden behind the noise of herself and her companions, there was…

She finally realized what it was. Birdsong. Even if they were very far away, she could hear the other world! The other world!

They all smiled at her, understanding. They had heard the same thing.

Rey covered the distance separating him from the phenomenon and grabbed the dagger he had strapped to his calf.

"Don't do that," Bowbaq begged.

The actor remained deaf to Bowbaq's pleas and delicately pushed the tip of the blade through the surface of the aqueous vision. Not feeling any resistance, he kept pushing all the way to the hilt. Then he started over, using a flower that appeared right at his feet as a target.

The results didn't satisfy him. It was all just an illusion with no substance.

Léti decided she wasn't going to be left standing there, and joined the actor. She faced the landscape and took a deep breath.

"Léti?" Yan called timidly.

Whatever she was trying to do, he didn't think it was a good idea.

The young woman suddenly took a big step that should have brought her onto solid ground in the other world, and disappeared.

At the same time, they heard a big splash followed by the sound of lapping water. Finally Léti appeared, walking back through the vision, soaked to her knees. It was as if she had fallen from a cloud.

"You could have warned me," she complained to her aunt.

"I assure you, I didn't know what you were planning to do," Corenn responded sincerely.

"I'm sure that on the other side, it's all black," Rey announced. "It's nothing but an illusion, a magic trick, a simple optical illusion."

He took his turn disappearing behind the phenomenon, only to return shortly after, grave and silent. Yan tried walking through the barrier himself.

He expected to feel something, but that wasn't the case. He walked straight forward, slowly, staring at a precise point in the landscape. An instant later he found himself facing the back of the cavern.

He turned around, curious to see what he was going to discover. There was still a magnificent valley in front of him, but not exactly the same. Or really, the same place, but seen from a different angle. Perhaps what you might see standing in the green valley on the other side of the door, if you turned around to look behind.

An enormous hand appeared from the sky, waved around for a moment, then disappeared. A foot, then an entire leg, came next, soon followed by the rest of Bowbaq's body.

The giant had a numb look on his face. He didn't know if he should laugh or cry. Whatever this thing was, it was beautiful. And impossible.

What they were doing was surely forbidden. He had the strange feeling he was violating a secret. And it reminded him too much of an unpleasant memory from his past, one he wanted to forget.

He returned to the other side of the cavern, leaving Yan alone with the landscape.

It all looked so peaceful. So calm. And as beautiful as it was inaccessible. As if nothing were real.

But he saw things. He could hear them. Squinting his eyes, concentrating, he could even make out the flowers swaying in a gentle breeze, or catch sight of a bird in flight.

He concentrated and leaned toward the vision, as if to caress the leaves of one of those strange and wonderful plants, but his fingers felt nothing but emptiness. It saddened him more than he'd expected.

He stood up and was about to join his friends, who were laughing on the other side of the gateway, when something caught his eye.

Someone was in the landscape.

"Come quick! Look!"

All his friends were soon at his side, rendered mute at his discovery.

Around two hundred yards away—assuming just one stride would bring them to the grass on the other side—a young boy walked about, admiring the sky.

He must have been four or five years old. He had the look of the people from the Upper Kingdoms, and could have been from Lorelia, Ith, or even Romine. Or from some other country; the blondness of his hair and his total nudity gave little hint as to his origins.

By instinct, Léti waved to him, before realizing that he wasn't looking in their direction. She began to call to him as loudly as she could, hoping to get his attention.

The child sat down on the grass a couple of hundred feet away, turning away from them. He hadn't heard her greetings, or perhaps just ignored them.

"Yan, help me!" Léti asked.

The young man nodded, and they yelled at the same time, with all their force.

The child lifted his head and turned toward them. He didn't seem joyous, or scared. He simply watched them with his big eyes.

Léti waved to him again. They all held their breath. Bowbaq forced himself to smile, not knowing why.

The child stood and came toward them at a lazy stroll. He stopped from time to time to contemplate one thing or another along the way, and didn't continue until Léti encouraged him.

He stopped only thirty feet from them and tranquilly stared at them, one hand in his mouth. Léti repeated her greeting for the tenth time at least.

The little boy smiled and clumsily imitated her wave, looking happy.

Léti felt an unbridled joy and couldn't explain why.

Yan figured something out. If the child could see them, just as they saw the other world, it was proof that he existed. It existed.

"Hello!" Léti began sweetly, still smiling, "What's your name?"

He looked at her without reacting. He soon focused his attention on Grigán, who had, up until then, kept himself from making any gestures. The warrior awkwardly waved, which seemed to be enough to satisfy the child, who responded to him as warmly as he had to Léti.

They all started to greet him with "hello" and "hi," and each of them got a response. But the boy never spoke.

Finally he turned his head to his left, his attention diverted by something else. Despite Léti's desperate efforts to keep him there, he walked straight out of the vision.

As if to signal the end of the performance, the image wavered and became opaque, before turning into a dazzling light that progressively dimmed, leaving them alone with the cavern's shadows. A whistle rose up, then went silent.

It was over.

They stood there, speechless, motionless. It was gone. The magic had disappeared.

Léti felt a tear roll down her cheek, then another, then even more. She cried silently, not knowing why. Turning toward her companions, she realized that many of them had glistening eyes. Even the proud, powerful Grigán.

Now she understood why all of the heirs returned from the island sad.

"Does it always have this effect?"

"Especially the first time," her aunt answered. "You get used to it eventually, as with anything. And then you only think about the beauty of it all."

"What did we see, exactly?" Rey asked. "Do you know where that place is?"

"So, you've finally come to accept it," Grigán said, scoffing.

"It's a wise man's strength to know his errors, the proverb says. I would add that you didn't really try all that hard to convince me!"

"The facts speak better on their own," Corenn said. "To answer your question, no, unfortunately, we do not know where it is. But that is where Nol the Strange brought our ancestors."

"And?" Léti asked, wiping away her tears. "What did they see there?"

Corenn sighed before responding. They could feel the regret in her voice.

"That part of the secret disappeared with them. They never spoke of it."

They all reflected on this revelation. Bowbaq was happy that nothing ominous had happened. Léti and Rey were frustrated they couldn't learn more. And Yan had the feeling that his life had just taken a new direction. He knew that from now on, his curious mind would know no rest, nor tedium, so long as he hadn't yet penetrated the mystery of the gateway.

"Did the Sages say how they crossed to the other side? I mean, I'm sure we wouldn't have needed much to do the same. Maybe an object, a magic formula..."

"The story goes that they simply held hands before crossing onto the grass," Corenn answered. "But we have already tried, in vain," she added, seeing the surprised looks of the youngest members of the group. "For all this time, the heirs have tried everything to pass to the other side. Unsuccessfully."

"Except for once," Grigán corrected.

"That's right, except for once. Queff, Bowbaq's own grandfather, offered a plon to the boy on the other side; the boy approached like the little boy just now, stuck out his hand, and took the fruit."

"You mean to say that a kid came out of the vision, that he took the plon and walked off without saying a word?" Rey exclaimed.

"Only his hand," corrected Corenn, "but I can't confirm it; none of us had been born at the time."

"Maybe the gateway only works in one direction?" Léti proposed.

"No, not if you consider that the Sages used it," Grigán disagreed.

"You know, we could make a mountain of gold with this thing," Rey said, grinning.

Five skeptical gazes turned his way.

"I'm joking, I'm joking. Rest assured, I truly intend to respect my oath."

"Did it reveal anything to you, Lady Corenn? I mean about our enemy?"

"Sadly, no, Yan. We were lucky enough to see one of the children, which is pretty rare, but nothing unique happened, as I had hoped."

"In my opinion," Rey said, "the guy who sent the Züu on our trail has found the way to pass through to the other side. And he wouldn't like it if we made it there too, for some reason that only he knows."

"That's also what I think. But I was expecting to see him tonight. Unless, perhaps, his discovery was even more incredible, and has allowed him to pass through this gateway, or another, at any given time…"

"Another gateway?" four voices repeated in unison.

Corenn looked at them one by one, and understood that, apart from Grigán, her companions had no idea what she was talking about.

"I obviously have a lot to tell you," she began. "We know that this one exists, and we suppose that a similar gateway is located on the other side. Which led our ancestors to think there could be other ones. So they began their search, as discreetly as possible—because their respective governments were still spying on them at the time. By rummaging through archives from geographical institutions throughout the known world, they found traces of two other doorways."

"The first one was found in Jérusnie, the far western province of the Romine Kingdom. But what little indication they had of its whereabouts was approximate, and they never found it. It was easier for the second one, renowned in the Upper Kingdoms: the Sohonne Arch."

"The Grand Arch?" Bowbaq said, surprised. "The Grand Arch of Arkary? A gateway?"

"What is it?" Léti asked.

"A sort of bridge in the middle of nowhere," Rey responded. "According to legend, it's one of the five ancient human wonders of the known world, along with Mount Crépel's stairway, the Kenz temple, the fossil pyramids, and the pillars of Corosta. But it's nothing more than a useless bridge above the snow!"

Corenn objected. "It's not a bridge. A bridge would have been designed differently, unless it were very poorly conceived. It's a gateway."

"I myself have been there," Grigán interjected. "In some parts, which are still intact, the interior of the Arch is adorned with the same marks as here."

"That's a bit much for tonight," Rey declared. "You make it sound like the supernatural is everywhe—"

"But it is everywhere! I am the Mother in charge of Traditions on the Kaul Matriarchy's Permanent Council," Corenn said portentously. "It is my job to be rigorous, logical, and intelligent. But can I explain the Ézomine stones? The Vines of Karadas? The Stone Tree? No. And yet these things exist, even if they escape our understanding. Can I explain the gateway of Ji? No. But it exists too. Just like the others."

Rey reflected before responding. "All right, I believe you. Why not, after all?"

Yan mused on all these mysterious names he had just heard. He promised himself to ask Corenn about all of these things sometime soon. The world suddenly seemed vast.

"I suggest we finish this conversation later," Grigán said. "We should leave the island before dawn."

A suggestion from the warrior had the same effect as an order. They regretfully turned toward the exit, after making sure they left no trace of their passage, and started on their way back.

"Aunt Corenn, in your opinion…the garden, the mountains, what are they?"

"I would say, maybe it's a thing that we find in every religion. Paradise?"

✸

They made their way out in a mournful silence. Rey couldn't stand it for very long. He was sad, inexplicably sad, much like his companions. So he made a token effort at cheer, devoting himself to his favorite pastime: annoying Grigán.

"Do we really have to walk so fast? That's twice now that I've almost fallen!"

The warrior taunted him in turn. "Once it's actually happened, let me know, Kercyan. The women aren't complaining."

"How sensitive of you," commented Léti. "May I ask why we should have more reason to complain than you men?"

The warrior didn't answer. He had learned to ignore the young woman's rebellions as much as the actor's barbs. It made life easier, but didn't soothe his sour stomach. Far from it, actually.

In any case, his priority for the moment was to get them off the island and return to the mainland before dawn. Which would be impossible if they continued to dawdle as they had in the cave with the arch.

What Corenn was expecting, which is to say an event even more spectacular than usual, or a meeting with their enemy, had not materialized. The visit to Ji didn't reveal any answers. It simply allowed them to eliminate a few hypotheses.

But Grigán's instinct didn't fail him. If there was no one in the cave, there would certainly be someone waiting for them at their exit. He couldn't explain it, even to himself, but he was sure. This was the kind of intuition that had saved his life more than once.

"Grigán, my friend," Bowbaq said, "it seems like you've spent your whole life on this island. You scurry between the rocks like you've known this path for years."

"Well, it's true, you know. That was the ninth time I witnessed the phenomenon."

He went quiet, hesitant to continue.

"I hope there are more to come. I've always liked round numbers," he added, to lighten the mood.

"Speaking of numbers, how many people have you killed?" asked Léti.

"I don't keep count like that," he snarled. "I leave that to the Züu."

"I just had an idea," she went on. "What if we hired a Zü to kill the other ones for us?"

"This little one's resourceful."

"I'm not little."

"My sincere apologies. But my compliment was sincere."

Rey could be charming and despicable at the same time. Léti never knew how to react to him—fall in love or detest him. At least with Yan she knew how she felt. But the young man was always so reserved.

"Snuff out your torches," Grigán asked. "We're getting close to the beach. From this moment on, I ask that you make as little noise as possible, and this time do it for real."

They complied. The warrior climbed on top of a rock and, looking toward their boats, watched attentively. Not long after, Rey did the same.

"Do you see anything?" Bowbaq whispered.

"I think we're on an island," Rey answered. "There's water all around us."

"I know we're on an island," the giant explained. "Rey, my friend, I don't understand you sometimes."

"It was a joke, Bowbaq, my friend," said the actor as he slid from his perch. "Just a joke. You can't see a thing."

"Which doesn't mean nothing's there," Grigán added. "Let's go. Very slowly."

They followed the warrior for a while, until he signaled a stop.

"I'm going ahead," he whispered. "Wait for me here."

He slipped away into the darkness, bow in hand, as he had done for his companions so many times before.

But this time, things would not turn out so well.

———— ✸ ————

He refused to admit it, of course. But he went much faster, more discreetly, and thus more safely, when he was alone.

Despite the goodwill and effort of—almost—all of his companions, the group made for easy prey. They were too numerous, too loud, and worse, most of them weren't fighters.

Grigán felt responsible for them, like a father with his children. And he had to do his best to keep them safe. He took this responsibility on himself and took a certain pride in it, despite the constant disagreements.

Like a shadow, he emerged through an opening a little bit larger than the others, walled in on either side by a large boulder stuck in the sand. The beach wasn't much farther. He could already hear the sea.

He crouched down and inched forward, hidden by a slanted boulder. He'd long ago stopped worrying about the ridiculousness of such postures. Many battles had been won by seemingly ridiculous people, or excessively cautious ones.

He leaned against the rock, all of his senses alive, and analyzed the layout of the terrain. Where would an ordinary person hide for an ambush? Over there, surely. In that corner formed by the two huge boulders.

He proceeded to circle around, using anything he could for cover, every relief, every spot blanketed in shadow. Soon, he neared his goal.

He set down his bow and quiver, arming himself with just a throwing dagger. Then he slowly poked his head out of his hiding place, just enough for a quick glance.

He was right, which brought him only a fleeting moment of satisfaction.

A man was hiding there, leaning against the rock, a sword in hand. He kept looking toward the path. The path that Grigán, Corenn, and the others would have taken.

He wasn't a Zü, more likely a low-level thief from the Guild, of the kind that Yan and Rey described. The man didn't do his job very well, anyway. Grigán was sure he could get rid of him in less than two heartbeats.

But where there is one, there are others, the proverb says. Maybe many more. Definitely enough for an ambush.

Under these conditions, a reconnaissance mission all the way to the beach was impossible. Opportunities for coverage were too few and far between. And he had to warn his companions, before they started to get noisy again.

The best thing to do was to lose their enemies in the labyrinth, maybe to eliminate them in isolated combat. At dawn, he would reassess the situation.

While figuring out this problem, he had started to return when a cry shredded the silence.

The voice was Léti's.

———— ❦ ————

Grigán had been gone for some time now, and Rey was beginning to get impatient. It was hard enough for him to bear the attitude of the old man, as he had disrespectfully nicknamed Grigán, and his obsession with controlling everything. But the fact that he was wasting time on top of that was tough for Rey to swallow.

The others waited obediently, their backs against rocks, or seated in the sand. They were all good people, sure, but far too timid for his liking. Apart from Léti, perhaps, they all seemed to accept the warrior's orders as if they had done so their entire lives. Rey couldn't go along with that.

He clambered on top of a boulder and attempted to pierce the darkness of the night. But all he could see was the sea, a slightly darker color than the island, and he gave up.

He was a city dweller through and through. Up until recently, he had only traveled between cities, taking the shortest route possible. On this deserted, desolate island, he was out of his element. As if he were closer to the realm of death. His death.

He tried to banish this unpleasant thought. In Lorelia, the streets were always lit and rarely deserted. The teeming city life, with its countless festivals and the impressive density of taverns and other entertainment establishments, didn't lend itself to pessimism. Whereas here...

Finally, he admitted it. Yes, he regretted the vision they had seen of the other world. He felt a kind of sadness and an inexplicable frustration he had never known before. He wasn't the only one, judging from the others' lost expressions.

So much for the old man's orders. He was going to break the ever-so-important silence. He needed to talk.

He went over to Léti, searching for an amusing way to strike up a conversation…and froze midstep, his eyes fixed in one direction.

A man had just appeared, right in front of him.

Rey lunged at him so swiftly that he surprised even himself. The stranger, just as surprised as Rey, reacted with much less agility and found himself with his back on the ground and a dagger to his throat before he could even draw his blade.

If he had been alone, Rey wouldn't have hesitated for an instant to slice his steel blade through the man's filthy skin. But some sense of decency, being in the presence of his naive companions, as well as the memory of the other world, prevented him from killing the stranger in cold blood.

It all happened very fast. Rey smelled the man's awful breath. He read the panic in his eyes. Then he heard Léti let out a dreadful cry, and something struck him brutally on the head.

As soon as Léti saw Rey bolt for no apparent reason, she stood up to find the actor subduing an armed stranger.

No one had heard the man approach. Yan, sitting close to her, was daydreaming, as he often did. Bowbaq was lost in his contemplation of the stars, and Corenn was resting with her eyes closed.

Léti's first emotion was relief. This stranger was clearly an enemy, but it was fine, since Rey had subdued him—and without Grigán's help, even.

Then she felt anger. Anger toward herself for not reacting as quickly as Rey. She hadn't even reacted at all.

Then hysteria overtook all of her other emotions when she saw the other men.

She heard herself yelling to warn Rey and watched, powerless, as one of the strangers clubbed the actor on the head.

She brandished her knife in front of her, in front of her enemies, in an improvised combat position. She didn't even remember grabbing the weapon.

Bowbaq placed himself between them and her, blocking the way with his massive body. Léti felt someone pulling at her clothes. She pivoted around, rage filling her body, ready to take on her assailant.

It was only Yan. She realized he had been calling her for a while now. She finally understood what he was saying.

"Come on! We need to leave! Léti, come with me!"

She followed him without knowing why. Maybe because it was Yan. Because he had called to her.

She couldn't think straight. All she wanted was to keep her grip on the knife.

She clasped the weapon, gritted her teeth, and started running as she never had before.

Bowbaq had spontaneously confronted the strangers without knowing what he was going to do next. He was overjoyed to hear Yan and Léti get away. Then he noticed that, among the group,

Corenn was in the most danger, so he leaped two yards to place himself in front of her.

There were several assassins. He counted at least five, but the shouts and clanging of metal that could be heard all around didn't bode well.

The giant didn't know what to do. The cluster of men standing before him remained still, encumbered by Rey's body lying on the ground and impressed by their new adversary's size.

He took a slow step forward, looking hard into the nearest man's eyes. He had often seen Mir do the same with his prey. The assassin unconsciously stepped back, forcing his fellows to do the same.

Bowbaq swung his gigantic arm forward and ripped the club from its owner's hands. He had taken an oath never to kill anyone, no matter who, but his enemies didn't know that. Regardless, he felt a little better armed than barehanded.

"Put it down!" he heard behind him.

Bowbaq shot a brief glance behind him, short enough to still keep his other adversaries at bay. But what he saw drained him of the meager hope that had vitalized him.

Men surrounded them on all sides, blocking all exits from the rocky passage. Several of them had bows.

He, Corenn, and Rey were trapped.

—⊕⊕⊕—

Grigán didn't like it, not one bit. Their enemies seemed to be legion, and he thought he could hear sounds of a struggle where he had left his companions.

In fact, all the assassins were rushing in that direction, and he was having more and more trouble making his way forward without being seen. Once already, he'd had just enough time to fling himself into a dark corner before coming face-to-face with three of the strangers.

Grigán was brave, very brave, but not foolhardy. If he kept running as he had been, it wouldn't be long before they captured him. If he waited, soon enough he really would be a solitary warrior, mourning the deaths of his friends.

He heard running; someone was coming toward him. Grigán melted into the shadows and gripped his dagger. At the last moment, he stuck his leg out, tripping the hurried man, and watched as the man's head smacked into a rock, knocking him unconscious before he could even cry out.

The warrior wished it could always be so easy.

But the assassin sprawled out on the ground gave him an idea. Somewhat ridiculous, surely very risky, but the best one he had for now. Actually, the only one.

He quickly undressed his victim and slipped the clothes on over his own.

Then he joined the band of assassins who were racing toward his friends.

Léti was going way, way too fast. At first, Yan intentionally let her go out ahead so he could protect her and stop her from turning right back around toward the heat of battle. But now she was too far ahead of him and was slipping out of his line of sight more and more frequently.

Forcing a swift pace wasn't the best solution: in the thick darkness, they could very well fall or run smack into a rock—or right into one of the assassins they were running from.

Earlier, running away as fast as possible seemed like it was their best option. Yan had understood that as soon as Rey was attacked, they were at a disadvantage. Their only chance at survival was to run; even Grigán would have agreed.

He tried not to think about Corenn and the others.

Not right away. First he needed to get his precious Léti out of danger, then he would turn back and help his friends. If he still could.

Yan slowed down, out of breath. The path he had been following began to slope down; their escape was altogether aimless, and now they were completely lost.

A few millidays had already gone by since Léti had faded from sight. She was several dozen paces ahead. He listened closely, trying to calm his panting.

He couldn't even hear her anymore. He concentrated hard, searching for the sounds of running feet in the silence of the night. Nothing.

He had lost Léti.

———

Corenn followed their enemies without resisting. It soon became apparent that any effort to escape would be useless against the imposing band of criminals and assassins whom had been sent after them.

These men hadn't slain them on the spot, which left a sliver of hope. Furthermore, Grigán's fate was unknown, and Léti and Yan had successfully escaped. Whatever they were planning, the best solution for now was to stall. By any means necessary.

Corenn immediately put this idea into action, faking a painful cramp. But after only a few millidays, the horrible man behind her violently pushed her forward, letting loose a string of curses which Corenn hadn't even known existed. That wasn't enough to stop her, and she made do with slowly hobbling along, crying out in pain every once in a while. She couldn't leave room for any suspicion.

Even limping, she managed to catch up to Bowbaq and get in front of him, before slowing down even more. The giant had been marching at his normal pace, which was far too brisk.

Their only chance was to stall their enemies, she repeated to herself. For Grigán, for Léti, for Yan. And to give her time to think.

The assassins had even brought Rey along on this forced march, even though the actor seemed more dead than alive. Two crooks had disarmed him and carried him along like a sack of grain. Corenn presumed it wasn't the intention of the men to kill them. Not right away, at least.

Nevertheless, they weren't treated any less like enemies. Not a single member of the Guild—that's who these men probably were—had spoken to them, except to deliver insults and menacing remarks. It was better not to have any illusions about their intentions.

"Where are we going?" she risked asking.

"Shut the hell up, old woman!" was the only response she received.

Corenn left it at that, not wanting to make things worse. Making one of the men mad would surely result in more violence and would eliminate any chance they had of escaping through diplomacy, if they had any chance at all.

"He's awake, I'm telling you!" a Lorelien voice shouted.

One of the men carrying Rey happily dropped him to the ground. Indeed, the young blond man had already regained consciousness, at least enough to protest his poor treatment.

"Well, sirs! I get the feeling you don't like me. This habit of dropping me without fair warning shows a flagrant lack of manners."

"Shut it! Stand up!" the scoundrel said, kicking him in the stomach.

Rey grabbed the man's leg and pulled him to the ground, then tried to take his sword. But it was stuck underneath its owner, and the actor's attempt to escape died in the womb. The second man booted him in the ribs before forcing him to his feet at bladepoint.

"I knew you didn't like me," Rey groaned in pain.

"Shut it!"

The little column started forward again. Corenn knew where they were bringing them: to the small beach where they had landed earlier that night.

Her worst fear was that they would be taken away immediately. That she would be separated from the others, without any way of knowing what happened to them.

Bowbaq had an exaggerated coughing fit. Corenn turned toward him, intrigued. To her knowledge, the giant wasn't ill.

Bowbaq stared back at her with eyes as big as saucers. He nodded to his left.

Corenn followed the signal as discreetly as possible. What, he wasn't thinking about trying to escape now, was he? It was too late for that.

But what the giant had seen was a trail sign. Grigán must have assembled the unique collection of branches, rocks, and seashells. Unfortunately, Corenn couldn't decipher it.

It didn't matter. Whatever the warrior's message, there was nothing he could do for them.

———— ⊶⊷ ————

Léti had cracked. Her mental balance, which had already been strained tremendously over the past two dékades, had finally tipped completely.

She had a strong urge to cry, but the tears didn't come. If it weren't for the bitter taste in her throat and the pounding headache that prevented her from reasoning, she would have thought she had become numb.

She felt as though she had been running her entire life. She ran from her dear ones' disappearance, from the love of the living, from challenges and joys, truths and lies.

She had run away yet again, just a moment ago. So quickly, so selfishly, that she had even lost Yan. When she finally noticed, it was almost too late.

Now, kneeling down in the grass, she shuddered at the memory. She had run and run, and still ran, as if she were trying to run from all her fears at once. She ran like a madwoman. Almost to her death.

She had only seen the danger once she was ten yards from the edge of oblivion. It had taken her seven or eight more to stop.

The path went no farther. Her aimless run led her to the top of a cliff overlooking the sea, 150 feet below.

Momentarily, she sat watching the waves crash against the rocks. She thought that joining them might be a solution, a relief.

But no, that would be another weakness.

She couldn't run any farther? Very well. Perhaps it was a sign of destiny.

Never again would she run away.

She tightened her grip on her knife and started back down the cliff toward the rocky maze with a confident step.

Three armed men appeared, blocking her way. One of them yelled something in Lorelien, likely an insult or a threat.

She calmly returned to the top of the cliff, turned around, and waited for them with a determined resolve.

Never again would she run away.

Grigán came as quickly as he could, but it wasn't quick enough. He finally reached his companions after the short battle, just in time to witness their capture.

The crooks already had them under escort. The warrior considered joining them, but it was too risky. Some of the men might know what he looked like; it was best that he stay back for now.

So he followed the troop from a distance, more powerless, tortured, and anguished than ever.

He figured they were taking them to the only place on the island where they could have landed: the little beach. Using this knowledge, he outpaced the group and left a sign for Bowbaq, hoping that the giant wouldn't pass by it without noticing.

It was all he could do for now—signal his presence not far from them.

It wasn't much.

Bowbaq wanted to be somewhere else. The more he thought about it, the more he was convinced that they wouldn't be in all this trouble if they had just avoided the cave. Once again, he had transgressed and was now suffering the unhappy consequences.

He didn't feel sorry for himself. He felt sorry for his wife and his children. The small group of heirs who had united failed to thwart their unknown enemy's plan. And now the Züu were going to carry out their despicable duty until they were completely finished.

Maybe he could have done something for them if he had stayed in Arkary. Or not. Anyhow, the past was the past and he couldn't do anything to change it now.

The line reached the beach. The heirs' skiff was still there, now joined by four other, larger boats. Bowbaq had expected this, just as he'd expected the more frightening events to follow.

No less than five Züu waited patiently on the beach. To a man, they looked just like the others they had already come face-to-face with: red cloak, shaved head, demented eyes.

Only one of them stood out from the others—his face, or rather his entire head, was painted in black and white. It mimicked the shape of a monstrous human skull, inhabited solely by two eyes that seemed eager to devour their prey.

Even the thugs seemed intimidated by these fanatics. Bowbaq noticed that none of them came near the Züu if they could avoid it. The majority of them preferred not to take their eyes off the assassins. Apparently, the Lorelien "brothers" didn't doubt the sinister reputation of the Züu.

Two of the Züu held their dreadful daggers. Two others were armed with crossbows, no less dangerous. The man with the painted skull was the only one unarmed. And yet he seemed to be the most threatening.

"Where are the others?" he asked one of the thieves.

He spoke perfect Lorelien, but there was something disconcerting about the sight of this enormous talking skull. The man swallowed painfully, cursing the gods for choosing him to answer the assassin's question.

"The two kids got awa—will soon be brought here," he immediately amended.

"And the Ramgrith?"

The man took a step back, and lowered his eyes in silence. Bowbaq noticed that the man feared his boss more than Bowbaq himself feared his abductors.

The Zü turned away and took a few steps.

"So your work is unfinished," he announced in a clear voice. "You know what you still have to do."

The thug didn't wait to be told twice and immediately left for the island's interior. Six of his comrades raced after him, all too happy to get away from the madmen with poisoned daggers.

The two men who held Corenn, Rey, and Bowbaq hostage moved to do the same, but the Skull constrained them with a simple furrowing of his brow. Then he approached the prisoners, walking slowly, very slowly.

Rey laughed uproariously. The Zü stopped dead right in front of him, his arms crossed, and stared him right in the eyes, which didn't seem to have the intended intimidating effect on the actor.

"This number, ha! I mean, honestly!" Rey jeered. "When I play bad guys in the theater, I always think they're so stupid, absurd, mad, and old-fashioned that I never imagined such sick people really existed. But it's true. Congratulations, really, well done," he concluded, with another burst of laughter.

The Zü smiled faintly for a moment, then thrust two extended fingers into Rey's throat so quickly the actor didn't even see it coming.

Breathing suddenly became impossible, and resumed only after a moment that felt way too long for Rey, as he tried desperately to draw air into his lungs. Then a gut-wrenching nausea took hold of him, and he turned to vomit, his throat convulsing in pain.

"You're lucky," the Zü declared. "Four times out of five, that's enough to kill any heretic."

Bowbaq couldn't believe it. These fellows were truly insane.

"Well," the assassin continued, "we're going to have a little talk. You, me, and Zuïa."

—◦◦◦—

Léti had never felt so alive. Three assassins were advancing on her, weapons drawn. She had no way to escape. No help was on the way, and all she had was a simple fishing knife to defend herself with.

But her rage was infinite.

All the hatred and anger toward the Züu and their henchmen, and the sorrow that had been welling up inside her until then, now flooded her entire being.

All she could feel now was fury.

Never had she felt so ready. So powerful. Her entire body was responding to her frantic spirit. So much so that her senses seemed amplified.

She heard each of their steps, every sound made by her approaching enemies. She noticed their changing expressions: from mocking, derisive, and curious to cruel. She felt the sand grinding beneath her feet, the wind caressing her hair, the knife's rough handle against her palm.

She had to force herself to unclench her jaw. While her body felt more agile than ever, her face was locked in a fierce grimace.

The three men were close to her now. She noticed every facial tic, every detail of their clothing. These images would forever be burned into her memory. But she forced herself to focus on everything else, which was of more vital interest for the moment.

Two of the men had swords. The third had a dagger. The bearded one carried his sword in his left hand. The man with the knife had only one arm. The bald one seemed the most menacing. She should get rid of him first.

"Just come with us, don't make a fuss," the bald one croaked.

Léti didn't respond, still threatening them with her knife.

"Come on now, just give it up, you'll hurt yourself."

She swiped the blade about a foot from his face. She didn't want to injure him. She still refused to start this fight. But surrender was out of the question.

The bald one cursed and took a defensive position, ready to respond to any attack.

"Wait," the one-armed man chimed in, "don't hurt her right away. This could be fun."

Léti faked an attack toward the man, who reared back and then continued forward with a stupid little laugh. Léti pushed back, but he drew even closer, laughing louder. The bearded one found the game to his liking and joined in, attacking her from the other side. Léti's blade danced through the air, still not connecting with her targets. The two men amused themselves by touching her and jumping back, the bald one enjoying the show.

Léti retreated a little farther up the cliff. The abyss was right behind her.

"Eh! I bet you can't undress her without getting bitten!"

"I'll take that bet!"

The two men took to their game again, a vulgar gleam in their eyes. The one-armed one tore a piece off Léti's tunic, crying out in victory.

The young woman fumed. A hand landed on her shoulder. She let her reflexes take over and her blade bit into the flesh of a wrist.

"Whore!" the bearded one screamed, clutching his wound.

He staggered backward and dropped his sword.

"Harlot! I'm bleeding like a pig!"

The game didn't seem so funny to him anymore. Nor to the others, who stiffened up in real combat positions before closing in on her.

Now it was for real.

The Zü paced back and forth, as if searching for words. But he must have already planned what he was going to say long before now, Corenn thought.

He stopped, and for a long moment contemplated the sunrise over the Median Sea. The Mother doubted he could appreciate the beauty of the sight. Finally, he turned to focus on them.

"For two of you, that's the last time the sun will rise."

Rey, Corenn, and Bowbaq exchanged looks. Although they more or less expected very bad news, the raw truth still shocked them. Rey attempted to say something, but the beating he had endured, especially the wound to his throat, left him speechless. The sarcastic comment he wanted to deliver died in a cough.

The assassin stared at them one by one before continuing.

"Zuïa will forgive the first one of you, and only the first, who asks."

No one moved. The Zü waited patiently before resuming.

"He who is forgiven must condemn his former accomplices. Which will essentially amount to reciting their names and where they're hiding, starting with the Ramgrith, if he isn't on the island."

There was still no reaction. The Zü looked irritated.

"We will get this information one way or another. It's simply a question of time and pain."

"You are truly the worst person I've ever met," Bowbaq commented. "Mir wouldn't even want you for food."

The Zü came over to stand right in front of him, fire in his eyes. The giant subconsciously covered his throat with his hand.

"I am worth one hundred of you," the Zü sneered, losing his temper. "Any one of Zuïa's messengers deserves more respect than all of your kings combined! The goddess's greatness flows through us!" he concluded, raising his arms to the sky.

"Look at yourselves, the 'heirs.' A farmer, a delinquent, a woman, two children. You're nothing compared to the Goddess. You're nothing in the face of her judgment."

Corenn had made her decision as soon as the assassin began his sermon. It was clear that there was no hope in negotiating with this maniac. Unfortunately, they had no choice but to take action.

It was best to act swiftly, before the others came back. While the Zü spoke to Bowbaq, she gave Rey a little nudge with her elbow, accompanied by a knowing look. The actor understood that the Mother was going to try something and prepared for action, though he was hurt and nauseous.

As best she could, Corenn closed her mind off to everything that surrounded her, devoting every ounce of her attention to the crossbow the nearest Zü was holding. She roused her Will, then let it grow on its own, easily controlling it as she had learned. Her body temperature rose slightly, and wild impulses invaded her mind. Then she unleashed her Will and the crossbow string snapped with a sharp ping, leaving the object useless.

Its owner leaned over to study it more closely, and everyone turned toward him out of curiosity. Rey swung around, caught hold of the guard behind them, and violently bit the man's hand before snatching his dagger.

No! It was too soon! Corenn didn't have time to disarm the other crossbow. The Zü was going to shoot him!

The magician couldn't call on her Will again so soon after releasing it once. Since she was out of practice, the feat cost her nearly all of her energy.

Horrified, she watched the assassin lift his bow and aim right at the actor, who didn't have time to take cover.

With surprise, she saw the tip of another arrow suddenly emerge from the Zü's eye. Then, after a moment, a second, then a third, hitting another Zü in the chest and the leg.

She searched the beach and the rocks surrounding them, not yet willing to believe the miracle. Grigán knelt at the top of a bluff one hundred feet away, firing arrow after arrow.

Corenn made her way toward him, still too exhausted by the recent use of her power to run or even think. She heard Bowbaq let out a cry behind her, and turned to find him on the ground, moaning in pain, his hands clasping the handle of a dagger stuck in his side.

The skull-faced Zü had just thrown the weapon. Toward her.

Just then an arrow pierced the leader's chest, and he fell to his knees. Rey, who had just finished off another crook, gave him a hard kick right in the throat.

The vermin coughed up a pool of blood before collapsing face-first into it.

Corenn gazed at the small beach that was once so peaceful. Now it wore seven bodies, one of which was her friend.

Rey hurried to Bowbaq's side and took out the little box that contained, perhaps, an antidote to the Züu's poison. He made the giant, still bellowing in pain, swallow it, and applied some to the small but deep wound.

"He threw himself in front of the dagger," Rey told her. "He threw himself in front of it to save you. It's the first time I've ever seen that. The first time."

The actor was truly moved. Corenn stared at him, still collecting herself. Rey had blood on his face, but he wore a boyish expression.

She gently pushed him aside and finished cleaning Bowbaq's wound. He was still conscious, although groaning in pain. He wasn't bleeding very much. The Züu's poison was known to spread quickly. If he wasn't dead yet, then it meant he was going to survive.

Grigán finally joined them.

"How is he?" he asked right away.

"I'm all right, my friend," the giant answered, out of breath. "I just wish I were somewhere else."

"You can count on me to get you out of here, my friend. Sorry for not stepping in sooner. But I couldn't do anything as long as the two crossbows—"

He didn't finish his sentence. Corenn threw herself into his arms. He clumsily embraced her, feeling more awkward than if he went for a walk in a Eurydian temple stark naked.

The Mother needed the embrace, but soon enough she regained her composure and broke free, feeling just as awkward as the warrior.

"Let's go look for Yan and my little Léti, shall we?"

It was almost a plea.

Yan felt more useless than ever. He had been walking around in circles for far too long without any sign of Léti. He could no longer even tell which direction would lead back to the skiff, or farther inland.

Everyone in Eza was right. He was good for nothing. He didn't know how to help his friends. He didn't know how to protect Léti. He couldn't even find the trail.

He would have been an awful companion for Léti.

Yan realized he had just thought about his proposal as if he had given up already. After all, even if the two of them survived this ordeal, he wasn't good enough for her. He didn't deserve her.

The Ancestress of Eza's council told him one day when he was thinking such thoughts that every person possesses a talent that makes him the equal of everyone else. But he didn't have any talent. He was only good at doing everything halfway. And the only reason he was still alive now, while his companions faced certain death, was because he got so lost that he disappeared in the center of the labyrinth.

He sat down to think about what he could do, besides feel sorry for himself. But as soon as he sat down, he jumped up and took off running.

He had just heard screams echoing in the night.

Among them, Léti's voice.

He didn't take any of the precautions from earlier. Get to Léti as fast as possible—that was all that mattered.

More screams. Threats. Sounds of a struggle. Léti was fighting for her life.

He scrambled to the bottom of the cliff, pausing only to grab a rock, before charging toward the bastards, screaming furiously.

A bearded man turned around to face him, sword in hand. The man's hand was bleeding, and he could hardly hold his weapon.

The other two turned around by reflex when they heard Yan arrive. Léti was still standing, but she was in a pitiful state. Even at this distance, Yan could see cuts on her arms and her legs. They had dared to hurt her!

Yan could hardly believe what he saw next. Léti thrust out her arm, and one of the men screamed out in pain, grabbing at his eye. He fell to the ground trying to stop the blood.

PIERRE GRIMBERT

The last man redoubled his effort and ferociously attacked Léti, who could only recoil to avoid him.

Then Yan watched with horror as Léti threw herself at her adversary, struggled with him for a brief moment, and then both tumbled off the cliff into the void.

He heard himself cry out, "No!" and he couldn't stop screaming.

He now found himself close enough to his own enemy. He threw the heavy rock right at the man's face, his strength increased tenfold by the horrible scene he had just witnessed.

The projectile hit its target with a heavy thud, but Yan didn't stop to judge the results. He ran to the top of the cliff and leaned over the edge, dreading what he would see.

"Yan!"

Léti was only two yards below. With a single hand, she desperately clung to a tiny rock outcropping.

"Yan, hurry! I can't hold on much longer!"

She wasn't kidding. She sounded panicked.

The boy frantically searched around him, but there was nothing—nothing—that he could use as a rope. Even his clothes weren't strong enough to hold her weight.

He got down on his knees and swung one leg over the cliff's edge. His foot found a hold and he started to move his other leg.

"No! No! We're going to die!"

Now she was really panicked.

Yan continued his reckless descent, hardly taking the time to verify the strength of each hold. But he couldn't make it all the way to Léti. The best he could do was lean over and reach out his hand to her, but he would never be strong enough to lift them both up with his other hand.

His foot slipped and Léti screamed, terrified.

Yan hesitated, trying to find some other foothold, some easier solution. But there wasn't one.

Suddenly, everything was clear, perfectly clear in his mind.

They were going to live or die together.

He reached out his hand, flexing his muscles as much as he could. Léti eagerly seized his extended arm and did her best to relieve Yan of her weight, grasping at the smallest handholds and footholds she could find.

But it still wasn't enough.

Yan couldn't lift her up.

One of his arms was weakening, and he was going to lose her or lose his grip on the cliff wall. One way or another, it was over. He could see the rocks, forty yards below, and Léti's pleading face right next to his. His arm began to shake.

No!

No, it was so simple: he had to do it. He needed to. He willed it to happen…

He gritted his teeth and concentrated his will on the strength in his arms. After a few moments, he was dripping with sweat; blood hammered in his temples like a drummer on the Day of the Earth. He couldn't feel anything except his own hand grasping Léti's and his will to pull her up toward him.

He gained a few inches, and kept pushing himself. Soon, he had pulled them up a full foot higher. Then, slowly, he straightened up and it got easier.

Finally, Léti was high enough that she could swing all of her weight up onto the little rock outcropping that had saved her life. She and Yan rested for a moment against the face of the cliff, gasping for breath.

"What you just did…was impossible, Yan," Léti whispered.

The young man didn't respond. He began to feel faint. He started climbing up right away, to avoid passing out in such a precarious position.

He felt completely drained and very cold. Léti reached the top before him and had to help hoist him up, where he collapsed. His head was spinning.

But he had saved her.

—∞∞∞—

For the first time, Grigán recognized that Rey had a place in the group. He had reacted well during the battle, and even before, from what Corenn said. He might have had a part in saving Bowbaq's life, and he was the one who spontaneously suggested they go looking for Léti and Yan.

Nevertheless, his biggest faults, namely, his disrespect and constant provocations, were hard to deal with. Even the Züu agreed.

But for now, Rey kept quiet and obeyed Grigán's every order. Their partnership proved effective: they had already come across three thugs working for the Züu in the labyrinth and struck them down with ease.

Finally, around a bend in the path, they stumbled right into the two young Kauliens. Yan looked feeble, and Léti was covered in cuts and bruises, her clothes torn completely to shreds.

The warrior sighed in relief. They had all been lucky. Extremely lucky, even. He promised himself to be more careful next time.

"Are the others all right?" Yan murmured with difficulty.

"Bowbaq is hurt, but not too seriously," answered Rey. "Let's get out of here."

Léti went up to Grigán and grabbed him firmly, but not aggressively, by his black clothing.

"You are going to teach me how to fight," she said clearly, fixing him with a solemn stare.

The warrior waited for Léti to let go of him before answering.

"Fine, if it will keep you out of trouble. But it won't be as much fun as you think," Grigán said.

"I don't think it's going to be fun," she answered, turning back to Yan, who wondered if he had understood this exchange.

They quickly made their way back to the beach. A few more thieves were waiting there, and threw a few insults their way, but Grigán held them off, threatening them with his bow.

"They must have already noticed the nice holes I made in their boats," Rey said. "My popularity must be at an all-time low today."

"What happened here?" Léti asked, seeing the bodies.

"We'll explain later."

Grigán motioned toward the boat, where Corenn and Bowbaq sat waiting for them near the shore. The sorceress brought the skiff to them, and they set out right away, relieved to finally be in relative safety.

Each told his or her story. Corenn was hardly taken by Léti and Grigán's new notion, but she put off discussing it in detail until later.

On the other hand, she was exceedingly interested in Yan's experience on the cliff.

After a long moment of reflection, she broke the silence they had all settled into.

"Yan, we're going to have to have a long talk, you and I," she said simply. "I'm sure you'll find it interesting."

SHORT ANECDOTAL
ENCYCLOPEDIA OF
THE KNOWN WORLD

A lt – The largest river in the known world. Its headwaters are located in the highest of the Curtain Mountains. It crosses the Ithare Kingdom and the Grand Empire before reaching its delta in the Ocean of Mirrors.

A Goranese legend claims that when the time has come, the dead will float down the river in gigantic phantom boats and take revenge upon those who have committed atrocities toward their living kin. Every once in a while, someone claims they've seen the vanguard of the dark army. Some harbors even refuse all embarkations after nightfall.

Apogee – The moment when the sun is at its highest point: noon, in our world. It's commonly accepted that the end of the third deciday marks the apogee.

Arque – Native of the Arkary kingdom. It's also the main language spoken in this land.

Bells (of Leem) – At one point in time, Leem experienced such a crime wave that the city seemed to be completely overrun by thieves, pillagers, arsonists, and murderers of all shapes and colors. Although the city doubled the guards' night rounds, and then tripled them, the criminals remained untouchable, since they were too well organized.

The provost at the time then came up with the idea of installing a bell in the house of each of the most prominent people in the city. When these important people were threatened by or witness to a crime, they could ring the bell and the city guard would come right away. Most of the time it wasn't quickly enough, with the villains fleeing the scene the moment the first strike sounded. But it was still better than before.

More modest citizens followed this example, and soon there were quite a few artisans and merchants who had equipped their shops with a bell. After a few years, there were so many bells in Leem that crime nearly disappeared.

Unfortunately, the criminals found a countermeasure: setting fire to each house that dared to ring its bell, as an act of vengeance and as a warning.

Today, there are still more than six hundred houses in Leem fitted with bells, but now the bronze only rings during the occasional festivity.

Brosda – A divinity whose cult is especially widespread in the Kaul Matriarchy. Brosda is the son of Xéfalis, and Echora's reflection.

Brothers (of the night) – What the members of the Grand Guild call themselves, as do members of any guild of thugs in general.

Some of them even go as far as renaming their new members, creating fake "families," etc.

Calendar – The one used in the Upper Kingdoms is the Ithare calendar. It contains 338 days, which are divided into thirty-four dékades and four seasons. The year begins with the Day of Water, which also marks the first day of spring. There are two dékades that contain only nine days instead of the usual ten: those preceding the Day of the Earth and the Day of Fire. Each day on the calendar begins with the sunrise.

Every day, as well as every dékade, carries a meaningful name originating from the cult of the goddess Eurydis; the moralist priests of the Wise One brought their nomenclature to the furthest reaches of the known world. But time and use brought about changes of varying degrees depending on the region. The Day of the Dog, for example, which the Grand Empire doesn't observe with any particular importance, was renamed the Day of the Wolf in the area around Tolensk, and corresponds to a feast day that all the locals really look forward to. Similarly, the Dékade of Fairs, kicked off by the Day of the Merchant, is well-known and will ever be so to the Loreliens, whereas it represents nothing to the Mémissiens.

Few know all the days of the calendar, and even fewer know what they represent for the cult of Eurydis—priests aside, of course. In the Upper Kingdoms, they use it very naturally, as they would talk of the day or the night, yet a lot of people are completely unaware of its religious origin.

Other calendars are used in the known world; they arise out of royal decrees, from other cults besides that of Eurydis, or quite simply out of tribal tradition. Many of them are based on the lunar cycle, like the ancient Roman calendar: thirteen cycles of twenty-six days.

Centiday – A unit of time of Goranese origin representing one-tenth of a deciday: approximately fourteen earthly minutes.

Council of Mothers – The main governing body of the Kaul Matriarchy. Each of the villages has such a council, presided over by the elected Mother and advised by the Ancestress.

Curtain – The Curtain is the mountain chain that separates the Grand Empire of Goran and the Ithare Kingdom from the countries to the east.

Dékade [pronounced "day-cahd"] – Ten days. A division specific to the Eurydian calendar. The days of each dékade are named in chronological order. The first day is prime, the last is term. The other days, from second to ninth, are: dès, terce, quart, quint, sixt, septime, octes, and nones.

The dékades of Earth and Fire, which only contain nine days, don't have an "octes" day. In these dékades, the calendar skips directly from septime to nones. The Maz have provided a religious explanation: the omission of octes symbolizes the victory of Eurydis over Xétame's eight dragons.

Deciday – A unit of time of Goranese origin representing one-tenth of a day: approximately two hours and twenty-five minutes in our world. The first deciday begins with the sunrise, the instant at which the tenth deciday of the previous day ends. The apogee generally falls around the end of the third deciday.

This unit of time is used crudely by the ignorant, but a lot more precisely by the learned people in all nations, who do not use a common sundial for reference, but rather consult calculations indicating the position at which the sun rises relative to the city of Goran, and make adjustments depending on the season. This is also the only method that enables one to discern precisely when the change between the night decidays, from the seventh to the eighth, occurs.

Dona – First and foremost, Dona is the goddess of merchants. The daughter of Wug and Ivie, legend has it that Dona created gold so that she could cover herself with it and thereby exceed her cousin Isée's beauty. She then gifted humans with her creation so that those like her, upon whom destiny endowed a less favorable

lot, could outshine others with their intelligence, with the possession of this precious metal acting as a testimony.

Unfortunately for Dona, the young god Hamsa, whom she
had chosen as referee, renewed his admiration for Isée. Dona then
resolved to disregard the singular opinion and became renowned
for her parade of lovers. And so she also became the Goddess of
Pleasure.

There's a Lorelien custom that requires a merchant who
has just made a lucrative deal to give an offering to a stranger,
and more specifically a young, impoverished-looking woman.
They call the offering "Dona's share." Unfortunately, the custom is dying out, since the members of the cult feel that the
share they routinely offer to their temples is in itself a sufficient
display of piety.

No successful merchant would ever forget to glorify Dona
with his gifts, if only to preserve the affection of a few "priest-
esses" who are particularly devout to the Goddess of Pleasure.

Emaz – The chief figureheads and high leaders of the Grand
Temple of Eurydis; in other words, the heads of the entire cult.
There are thirty-four Emaz. Each Emaz reserves the power to
pass on his or her title to a chosen Maz.

Erjak – An Arque title given to an individual who has the
ability to communicate with animals from mind to mind.

Eastian – A Levantine. A native of the lands that lie to the
east of the Curtain Mountains.

Eurydis – The chief deity in the Upper Kingdoms. The cult
of Eurydis has spread to even the most remote areas of the known
world, at the instigation of Ithare "moralists."

The legend of the goddess has forever been tied to the history of the Holy City. During the sixth Eon, the Ithare people—
who didn't yet carry this name—were merely a colorful grouping
of more or less nomadic tribes, assembled at the foot of Mount

Fleuri, one of the old summits of the Curtain Mountains. It is said that the people first came together thanks to the vision of one man, King Li'ut of the Iths, who wanted to create a powerful new nation by bringing together all of the independent clans residing east of the Alt river.

King Li'ut dedicated his entire life to this dream, but the building of the city of Ith—the Holy City, as it is now more commonly called—took more time than he had. With Li'ut gone, ancestral divisions sprang up again, and stronger than ever: without Li'ut's art of diplomacy, the beautiful dream would crumble.

It is then that the goddess is reported to have visited Li'ut's youngest son, instructing him to finish the immense work his father had begun. Comelk—as he was named—thanked the goddess for her confidence, but explained that given the severity of the tribal quarrels, he didn't believe he could succeed. Eurydis then asked him to bring all of the clan chiefs before her, which Comelk promptly did.

Eurydis spoke to each one of them, demanding that they follow the path of wisdom. Everyone listened respectfully, for as barbaric and unruly as they were, their superstitions and traditions made them fear divine power.

Once Eurydis had left them, the chiefs spoke for a very long time, consulting the elders and the oracles. All problems were brought to the table, and all of them were resolved. They swore to keep peace forever, under the name of the Ithare Alliance.

Years passed, and little by little Ith became a city of reputable size, and eventually a truly grand city. At the time, Romine alone could still rival the young kingdom's capital. The tribes mixed among themselves, and the old quarrels became nothing more than a memory of the past. Ith had everything in its favor to become the leading power in the world...which it became, but not as it should have.

Blinded by their new power, which was so easily obtained, the descendants of the first tribes started to boast of their superiority over the rest of the known world. Eventually, a few wanted to demonstrate it. The Ithares launched small-scale war raids, and later small border disputes, which finally escalated to full-scale conquest campaigns that progressively became more frequent and deadlier.

At the end of the eighth Eon, they had made themselves masters of all the territory stretching from the Curtain Mountains in the east to the Vélanèse River in the west, and from the Median Sea in the south to the Crek region in the north. The Ithares behaved like genuine conquerors: they pillaged, burned, and ravaged shamelessly, massacring thousands...

One day, as the war chiefs gathered once again to consider an invasion into Thalitte territory, Eurydis appeared for the second time.

It is said that she came in the form of a young girl, hardly twelve years old, the way she is most often depicted to this day. Still, many of the seasoned warriors present thought they might die of fear, the goddess's ire was so great.

She didn't speak, feeling that a piercing look was sufficient. She simply bored her gaze into the eyes of every one of the powerful individuals in the Ithare Empire, as it was called at the time. The war chiefs understood her warning, immediately gave up all their plans for conquest, and made every resolution possible to put an end to the battles and the occupation of foreign lands. Each of them felt personally responsible for the major changes that needed to be brought to the Ithare way of life.

The next generation of Ithare people turned toward religion. At first, they experienced great tragedies. Their former victims, such as the young Goranese people, in turn became the executioners.

The Ithare territory shrunk back to about what it was to start with: Ith and its surrounding area, and the Maz Nen Harbor.

But the years went by, and the Ithares launched into a new form of conquest, one that was surely more in line with what the goddess had in mind: the Maz left in all directions to the most distant reaches of the known world, with the aim of bringing the "Eurydis Ethic" to all the people of the known world. These excursions were very beneficial to the less evolved peoples, since the Ithares also brought their civilization with them: the calendar, writing, arts, and skills…everything they had learned over the course of their past conquests.

Some theorists are now proclaiming the third appearance of the goddess. She will come again, of course, since she has appeared twice already. But the main question the Ithares ask themselves is this: What will be the next path to follow?

Gisland River – River that partially draws the border between the Kaul Matriarchy and Lorelia.

Grand Guild – This term designates the loose collective of practically all the criminal organizations in the Upper Kingdoms. There is no formal structure or hierarchy to the Grand Guild; it is more like an agreement among gangs that guarantees the respect of one another's territory and activities, just like the kingdom-wide and citywide guilds.

Despite their numerous internal quarrels, the groups sometimes manage to agree to conduct an operation together, notably with contraband.

The Grand Guild does not officially deal in hired killings, but more often in extortion, kidnapping, fraud, contraband, and of course any form of stealing. However, it should be noted that any newcomer organization that doesn't respect the agreements doesn't last long.

Grand House – This is the seat of power of the Kaul Matriarchy, where the Mothers hold their council. Their living quarters are also located here, as well as their study chambers. Anyone can come to the Grand House to express their grievances; fifteen or so Mothers are permanently present to accommodate them. At various times during the year, the study and council rooms of the Grand House are open to any curious visitors.

Holy City – Another name for Ith, the capital of the Ithare Kingdom. This term is most often used to describe the religious quarter, an enclave with its own walls, laws, and citizens, constituting a veritable city within the city.

Ithare dice – A very popular game throughout the entire known world. While its origin remains uncertain, it is nevertheless known that it spread at the same time as the Ithare Empire, during the seventh and eighth Eons, and was quickly adopted by all of the conquered territories.

The Ithare die has six sides, with four depicting the elements Water, Fire, Earth, and Wind. The two remaining sides represent a double or triple of one of the four elements. There are four kinds of dice: one for Wind, generally white; one for Fire, red; one for Earth, green; and one for Water, blue.

The number of dice used in a game varies depending on the rules of the chosen game and any specific arrangements decided upon between participants. While a set of four dice—a soldier— is generally all that's needed, it isn't uncommon to see games requiring several dozen dice. The star, the prophet, the emperor, the two brothers, and the guéjac are the most popular variations of the game. However, there are many more.

Jez – A native of Jezeba.

Kauli – The native language of the Kaul Matriarchy.

Kaulien(ne) – A native of the Kaul Matriarchy. Kaulienne indicates a female, while Kaulien indicates a male.

Kurdalène – This Lorelien king is celebrated for having fought long and hard against the Züu during his reign. The cult of the Goddess of Justice, Zuïa, through threats, extortion, and murder, then exercised such strong influence on the kingdom's nobles and bourgeois that the king couldn't make the slightest decision without the endorsement of the Züu.

At his wit's end, one day Kurdalène decided to put an end to it, and from then on he dedicated all his energy to the annihilation of the cult—at least in Lorelia.

He survived for almost two years cloistered in a wing of his palace, surrounded by handpicked guards, before the Züu finally assassinated him.

Lermian (kings of) – Five centuries ago, Lermian was still the capital of a rich kingdom that had nothing to envy in the nascent Grand Empire, or in the expanding Lorelien land. The royal family had controlled the throne for eleven generations, and the dynasty didn't seem anywhere close to dying off, since Oroséléme, the monarch at the time, had three sons and two daughters with his wife Fédéris.

Lermian had endured the Rominian invasions, the domination of the Ithare, and later on the Goranese expansion, all with relative ease. It seemed that she would just as easily resist Blédévon, the king of Lorelia, and his attempts to exert his influence. Blédévon wanted to incorporate Lermian, which was practically an island within his own kingdom, into his realm. But it wasn't in his interest to launch an assault against Lermian's walls, since the city acted as a buffer zone between his kingdom and the Goranese border; Oroséléme was well aware and teased the Lorelien king with games of intimidation, promises, and intrigue.

Lermian could have become—more than it is today—a leading city of the Upper Kingdoms if misfortune hadn't struck its rulers. Oroséléme died from food poisoning; his oldest son had been on the throne for only six days before perishing in a fall from the city's high walls. The younger son reigned for a little more than eight dékades before he just vanished. Since the last son was too young to rule, the prince consort was given the title of regent, but not one year later he had to be relieved of this title because he went mad after falling off his horse. The husband of the second princess refused the honor of ruling the kingdom, choosing a life of exile with his wife. Queen Fédéris asked her councilors to elect one of their own to be regent. Only one came forward, but he perished just a few days later, stabbed to death in the street by thieves.

After that, no one wanted to volunteer to be regent. The queen, feeling unable to rule alone, finally accepted the deal King Blédévon offered her, making Lermian a simple duchy of Lorelia. In return, the merchant kingdom offered the protection of its army.

The curse that weighed on Orosélème's dynasty seemed to stop there; Queen Fédéris and her last son escaped death.

Rumors spread that the deaths were a series of assassinations; some even said that Blédévon was behind it all. But the theorist of the Lorelien court managed to dispel any doubt by revealing that it was the will of the gods to join the two kingdoms under one crown.

From this tragic episode sprang the popular expression "as dead as the kings of Lermian."

Lesser Kingdoms – Another name for the Baronies.

Lorelien Fairs – One of the oldest Lorelien traditions. During the tenth dékade, from the Day of the Merchant to the Day of the Engraver, the entry and exit of all goods into and out of the city—whose trade is authorized by the kingdom's laws—are tax free.

Obviously, this is the time of the year when the majority of occasional traders, faraway artisans, foreigners, and rare-goods sellers decide to find buyers.

The fairs draw in a lot of people. In fact, about a third of the participants don't come for business at all, but to simply enjoy the numerous attractions that come along with the fairs—street shows, games, banquets, and more. Some of them are generously paid for by the Crown, which sees it as an opportunity to affirm its prestige.

Anyhow, the kingdom's coffers hardly lose out in the deal: each seller has to pay a three-terce fee before he can set up even the smallest stand in the street. The process is tightly monitored and violators are severely punished: no more and no less than the immediate confiscation of the entirety of the violator's goods.

Fairs also take place in the other large Lorelien cities, Bénélia, Lermian, and Pont. Here the fairs enjoy a relative local success, but they remain insignificant in comparison to the capital's fairs.

The Louvelle – River marking the border between the Baronies and the Lower Kingdoms.

Lower Kingdoms – Case dependently, this term designates either the territories stretching south of the Louvelle or the land collectively formed by these same territories *and* the Baronies.

Margolin – A medium-sized rodent. Adults can grow up to two feet long. There are several species: the copper, the screamer, and the glutton, among others.

Margolins are well-known in the south and central areas of the Upper Kingdoms, and thrive just as well on the plains as in the forests or along riverbanks. Generally considered to be pests because of their rapid proliferation, their occasional aggression, and their unpleasant-tasting flesh, they are sought after only for their skins, which artisans use for all sorts of furs, bags, and leathers.

Maz – Honorary title used primarily by the cult of Eurydis, but other religions have borrowed the title as well.

The title can only be transferred—with exactly one exception—from a Maz to one of his or her novices who, as shown by work and devotion, deserves the position. The Grand Temple must approve the transmission, which takes effect either immediately or at the death of the granter, depending on the arrangement. A rule forbids any Maz from passing on his or her title to a family member.

The one exception involves the spontaneous "elevation" of a novice as a thank you for a service deemed particularly noteworthy. The title is often bestowed posthumously—and therefore cannot be transmitted—as a sign of gratitude for a lifetime of service to the cult. The Emaz reserve the exclusive power to elevate novices in this way.

The tangible advantages of a Maz are not defined, for they vary greatly according to the particular priest's "career." Some have many responsibilities in the cult's main temples; others are entrusted with the occasional apprenticeship of a few novices, and still others are never called upon.

The number of living Maz is unknown, except by the archivists of the Grand Temple, who keep a continuous count. Many priests in foreign lands grant themselves the title without actually earning it, which doesn't help the estimates. But legend has it that the Maz were originally only 338, as many as there are days in the year; similarly, there are as many Emaz as there are dékades.

Mèche – A small river that is completely contained within the borders of the Kaul Matriarchy, whose capital sits on her banks. A tributary of the Gisland River.

Milliday – A unit of time of Goranese origin representing one-tenth of a centiday: approximately one minute and twenty-six earthly seconds. Most people consider it useless to measure anything that takes less than a milliday; however, the unit is itself fractioned into "divisions," representing about eight seconds, and then "beats," which are less than a second.

Mishra – The cult of Mishra is at least as old as the Great Sohonne Arch. She was the Goranese people's chief goddess before the Ithare army finally overcame Goran's defenses, sometime during the eighth Eon. She reclaimed her role as chief goddess of the Goranese after the Ithares completely abandoned their warrior ways for religion. In the period that followed, the city of Goran progressively became the empire of Goran, then the Grand Empire, and Mishra's cult developed at the same time.

Mishra is the Goddess of Just Causes and of Freedom. Anyone outside of Goran can appropriate her. And so it has happened that the people conquered by the Grand Empire have called upon the goddess for help, just as their conquerors did.

She has no known divine parentage; a few theologians present her as Hamsa's sister. There are very few Grand Temples dedicated to her—apart from Goran's impressive Freedom Palace, of course—but there are many followers who individually revere miniature idols of the goddess or her symbol, the bear.

Moralist – The moralist priests use the writings and narratives from all religions and combine them to find the morals that are most common and important: pity, tolerance, knowledge, honesty, respect, justice, etc.

They are often teachers and philosophers who humbly limit their task to the education of a small community. The most recognized of moralist cults is that of the goddess Eurydis.

Niab – A Kauli term. The niab is a deep-sea fish that only comes to the surface at night. Kaulien fishermen use a large dark-colored cloth to lure the fish by stretching it out on the surface of the water between several boats, thereby fabricating artificial darkness. Then all they have to do is dive in and "pick" them like fruit, since the fish enters into a state of drowsiness near the surface.

From this, the term "niab" is used as an insult for someone who is gullible, or acts without thinking.

Odrel – Divinity whose cult is widespread in the Upper Kingdoms. According to legend, Odrel is the second son of Echora and Olibar.

After a lifetime of work, a single Odrel priest managed to assemble more than five hundred stories that centered on the god of Sadness, as he is sometimes called. None of the stories finish well. The most famous story by far is the one that tells of Odrel's complicated love affair with a shepherdess. It ends with the dramatic death of the woman and their three children, and Odrel's agonizing realization that he can't follow them into death, the only thing in the world beyond his reach.

The priest-historian finishes his work with these words: "No one has experienced such misfortune as Odrel. It's surely because of this that all the ill-fated, unlucky, and destitute; those who carry the burden of mourning, regrets, and of memories; those who have known injustice, despair, disgrace, misery, all of life's trials; all have come, do come, and will come one day to seek comfort beside Odrel. He's the only god capable of understanding them, because he's the only one who himself inspires pity."

Old Country – Another name for the Romine Kingdom.

Queen moon – A small, smooth seashell, almost perfectly round in shape. Precious because of its rarity, the shell exists as three known types: the white, the most common; the blue, less common; and finally, the multicolored, a rarity. At one time, the last two varieties were used as money in some isolated parts of the Kaul Matriarchy. Elders may still accept a few shells in a transaction.

In fact, the seashell is still represented on every coin minted by the Treasury of the Matriarchy, and the Treasury adopted its name for its official currency, the queen, which exists in denominations of one, three, ten, thirty, and one hundred. The hundred-queen coins, as large as a hand, are not in general circulation, and are only used as a guarantee in transactions with the Matriarchy and other kingdoms.

Ramgrith – Native of the Griteh Kingdom. Also the primary language of this kingdom.

Ramzü – The language of the Züu.

Terce – The terce is Lorelia's official currency. There is a difference between the silver terce, which is most commonly used, and the gold terce, which is minted with an image of the king's head. Gold terces are known to have a level of purity unrivaled by similar coins. The denomination of official currency is the tice; one silver terce is worth twelve tices.

Theorists – A caste of priests devoted to all of the gods in general or, less frequently, to a few, or even just one. The theorists work to reveal the will of the gods through divine omens. Although the Grand Temples view them rather dimly, the royal courts and lords prize them, and they often act as astrologists and advisors.

The Wise One – Name sometimes given to the goddess Eurydis.

Three-Steps Guild – Name given to the circle of prostitutes in Lorelia. The name originates from the fact that this "business" used to be confined to the part of town known as the lower city. These merchants of charm were so numerous that the pimps, tired of arguments that frequently devolved into fights, finally gave each one of them a portion of the street measuring exactly three steps.

Some pimps have held on to this tradition, even though the majority of prostitutes now gather in the harbor neighborhood, which is much larger.

Upper Kingdoms – Term used to designate the group of kingdoms comprised of Lorelia, the Grand Empire of Goran, and the Ithare Kingdom, and sometimes Romine. In the Lower Kingdoms, however, the term is used to indicate *all* of the countries north of the Median Sea, meaning the kingdoms listed above, with the addition of the Kaul Matriarchy and Arkary.

The Vélanèse River – A Lorelien river. The town of Pont was built at its headwaters.

White Country – Another name for the Arkary Kingdom.

Zuïa/Züu/Zü – Called the Goddess of Justice by her followers, Zuïa is the goddess of the Züu assassins. A single follower of Zuïa is called a Zü, with the plural form being Züu.

ABOUT THE AUTHOR

A native of France and a lifelong fantasy enthusiast who numbers Jack Vance, Fritz Leiber, and Michael Moorcock among his heroes, Pierre Grimbert has been awarded the Prix Ozone for best French-language fantasy novel and the Prix Julia Verlanger for best science fiction novel in any language. He is the author of thirteen widely admired novels of the Ji mythos, including the series The Secret of Ji, The Children of Ji, and The Guardians of Ji. He lives in northern France with his wife and two sons.

ABOUT THE TRANSLATORS

This is Matt Ross and Eric Lamb's first collaborative translation. They were both working as English teaching assistants in France when the project was born. As friends who share a passion for the French language and its literature, they are very excited to introduce Pierre Grimbert's gripping Ji series to the English-speaking world.

Matt has been losing himself in fantasy books for many years, but only discovered the wonders of the French language while studying at CU Boulder. These combined interests sparked his interest in the Ji series, which a friend in France described as the "best French fantasy." He is pursuing a doctorate in ecology at Duke University in North Carolina.

Eric received his bachelor's degree in French from CU Boulder in 2010 and a certificate in applied literary translation from the University of Illinois in 2011. His first book-length translation, *My Beautiful Bus* by Jacques Jouet, was published in January 2013 by the Dalkey Archive Press. Eric teaches French at Aspen High School in Colorado.